KONA

ERIK DANIEL SHEIN
MELISSA DAVIS

World Castle Publishing, LLC
Pensacola, Florida

Copyright © Arkwatch Holdings, LLC & Erik Daniel Shein 2021
Coauthor: Melissa Davis
Hardback ISBN: 9781951642242
Paperback ISBN: 9781951642259
eBook ISBN: 9781951642266
First Edition World Castle Publishing, LLC, February 1, 2021
http://www.worldcastlepublishing.com

Licensing Notes

Arkwatch Holdings, LLC
4766 East Eden Drive
Cave Creek, AZ 85331

Cover: Karen Fuller
Editor: Maxine Bringenberg

DEDICATION

This book is dedicated to my young friend Rissy, who is a survivor of medulloblastoma. Rissy, never underestimate the power of perseverance. Always have the courage to push past any barriers that keep you from your dreams. Heroes come in many shapes and forms, and you are the fiercest of them all.

And to Kelly, who has walked beside you every step of the way. From one mother to another, I am amazed at your courage and just know our girls are gym sisters for life.

A SPECIAL THANK YOU

I would like to thank my friend, Mare, who was a sounding board when I was writing. She let me read it to her when I wanted to see whether or not I was on the right track—also, a big thank Courtney Vail from Lightkeepers Foundation for her infinite knowledge of dolphins. A big thank you goes to our readers and fans. And last but not least, I would like to thank Erik Shein, my coauthor and our publisher, World Castle Publishing.

Melissa Davis

CHAPTER 1

"Sorry, River. There's no room on my lap for you too." The Labrador retriever was always whining at her as if she could fit him on her lap the way she did the black cat, who was almost dozing. River had not been able to fit on any lap for quite some time, but he still had not figured that out. In his mind, the dog was just like their cat, Nite. He chased red lights and used every piece of furniture as a scratching post. He had even tried to use the litter box, which had never gone to plan because his butt was way too large for that tiny thing.

As his cold nose touched her arm, Melanie sighed, and her shoulders dropped back. She could not even sit at the table in peace. It was as if she were some kind of magnet for their neediness. Some days she did not mind. This was not one of those days, for Melanie was way too distracted with her own thoughts. She did not have time to deal with their four-legged drama. Where was Kimmie? Maybe she could play with them.

The whimpers got so loud that Melanie could no longer ignore them. Reaching down to scratch behind his ears, she gave in to his pathetic whine. His paw reached up as he tried to get the leverage to hop on her, but the hissing cat in her lap shot him down before he could even try. Melanie giggled when River tried to push enough air out of his nose to make his irritation known. This was his way of hissing, even though it sounded much like a balloon deflating.

"I tried to tell you, silly goose."

River plopped down on the floor with a loud oomph. The dog whimpered and put his head on his paws. Nite heard his complaint, and her belly seemed to rumble in reflex, her warning sign before she went on a hissing rampage. Nite was not in the mood to tolerate him. Then again, Nite hissed at her own shadow, so it could be nothing at all. While Melanie was usually irritated by their rivalry, today nothing could touch her, for she was about to start a new chapter in her life. Today, she would contemplate much more than why her dog had decided that he would ditch his canine ways and hone his feline skills, none of which existed in any mind but his own. And why would he want to be like the black cat? Like most cats, Nite barely tolerated any living being in the Parker household. She was the essential queen bee, ready to eviscerate anything of value with her claws.

The dog whined, and Melanie reached down to stroke his fur despite the hiss that left Nite's mouth, followed by the snarling grumble in the pit of her belly right before she hopped off Melanie's lap and sauntered away. Every sway of her tail punctuated her mood. Melanie just shook her head at the cat's antics as she continued to pet River. The crazy dog did not start wagging his tail as he would have years ago. No, not River. Instead, he arched his butt high in the air as if giving her the blueprint for where to start. When she did not comply, he inched forward under her hand and forced her to focus her hand down the length of his spine to the tip of his tail, full diva style, just like his nemesis. He now stood there with his tail, slowly stroking the ground in gentle movements that were a feline conducting a

6

slow ballad.

She giggled at his antics. "You're weird. You know that, River?" Nite turned around and gave her the evil eye. Melanie shook her head. "I'm not even talking to you!"

Nite meowed back at her before scampering off. That was when River decided to scoot even closer to her as if Melanie would suddenly have room for him now that the cat was not on her lap. "Stop, River. Down, boy. You are not getting on my lap. You're a dog...D-O-G...dog!"

Grandma Mimi, who was stirring a pot of noodles on the stove, stopped long enough to comment on the antics around her. "That lab is bonkers. Why do you treat him like a cat?"

"Hey, don't blame me. That's all on Kimmie."

"And she'll say it was Amber, who will then say it was you. You girls like to pass the buck sometimes." Grandma Mimi shook her head and went back to the pot. She pushed her brown curls behind her ears as the steam from the pasta made them curl even more. Melanie noticed the grey that was working its way into Grandma Mimi's hair and wondered if it was age that had put it there or the fact that she had been everyone's rock for so long. Grandma Mimi had moved in when Melanie was much younger. That had been right after her father had died in the line of duty. Grandma Mimi had given up her home in Scottsdale to help her mom take care of their entire world. With all they had been through over the years, it was a miracle that Grandma Mimi was just now getting grey hair.

Melanie opened her mouth to reply, but at that moment, her older sister Amber walked into the room. "That's because he is a cat, aren't ya, boy?"

At seventeen, Amber was tall, thin, and wore her long blonde hair pulled back into a ponytail. As she bent down to pet River,

Amber handed him a piece of bacon she had brought home from the diner where she worked. The dog raised his head and acted like a dog for the first time in ages, thumping his tail and swallowing the bacon in one bite as if his dog mode had finally been activated. Bacon was the ultimate treat for him.

Amber patted the dog on top of his head, then made her way to the refrigerator. "That smells delicious, Grandma."

Grandma Mimi favored Amber with a smile. "Did you eat already?"

"No. We were way too busy for that. Besides, why would I want to miss your cooking?" Amber smiled affectionately at their grandma before walking over to kiss her on the cheek.

"Flattery will get you garlic bread. Hand me the mitts, will you?"

"Sure."

Amber reached over to grab the oven mitts that had seen better days. The tips of them had scorch marks from when the girls had tried to make cookies on their own. Thankfully nothing but the cookies had been burned, although that was a smell Melanie never wanted to experience again.

"How was work, Amber?" Grandma Mimi asked her as she put the oven mitts on to put the garlic bread into the oven.

"Not bad. I got a few tips today. There was a large party from out of town. They make the best tippers. Not like the locals." Amber grumbled a bit as she took the jar down from the top of the refrigerator and opened the lid. She put her extra tip money inside and put it back.

Grandma Mimi shook her head slowly. "It's a shame that today's youth has no idea how to treat the service industry. Someone needs to teach them some manners."

"Should we send you out to conquer and destroy?" Melanie

teased her grandma.

Grandma Mimi held her wooden spoon up in the air like a sword and swished it back and forth. "I could teach them a thing or two."

"Down, Grandma." Amber held up her hands and pretended to back away from her. Grandma Mimi advanced on her with a few slashes, and Amber pretended to fall back against the refrigerator at her attack. She held up a few more bills in front of her. "Here, here, take some more."

Grandma Mimi grinned at her and withdrew the spoon. "No, child. You have to keep some for yourself. Being a teenager is expensive."

"You got that right," Amber agreed with her.

"That's only because you're so addicted to makeup videos," Melanie added. When her sister wasn't working, her face was stuck on a screen watching every makeup tutorial she could find. It wasn't that Amber was vain, but that she enjoyed the artistry of it all. Melanie would not be surprised if her sister joined the cosmetology field when she graduated from high school.

"Hey, those videos helped me do your makeup last year, remember?" Amber tilted her head and narrowed her eyes on Melanie.

"That was the scariest zombie I've ever seen," added Grandma Mimi.

"Yeah, but I was supposed to be a post-apocalyptic vampire," Melanie teased her sister.

"That's not a thing!" Her sister shot back.

"It is in my mind."

Melanie had come up with that idea after watching a few steampunk videos. She had imagined a world where people were sparse, and vampires were starving because they could not find enough food. Amber had captured her idea to the best of her ability. Melanie could not fault her for lack of vision when Melanie had conjured an impossible character like she usually did. That's what happened when Melanie decided to be unique. She had always stood out at Halloween, not wanting to wear any cookie cutter costume that everyone else wore.

"Whatever!" Amber rolled her eyes.

Melanie did not take it personally, though. While most siblings were at odds with each other, the Parker sisters were extremely close. Maybe it was the fact that they had lost so much early on when their father died or the fact that they had to fight so hard to keep themselves afloat. Whatever the reason, Melanie would always be thankful for her sisters, even when she was annoyed with them. Melanie and Amber had always been thick as thieves, and although their younger sister, Kimmie, was only nine, they often involved her in their hijinks as well. Her innocent face was a bonus, for Kimmie had managed to talk her mother out of punishment several times over.

"A few more shifts and I can start paying for my insurance." The moment Amber had turned sixteen, she had become obsessed with driving everywhere. Now that she was almost eighteen, she was dying for her own car. Their mother had told her that they could look for one as soon as she was able to pay for her own car insurance. While their mother had been able to cover almost everything else in their lives, underage car insurance was very expensive. Melanie was glad she didn't have to worry about that for a little while longer.

Grandma Mimi turned to her granddaughter with an approving smile. "Every little bit helps."

"I'm going to start saving up as soon as I start my job," Melanie piped in. She couldn't wait to start her first summer job, which put her well ahead of her sister, who had just gotten her job when she turned seventeen. Amber's motivation was having the freedom to take the car when her mother wasn't using it. Melanie's reason was different. She wanted to save up for college so that it would be less of a burden for her mother. Not all sixteen-year-olds were obsessed with planning their futures out, but it was what drove her forward. The future was never a guarantee, a lesson she had learned a few times over already.

Melanie closed her eyes and tried to redirect her thoughts. The doubts inside her were like dark clouds that she had to evacuate daily. Today, all she wanted was to keep herself focused on the good things that were happening for a change. Although she was only sixteen, her mother had gotten her a position at The Oasis Aquarium, the one place that had inspired her to follow her dreams. Even at her age, Melanie knew what she wanted to do with the rest of her life. Becoming a marine biologist was the only thing she'd ever wanted to do. Working at the aquarium would put her even closer to that goal, especially if she could join their junior trainer program while she was still in high school. Melanie would only have part-time hours, but that didn't bother her because everyone had to start somewhere.

She had spent a lot of her childhood at the aquarium, especially since her mother, Linda, was the assistant manager. Her sisters weren't nearly as fascinated by the marine life, but they had all spent plenty of time there. Sometimes when their mom had to work all weekend, she would take the girls with her. They would have free run of the aquarium while their mother finished her shift inside the main office. As long as they were out of sight and kept out of trouble, no one even knew they were there. Melanie had become a master at blending in with the crowds. She often pretended she was there with another family altogether as she stuck close behind different groups of people. It had become one of her favorite past times.

Grandma Mimi put the lid on the pan before taking it off the burner. Then she turned to face Melanie. "That's right. You start next week, don't you?"

Melanie could feel the silly grin slide across her face and didn't bother to hide it. She was too excited to worry about how juvenile that might make her. "I can't wait! I'm so excited!"

It was true. She was more than ready to get on to a normal life for a change. Her world had been off-kilter for far too long. Finally, she would feel like a regular teenager, no longer limited by the label that had been on her head for far too long. Two words that no one voiced aloud, even though Melanie knew everyone was thinking them. Melanie didn't have to be a mind reader to know where their thoughts turned. Cancer Kid. Those two words had haunted her for far too long now. Some days she tried to outrun them, racing as far and fast as she could from the reality of her life. That only ended up making her sides twist painfully, though, because Melanie was not much of a runner. Cancer had nearly ruined her life. It was just under the surface slithering deep below, waiting for the right moment to strike and steal every last hope she had for a normal life. Even though she had won the battle earlier, it was a foe that could return at any point and ask for a rematch.

Once a cancer kid, always a cancer kid. At least that was what it felt like, especially when she had to deal with kids that had no idea how to treat her. Even after all this time, she knew her friends were afraid to connect with her. It was as if her diagnosis had thrown up a wall between them, one they were too scared to break down. And why was that? Because they were afraid of loss? Were they worried they could catch it? Or had they simply

12

thought she was not worth the effort anymore? Melanie had gone from having best friends for life to spending sporadic amounts of time with them here and there. She had watched them move on from her and band together without her, leaving her to find her comfort in the silence of rejection. Knowing all this had not only made school even more awkward for her, but it had also made her feel isolated from the rest of the world. Melanie's only friends now were the other cancer kids from her survivor group. The time they spent together was limited to monthly meetings and text messages here and there.

Melanie sighed as the thoughts swirled around inside her head. Even now, when she should only be excited about her new job, happiness eroded way too fast as the past echoed inside her like ghosts trapped in time. At nine, what had first felt like the common cold had quickly amplified to such an extreme that she thought she had the walking plague. Her mother had refused to let the doctors stop with just the routine tests. Linda Parker had pushed the doctors to explore every route possible to find out what was wrong with her daughter. They often say a mother knows her child better than anyone else. It had indeed been true in this case. Her mom had been like a hound snapping at the doctor's heels until they had finally gotten real answers. Thankfully, her pediatric oncologist was well versed in dealing with parents who had been stretched to their limits. Dr. Rebecca Strand was a godsend with her patience and understanding. Dr. Strand had held their hands through it all, making them feel hope when everything had seemed so dark. That felt like almost a lifetime ago. Almost.

Three years ago, Melanie had received the best news any cancer kid can. NED—no evidence of disease. The cancer had been kept at bay ever since, so well that sometimes Melanie hoped it had just been a dream. A nightmare was more like it, though, one that she was afraid would recur at any point, even though she had felt totally fine. The moment she was cleared, Melanie started to live a normal life. Well, as normal as she could, for nothing ever stayed the same. A voice was always there in the back of her head, telling her that nothing was ever permanent. No one was guaranteed forever. Infinity did not exist for the human race. All anyone could do was leave their mark in history while they lived the only life they were given. That was what Melanie wanted to do, to make a mark on the world that would make it clear she had been there, for whatever duration that was.

Melanie's thoughts faded away as the humming nine-year-old came skipping into the kitchen. With curly brown hair and blue eyes, she was the spitting image of Grandma Mimi and just as rambunctious. Kimmie reached her hand out in her best attempt to ninja a cookie from the jar on the counter. Her eyes met Melanie's, and Kimmie gave her the "Be quiet, and I'll make it worth your while" nod that the siblings had perfected over the years. Melanie saw her mother, Linda, shake her head as she followed the nine-year-old into the kitchen.

"Excited for what?" Kimmie joined the conversation without skipping a beat.

"She's going to go to work with me next week." Kimmie's head whipped around in surprise that her mother was right behind her. "And don't ruin your dinner, Kimmie."

"I just took one...." Kimmie gave her the innocent look she had perfected as the youngest member of the household.

"Kimmie...."

Kimmie opened her hand and grinned, as she knew she had been caught taking more than one cookie. "Okay, two."

Melanie sneezed into her arm, wishing that it would have

happened ten minutes earlier. Any little sniffle, cough, or headache immediately put her mother in protective mode. It took Linda just two steps to get to Melanie's side, where she put her hand on her forehead. Melanie rolled her eyes and let out a slow sigh, knowing what was about to come.

"Are you feeling okay? Maybe we should get you in to see Dr. Strand." Linda smoothed some of Melanie's brown hair away from her forehead.

Melanie shrugged away from her mother's touch. "Mom! Stop fussing. Sometimes a sneeze is just a sneeze."

Melanie said the words, she knew that she did, but it was clear from the way that Grandma Mimi and her mother exchanged a silent glance that they were immediately worried. One tiny sneeze, and they were already imagining the worst. She was tired of being treated like she was fine china, something that was fragile, breakable. Melanie was tired of feeling broken. Couldn't she just feel like she had everything together for once in her life? Would that be too much to ask?

Melanie's shoulders slumped in defeat as she realized this was a fight she would not win. "I hate doctors."

Grandma Mimi winked at her. "Don't we all?"

Melanie was desperate to change the subject. It was bringing the atmosphere in the kitchen down to the point that a sad clown could walk through with a withered bouquet at any moment. She looked around, half expecting that to happen, but even that would be preferable to the silence that hung around them.

"Can we just focus on the fact that I'm going to have a summer job? I've wanted to work at the aquarium ever since Mom started working there."

Linda smiled softly as she sat down next to Melanie at the table. She patted her hand as a mother tended to do when they were trying to console a child, while still rambling on with their agenda regardless. It was a move her mother had done several times before. Even Grandma Mimi knew it was coming, for the older woman turned away from it so that she was no longer involved. Chicken. Sure, pull out the plates and pretend to ignore the depressing soap opera that was flooding the kitchen. Any moment now, a sad violin would start playing with a haunting piano refrain. Melanie waited for the setup before her mother drove her point home.

"I'm glad you're excited." Those few words were trouble. Her mother was definitely going to follow it up with something else.

"I get to be with the dolphins…well, almost. But I do get to watch people feed them all day."

Melanie saw her sister Amber smirk at her as she held a plate out for her grandmother to fill. Even Amber knew what was coming. Hook, line, sinker. Amber tried to deflect the shot, though.

"Yeah, sounds great if you want to walk around smelling like fish all day," Amber teased her sister.

Melanie smirked at Amber. "Better to smell like fish than fried food. You smell like you swam in an oil vat."

Amber rolled her eyes and tossed her ponytail. "If you say so."

Kimmie sat down at the table and giggled at her sisters. "You'll both stink."

Melanie stuck her tongue out at Kimmie, which was a big mistake. The girl started to snort and giggle as if someone was tickling her hard in the ribs. "Bet you think you're funny, don't you?"

"No, just not smelly like you two," returned Kimmie.

"I still think I'll make a call to the doctor." Her mother was not going to let this go any time soon.

"Mom! Ugh. You worry too much." Melanie shook off her concern. She did not want to hear it right now. Things were just starting to settle down in her life.

"It's my job to worry. Besides, your six-month scans are just around the corner. We could just bump them up a bit." Linda's face looked weary from work and life in general.

Melanie hated to see her looking that way. Her illness had taken such a toll on her mother the last time. Guilt crept into her consciousness, and she tried to shove it down. If only she could control the blood cells in her body and make them behave so that she would never have to see the fear of loss in her mother's eyes ever again. It was hard enough trying to fight an unseen attacker, but doing so at a great personal cost to the rest of her family was something no child should ever have to shoulder. It had made her grow up way too fast, as mortality made itself evident. Maybe that was why Melanie had fought so hard to stay positive through it all. Even when she had been terrified, Melanie had done her best to broadcast a strength she didn't always feel. "Fake it until you make it" had become her motto for much too long.

"Why don't you all wash up? Dinner's ready. Amber, be a dear and help me get the food to the table," interrupted Grandma Mimi as she pulled the garlic bread from the oven.

"Yes, ma'am." Amber was the first to answer as she headed for the bathroom just off the kitchen.

Not far behind her, Melanie got up from the table to go wash her hands. All the while, her thoughts turned back to things best left forgotten. When Melanie approached the sink, her sister gave her a weak smile, as if she knew where Melanie's thoughts had turned.

"She means well, Mel." Amber pulled her hands out of the water and started to dry them.

"I know, Amber. I know." Melanie sighed softly as she washed her hands. "But could I have just one happy moment?"

"You'll have plenty of them." Amber checked herself in the mirror. "Ugh. Why didn't you tell me I had sauce on my cheek?"

"You do? I thought it was just part of your face now," teased Melanie.

"I hate that place!" grumbled Amber.

"It's only a high school job, right? Aren't they all supposed to be disgusting?"

"Well, here's to hoping yours is better than mine." Amber smiled at her. "I'm happy for you, Mel."

"I know. There's a 'but' though, right?"

"Yes…make sure you don't overdo it, okay?" Amber was worried too.

"Promise," Melanie mumbled. She finished drying her hands and walked away from her sister. All Melanie wanted was to forget the things that everyone else in her family seemed to worry about all the time. She was fine. Everything was fine. They needed to back her up.

CHAPTER 2

While she had tried to talk her mom out of dragging her to the doctor's office, Melanie had lost. Funny how quickly they could make an appointment. Melanie thought she would have at least a few days before she had to deal with anyone in scrubs. Fat chance! When her mother called the next morning, demanding to see Dr. Strand, it was almost as if they had cleared their entire schedule. Of course, they had.

Melanie's shoulders slumped, and her head fell back, so the base of her skull rested on her back. Closing her eyes, she tried to keep her thoughts from attacking her, but the four walls of the exam room were closing in on her with memories that were hard to keep at bay. First diagnosis, first scans, first treatments. They were never far from the surface. Every doctor's office was plagued with the same thoughts, even if she had never stepped foot inside it before. Melanie was afraid she would have that problem for the rest of her life. Even though this doctor was the one who had saved her life, the fear was still there.

Cancer felt like lice sometimes. Any time either one was mentioned, she started to think she had it. Any time she had heard there was a lice outbreak at school, Melanie would immediately begin scratching her head as imaginary bugs crawled all through her hair. It was the same exact thing with cancer fears. A slight cough, a bad headache, low blood sugar—all of those things were like an instant replay of the past. When her mom started to worry about the slightest cough, even Melanie had trouble not imagining the deadly cancer cells multiplying through her body. At this point, they were nothing more than imaginary, though, a figment of the past that had no place in the present. Crossing her arms over her chest, Melanie tried to deny the dark thoughts that circled through her head.

As she sat, she let her eyes roam around her, taking in the long exam table with the white strip of paper she used to color on while she waited. Many a tic-tac-toe game had been played on them. Sometimes her mother had let her win just to make her feel better. Other days they had created an ocean of animals, much like the ones that lived at The Oasis. Her mother always had pictures of them on her phone, ready to pull up at any time. The two of them would make up fantastic stories of the things all the animals did when everyone else had gone home for the night. Melanie smiled as she remembered the story of the black cat who had tried to ride on one of the dolphin's backs. It had never happened anywhere else but her imagination, but it had seemed so real all those years ago.

Melanie smiled to herself as she looked over at the swivel chair near the counter that was a makeshift desk. How many rodeo spins had she taken on that thing? Well, the one before it, because this one was even fancier than the one that she remembered. Melanie remembered spinning around and around until she felt like the whole world could not keep up with her. The blur around her had made her feel like she had found her own piece of the universe to hold on to. The more she thought of the happier memories, the more her brain started to settle down.

On the counter near the sink were the jars filled with cotton balls and other various odds and ends. Melanie felt the urge to rifle through them the way she had before, but only children got away with being so rambunctious. Growing up was never easy. When she was younger, there had been at least a handful of childish innocence left. The world had so many possibilities, or it had before she'd gone through so many rounds of chemo that she lost track. Before her life had completely imploded, she would pretend she was in a candy store, looking for the right piece of candy. How many cotton balls had she tried to convince her mother were gumballs? Hundreds? It was a small game from a child who was desperate to hang onto childhood, in a world filled with needles and masks that always seemed to bring her back to the reality of her life.

At least they had changed the artwork. Gone was the rainbow hot air balloons. In its place was a colorful African sunset with the dark silhouettes of the majestic animals that roamed the savannas. Her preference would have been the sea, but jungle animals were probably more relatable with all the cartoons fashioned after them. Unless it was a cartoon about a mermaid, most kids didn't seem to care about the ocean—their loss.

"I know you didn't want to come," her mother tried to console her.

"I've seen enough doctors' offices to last me a lifetime." Melanie let out a slow breath as she tried to get her attitude in check. This was hard for her mom too, Melanie knew that. None of this was a picnic.

"I know, baby. I know." Linda reached over and patted her knee as if that would be enough to keep her fears from creeping up on the both of them. If only it were ever that easy.

Melanie heard the shuffle of feet outside the door right before

21

the small knock that felt like a mallet hitting a gong, that tiny tap punctuating the moment in ways no one would ever understand. The door opened, and Dr. Rebecca Strand entered the room. She was wearing her white coat like most doctors, but on the lapel, a small bunny was held in place with a safety pin. Dr. Strand had always had a thing for rabbits since she had a few of them at home. Even now, Melanie was sure there were several pictures on her phone, not that she planned to ask if she could see them.

"Good morning, you two. Has it been six months already?" Dr. Strand's face was filled with a genuine smile. How she still smiled through all the tears and hand holding she had to do was a mystery to Melanie. This had to be one of the hardest jobs in the universe.

"Yes, we're really close to it, so I just thought we might as well get her in. She had a cold the last few weeks that seemed to linger." Her mother gave the doctor a worried smile.

Mom! She wanted to shout. It wasn't anything to worry about. Normal kids got colds. Melanie was perfectly fine. At least those were the words on the surface. She would be lying if she said none of it made her worry because deep down it probably always would.

Dr. Strand seemed to catch on fast. Her eyes went from Melanie to her mother with an understanding that did not need to be vocalized. "Always better safe than sorry. Let's take a look at you, Melanie."

Melanie squinted when the doctor used her light to check her eyes with its blinding flash. As her eyes adjusted, Melanie moved through the next check. Tilting her head back, Melanie fought the urge to sneeze as the scope touched the inside of her nostrils. Closing her eyes, she tried to pretend she was anywhere but there as all the memories she tried to keep at bay made their presence known with an angry roar inside her.

"How've you been feeling, Melanie?" Dr. Strand was checking her pulse now.

"Good, mostly. Every once in a while, I get a headache. Mom tends to treat any cold like the plague."

"I can't help it. I'll never stop worrying about her." Her mom sounded a little piqued.

"Leukemia takes a nasty toll on families. Let's take a look at your glands, shall we?"

Melanie laid back on the table and took a deep breath as the doctor used her fingers to softly mold over her skin as she checked for swelling in her stomach. As Dr. Strand continued to check her glands, Melanie saw the concern on her mother's face and gave her a small smile to make her feel better. She was often smiling through her fear, not because Melanie needed to pretend that she was okay, but because she knew how much her mother needed to think she was. The truth was sometimes she did worry it was coming back, not that she would ever admit it out loud. Her fear was not something she needed to broadcast to the world. That would only multiply the fear in everyone else. Instead, she put on the brave face that kept her family from falling into the black void of hopelessness that took over many cancer families.

"Up you go, then. I have just one more thing to check." Dr. Strand waited for Melanie to sit up. When she did, her doctor started to feel the lymph nodes around her neck. Dr. Strand stepped back with a thoughtful look etched across her face. "Hmmm...."

Her mother sat as straight as a rod in her chair at that one syllable. "Hmmm? What does that mean?"

"Nothing to be alarmed about, but I would like to get a blood panel just to be sure. Your lymph nodes are just a little swollen here. It doesn't always mean bad news, though."

Blood panel? Melanie felt her heart drop to her stomach. That meant she was about to be jabbed with a needle yet again, and then she would do the bloodwork tango where she danced around her emotions for days until the results came back. "So, I get to be a pin cushion again?"

Dr. Strand patted Melanie's hand. "Don't worry. Olivia is very good at what she does. You won't feel a thing."

"When will you have the results?" Linda Parker looked as if a thousand bees were stirring inside her. Mild panic crossed over her face before her mother finally got it under control.

"A few days. Don't worry. This is really precautionary, just the labs we would have done soon anyway." She favored them both with a reassuring smile, the one that she probably had to plaster on her face every day. Melanie could not imagine how hard it would be to keep that up when she dealt with such sick kids all the time. Maybe that was why Melanie felt the need to return it.

"Thank you," Linda called to the doctor as she was about to leave the room. Dr. Strand turned and nodded her head politely before she walked out the door.

Melanie crossed her arms over her chest again. "I'm still going to work."

Linda smiled at her daughter. "Yes. You are."

Melanie saw the tears that were pooling in her mother's eyes as she turned to look out the window. Closing her eyes, Melanie tried not to take on the fear her mother was feeling right now. The toll cancer had already taken on their lives was massive. It had stolen years from her already, sucking out the life from the happy moments that should have been hers to keep for years to come. Instead, she would remember having to fight through the

24

nausea and pain that came with her treatments. Melanie was not about to let those things cloud her mind right now, though. The fight to stay focused on the present was the only thing she should spend her time on. There were many good things in her life now.

Shaking off the melancholy, she decided to think about the summer she was about to have. Melanie would even be working near the dolphins...well, almost. She would be working at the fish stand right near the feeding exhibit. While she would not be interacting with the dolphins, it was the next best thing.

"Nothing's going to keep me down, Mom." Melanie held her chin up, taking on the fighting pose she had assumed so many times before even though there was no need to do so right now. She was not sick. Not again. Her mother was just overly concerned. That's all this was. End of discussion."

"I know, Mel." Her mom patted her arm and smiled at her. "Ice cream?"

"A scoop for every time she misses?" Melanie suggested. It was only fair. If she was going to be a pin cushion, she should at least reap the rewards.

"You got it."

Melanie had a feeling this was just the beginning of another very long day. She rubbed her arm and tried not to think of the pain that was about to come. Needles were at the top of her least favorite things in this world. Chemo was just above it. The list was growing to include overprotective mothers too. Melanie clenched her teeth together and waited for the worst part of her day.

She wished she could say the rest of the visit was a blur, but the truth was it had gone in slow motion from the misplaced needle sticks to the scans that seemed to take forever. By the time it was all over, Melanie barely had an appetite for ice cream, although she made sure to keep her mother at her word. This was the only time her mother did not give her grief for wasting her food, as the ice cream had melted in her bowl before her. Melanie wanted to eat it, but her stomach was just too upset to let her.

It was early evening before Melanie could find sanctuary on the porch of their two-story stucco house. Her sister had barely said a word as she shot past her to get her scooter. Now, Kimmie was riding the scooter in the circle drive out front without a care in the world. Melanie watched her stumble slightly, catching herself before she landed on the large cactus in the middle of the small circle.

"Watch out there, squirt," Melanie cautioned her.

"I'm not a squirt," her sister grumbled as she took off again.

Oh, to be innocent enough to not worry about injury and illness. Kimmie had been there through it all, but she had not really understood what was going on at the time. Grandma Mimi had spent a lot of time distracting Kimmie. It had been for the best, considering Kimmie had been too young to visit her in the hospital those first few years. That did not mean that Kimmie had not missed her or worried about her; it had just distanced her from it a bit.

At that moment, Amber walked up the drive shaking her head at Kimmie, who almost ran over her foot. "Watch it."

"Move it, or lose it," Kimmie taunted her.

Amber rolled her eyes and sighed. "Kids."

Melanie snorted as she watched Kimmie stick her tongue out at Amber, something Amber probably saw out of the corner of her eye but chose to ignore as she sat down on the steps next to Melanie.

"Hey."

"Hey, Mel." Amber nodded to the bright neon green Band-

Aids on her arm. "How many scoops?"

Melanie sighed and rubbed her arm. "Three."

"What's the record again?"

"Six. No wait, there was that one time they did seven."

Not that Melanie wanted to remember all of them. She was surprised that she didn't have more scars considering all the times she had been poked and prodded. From the IVs to port lines, Melanie had pretty much seen it all. And let's not even talk about the catheter. She winced, just thinking about it. Yeah, there was not enough ice cream in the world to make up for the things she had already been through.

Amber winced as she imagined each one. "Ouch. It's going to be all right, Mel."

Melanie leaned against her sister and put her head on her shoulder. "I know. I feel fine. Mom just worries a lot."

"I know she does. We all do." Amber tried to explain away their mother's fears. Melanie knew them all too well, though. They would forever be tattooed in her memories.

"Well, there's nothing to worry about. No evidence of disease, remember?" Melanie knew that her voice did not sound nearly as confident as she wanted it to, but she could not summon the will to hide in front of her sister. Amber had been her rock, the one person who held her hand through the worst of it and stood over her like her very own protector from the kids that asked too many questions.

"Yes, but…." Amber looked away from her sister as if her deepest thoughts would be too much for Melanie to take.

Melanie quickly changed the subject. She knew that look all too well. "Can you believe I get to bust out of here tomorrow?"

"First day, huh?" Amber grinned at her.

"Yep. No more babysitting for me."

Kimmie brought the scooter to a standstill and turned to glare at Melanie. "Hey! Who you callin' a baby? Do I look like I'm in diapers?"

Melanie and Amber took turns snorting loudly between their laughter. Melanie laughed so hard, she almost coughed. "If you say so."

Kimmie stuck her tongue out at her sisters, then pushed the scooter forward. She called their dog to her side. "Come on, River. At least you love me."

The dog let out a slight huff as if he knew he should protest as the cat-dog he was, but when Kimmie whistled, his thumping tail could not be denied. He hopped up from his spot on the ground and started to chase her. Melanie watched him tackle Kimmie from the scooter and burst out laughing. "Good boy, River!"

Kimmie pushed the dog off her as his tongue tried to lick her face off. "River! Stop! Down boy! Can you just go back to cat mode already?"

"Hey, you asked for it," Amber pointed out.

"Whatever. Don't you need to go peel your face off or something?" Kimmie shot back at her.

"A peel is something you put on your face to clean your pores out, Kimmie," Amber attempted to explain.

Melanie put her hand on Amber's arm. "Just quit while you're ahead. She'll just find some way to talk you in circles, Amber."

"Good point." Amber snapped her fingers and pointed to Kimmie. "Lick her face off, River. She needs a good peel herself."

"Whoa, whoa, whoa...."

Kimmie put her hands over her face and shrieked with laughter. Before long, they were all giggling uncontrollably. Melanie had to admit this was much better than the rest of her day had been. She was laughing so hard she was afraid she might pee herself by the time it was all said and done. Melanie was thankful for it.

CHAPTER 3

The morning had not come soon enough. Her emotions were so mixed up. She was equal amounts excited and worried. Melanie tried not to worry about the doubts that lingered inside her, but they were cemented in. The only thing that kept her from completely freaking out was the fact that she started her job the following morning. When she finally did fall asleep, her dreams were filled with large needles and dancing stethoscopes that dove through the water like dolphins. When she awoke, Melanie was more than confused — she was almost traumatized.

"That was crazy!" She muttered to herself.

"Mmm? Did you say something?" Amber mumbled from her bed as she covered her eyes with her arm as if to shut out the morning.

"Sorry. I didn't mean to wake you."

"It's all right. I have to get up eventually anyway." Amber pushed up on her elbows and looked at her through sleep laden eyes. "What's up?"

"Just a weird dream." Melanie threw the covers off and sat up in bed.

"Well, spill. I'm already up." Amber turned to her side and propped her head up on her arm. Her eyes were now completely open, and her face was fighting her annoyance at being woken up. Amber was not the most patient person in the morning.

"Just my mind racing, really. I was being chased by large needles."

"That sounds like a nightmare." Amber's eyes filled with concern. "You okay, Mel?"

"Yeah. I guess." Melanie's eyes locked on the floor under her feet. She saw the tiny drops of nail polish that had dripped onto it years ago. Counting every little speck, she ended up with the same fourteen she always had. Sometimes it was easier to distract herself with the small things than focus on the really big thing that was eating at her.

"It's going to be all right. Besides, today you start your job. I'm sure that will keep you distracted." Amber attempted to help deflect Melanie's feelings.

"You're right. It was just a stupid dream." Melanie attempted to smile, but the corners of her mouth barely turned up. As much as she wanted to draw the happiness to the surface, the sleepy haze was still taking over. Melanie squeezed her eyes shut and took a deep breath. Today was a new day, a new adventure. There was no time to dwell on some stupid dream.

"When do you go in?" Amber asked her.

"At eight. I'm going in with Mom when she starts her shift. Mine doesn't start until nine."

"It's six in the morning, Mel. Go back to bed." Amber looked as if she were digging even deeper for patience.

"I can't. I think I'll just get ready. Go back to sleep, Amber." Melanie gave her an apologetic smile. "Sorry for waking you."

"Don't mention it." Amber plopped back down on her bed and pulled the covers over her head to shut out the early morning light.

Melanie got out of bed, moving as fast as her sleepy brain would let her. By the time she had showered and gone downstairs, ready to go, she looked over at the clock to find it was only seven. A low groan left her mouth. "Come on!"

River heard her voice and came barreling around the corner. Mornings were just dog time because if River were a true cat, he would still be sleeping on someone's head like it was some kind of pillow. Melanie saw the tongue come lolling out of his mouth as if waiting for Melanie to scoop up some of the yummy goodness into his bowl. Melanie shook her head at him. "Hold on, boy."

Melanie dumped a small cup of dog food into his bowl and scrunched her nose together as the smell teased her nostrils. "Yuck! No wonder your breath smells so bad!"

Thankfully, the rest of the morning did not drag on so slowly. When her mother came down for breakfast, Melanie was more than ready to hop in the car and take off. Melanie just wanted to push all the noise deep inside her as she tackled the next stage of her life: a summer job. She was thankful that her mother had signed all the waivers to let her work early. Most people started working at sixteen, but Melanie had begged her mother to give her a chance once she had learned there were summer openings. When the school year started, she would have limited weekly hours. High school was going to require even more focus than in middle school. Melanie had seen the homework her sister brought home. Some days she wondered how in the world Amber did not have a hernia from carrying all those books home every night. Melanie was not looking forward to that.

When her mom parked the car, Melanie nearly banged her head on the car door; she was so excited to get moving. She turned to find her mother giving her a teasing smile. "I'm all right."

"Slow down a little, Mel. I don't want to write an accident report before you even get started."

"Mom! Ugh!" Melanie rolled her eyes and let out an irritated breath. "I'm fine. Missed it by a mile."

"Be more careful, though, will you?"

Melanie pushed the door closed with her palms. "See... missed my fingers too."

Her mother smirked and shook her head slightly. "Behave."

"I am. I'm sorry. I'm just too excited." Melanie swung her backpack over her shoulders.

"I can see that. I'm glad."

"Let's go." Melanie started to walk through the parking lot, not even bothering to look back to see if her mother was behind her. Her mom needed to kick it into gear. Daylight was wasting.

As Melanie walked down the long white hallway of the main office building, she took in the aquatic artwork on the walls and smiled. The images had been there forever, it seemed. To Melanie, they had been like old friends to her when she was younger. She had given each of them a name and a personality, creating many stories of adventures in her mind. Back then, she'd had a lot of time on her hands. Cancer had made it difficult for her to keep a regular public school schedule. On the days when her grandmother had to work, Melanie would go to work with her mother, taking all her homeschool work with her. When most of her assignments were finished, her mother would let her follow her around the park as she completed some of her duties. At times she would sit in for all the shows near the back where no one ever wanted to sit. A few of the workers would keep an eye on her, but Melanie had never been much trouble. She had been far too occupied with the animals in the shows to ever run off and get into anything.

Linda stopped just outside her office. "We have to check in with Mr. Marcus first."

Melanie felt her stomach flip over nervously. Raymond Marcus had always been kind to her, but this was a different situation altogether. Then, he had to be nice to her because she was Linda's daughter. Now, she would be working here too. There would be expectations to meet, and if she didn't meet them, she could lose her job. Even though her mother had a little pull over the situation, she could not count on her to keep her job. Melanie had even more to prove than other employees. She didn't want people to think she had just been handed this job, even though in a way she had been.

"Okay."

"Relax, Mel. You've known Mr. Marcus most of your life. It'll be fine."

Easy for her to say. Her mom had been working with him for quite some time now. Linda Parker did not have anything to prove. As a sixteen-year-old just starting her career at the aquarium, she had to make a good impression, especially if she wanted to use this on her resume later in life. Melanie was bound and determined to apply to be a junior trainer as soon as she could. The junior trainers at The Oasis Aquarium got to work with the animals one on one, under the direction of the aquarium trainers. Since this was what she wanted to do with her life, she would take any experience she could get. Her goal was to get a degree in animal science or zoology. Those were paths that could allow her to work with marine mammals.

Mr. Marcus must have been expecting them, for the moment they came into the main office, he stepped out of his small office to greet them. "Good morning, Linda. So this is our little Melanie."

Melanie fumed inwardly. She had not been little in quite

some time, and was a teenager, for crying out loud. Why did everyone always treat her like a child? It was beyond frustrating. Nevertheless, she kept her thoughts to herself. What was most interesting was the fact that Mr. Marcus was acting as if he hadn't just seen her in the aquarium last week with her mother. Was his attention span really that short?

"It's her first day as an official employee."

"Well, welcome to The Oasis Aquarium, Melanie. We're so happy that you can join our team. Has your mother given you the grand tour?"

"Mel, please, and I don't need a tour. I know this place inside out." Had he forgotten all the time she had spent here? Was he really that distracted?

"Mel's been coming with me since she was only four feet tall," Linda reminded him. She turned to see the irritation on Melanie's face and gave her a half-smile.

"Well, be sure to let me know if you need anything, Mel. We're a family here at The Oasis."

Were they? Were they really? Melanie doubted that. If they were, he would have remembered her. And then there was the overtime he had been making her mother work lately. Family should make lives easier for each other, not harder. Melanie hated to see the exhaustion on her mother's face. She worked far harder than she should have to. Add in the worry lines, and it completed the full package of a single mother who was just trying to juggle all the balls in her life.

"Mel, why don't you wait in my office until it's time for you to clock in? Mr. Marcus and I need to get our morning started," her mother suggested.

"Sure."

Melanie turned away from them and went into her mother's

office, which was just next door. She left the door open because she was far too curious about what office affairs they would be talking about this early in the morning.

"Your daughter's a go-getter, isn't she?"

Melanie shook her head. A go-getter? How did he know, considering he was acting as if he had never seen her at the aquarium? Was he always that preoccupied? Melanie continued to listen, even though she was tempted to put her earbuds in.

"That's my Mel."

"Well, on to our morning meeting. We need to talk about our new requisition."

"What's he done now?"

"Mr. Fillimore means well, but he has no idea how to run an aquarium. He's purchased a new dolphin. This one's going to need a lot of care from what I understand."

"Why's that?"

Mr. Marcus cleared his throat before he answered. "He called her wild and unruly."

Melanie heard those words and wondered what in the world that could mean. Was the dolphin violent? Did it attack others? Was it hard to manage? She was instantly curious, for she knew most of the dolphins at the aquarium. Stepping closer to the doorway, Melanie wanted to hear everything possible about the dolphin.

"Oh no, tell me it's not so. He didn't...." The irritation in Linda's voice was easy to hear.

"Yes, he bought a wild dolphin for the aquarium."

A wild dolphin? Melanie couldn't have heard that right. They'd never had a wild dolphin at The Oasis before, probably because it was a very bad idea. Melanie wondered what in the world they were going to do with it.

Her mother continued talking. "That man has no idea what he's doing. That poor thing. I'm sure Julia will do everything she can to make her comfortable here."

"We have our work cut out for us. Let's go over our numbers for the week, shall we, Linda?"

"Yes."

Melanie stepped away from the door and slid into the chair near the wall. Glancing down at her phone, she blew out a frustrated breath. Still, a half-hour before she could clock in. If only she could clock in earlier instead of being caged inside this room. Melanie was usually pretty patient, but today she was too anxious to sit still. While she could be dwelling on the tests done the day before, all she thought about right now was the day that loomed ahead of her. Would she still love her job at the end of the day? Or would she want to run the other way?

For the next several minutes, she tried to distract herself with her phone. When her mother came back into her office, she almost popped out of her chair. "Can I go now?"

"Yes, you can." Linda pointed to the door. "Have fun!"

"Great. See you later!"

Melanie turned away from them and fought the urge to race out of the room. There was no time to waste. Today was going to be the best day ever, even if she ended up smelling like rotten fish by the end of the day. Melanie was determined to make the best of it.

Melanie barely took in the world around her as she made her way across the aquarium to the dolphin feeding exhibit. She stood in front of the small booth where they sold fish at different times throughout the day. Melanie had fed the dolphins many times over. The dolphins were always hungry for fish, but there were select times that the exhibit was open, because otherwise they could become overfed. The number of trays sold were also monitored for the same reason. Melanie imagined the job would not be that difficult. Then again, she had never had to do it before, so there was no real way of knowing.

Taking a deep breath, she opened the door and found the day was already getting started. Two people were already inside the booth, busy with early morning preparations. Melanie had seen one of them before. Julia Makenzie was one of the animal trainers in the dolphin exhibit. Julia was already dressed in her wetsuit and had her long blonde hair pulled into a tight ponytail at the back of her head, her usual hairstyle, as she had to spend a good part of her day near the water with the marine life. Julia was her favorite trainer at The Oasis, even though there were two others. Julia seemed the more approachable of the three. One day, Melanie hoped to work with her as a junior trainer. She just had to make a good impression and prove that she deserved it. Not every person who applied got the chance, and even though her mother was the assistant manager at The Oasis, she did not want to be handed a job because of it.

"Hello?"

Melanie's voice was hesitant at first. Maybe it was because she had never had a conversation with Julia before. Or it could have been the boy who stood beside her? He had the same blond hair and blue eyes as Julia, making her wonder if the two were related. When he turned to find her staring at him, she felt a small hot flush climb up her face. Melanie had never really talked to boys her age before, not since she had hit puberty. She found the whole process embarrassing and awkward. Other girls her age had already been boy crazy for years. Melanie had never much thought about them, not until she saw the one standing in front of her. Now that she had, she was having trouble remembering what it was she had come here for.

Julia's face brightened with a smile. "You must be Linda's girl. Melanie, right? You're just in time to help Chase get the fish ready."

"Hope you're not squeamish," he teased her.

If she had not been blushing before, she was sure blushing now. Did he wink at her too? She started to feel like she had swallowed a handful of Red Hots, for her face was on fire. Melanie dug deep to find a voice that wasn't shaking. "Not at all. So, what do you need me to do?"

Chase pointed to the front. "I'll be manning the registers, and you'll make sure we keep up with the orders."

"Remember, no more than a hundred trays. Can't let them overeat," Julia reminded them.

"This isn't my first rodeo, Mom." Chase shook his head at his mom.

Julia let out a small sigh. "No, but it is hers. Chase knows this job inside and out."

"Yes, I do. We got this. Don't you have a dolphin to train or something?" Chase waved her off with his hands.

Julia rolled her eyes at her son. "Teenagers."

"Mothers," Chase shot back at her.

Julia shook her head at him. "Well, good luck. Looks like we're going to be at peak today."

Melanie watched her leave the booth and turned to look down at the trays. "So how many fish per tray?"

Chase pointed to a small poster. "The chart is right by the wall there. It's pretty easy. Stinky, but easy."

Melanie snorted. "Bet you're glad you graduated to the cash register."

"Maybe." His grin told her more than his words. He was

definitely glad to be manning the register instead of sorting the fish. Of course, he was. Who wouldn't be?

In the back was a refrigerator filled with fish. Several paper containers were already lined up on a long table behind the counter. Some of them were filled with small sardines that people would take to feed the dolphins. Melanie wrinkled her nose at the smell and grimaced slightly. "So how long will it take to get the stench off me?"

"Years," he teased her.

"Great. My cat and dog will be following me around forever." She sighed dramatically.

Chase looked stumped. "Dog? I get the cat following you, but the dog?"

"He thinks he's a cat," Melanie attempted to explain. She knew that it would not make sense to anyone who had never seen River before.

"A dog that thinks he's a cat? Now I've heard everything." His grin showcased the two dimples at the corners of his mouth.

"It's true. He even tried to perch on Nite's cat tree. After it crashed down for the tenth time, we had to make one that he could climb on. It's in my sister's room." Melanie pulled out her phone and showed him a picture of the cat tree, where both animals were lounging on it in her sister's room.

"That's not something you see every day." His eyebrows rose in surprise.

"Told you. Cat-dog. It's a thing." Melanie pointed to her phone.

"So, do you go to Montgomery?"

Melanie wondered why he was asking that. Just to be nice? "I do, I'll be a junior."

"A junior? I wonder why I've never seen you in the halls."

She hadn't seen him either. There was no way she would have missed noticing him. "It's a big school." She shrugged, a bit selfconscious. "I prefer to blend in with the masses."

"I believe I would have still noticed you."

Melanie felt the heat rises to her cheeks. Would he really? She clears her throat uncomfortably to get the topic off herself. "So, are you a junior too?"

"I'll be a senior this year. Just got my license." He held his head higher as if having a driver's license gave him a sense of superiority.

"Nice." That meant he was at least seventeen, not that Melanie would be asking him anytime soon, even though she was deeply curious about it. Her sister would tease her endlessly if she knew she was already developing a crush on him if that's what this was. Did thinking a boy was cute make it a crush? Or was it just a reflection? Melanie tried to shove those thoughts away, but her whole brain seemed stuck on them. Ugh, yes, this was a crush. She didn't even know him. But she wanted to, her inner voice told her.

"It would be if I had a car, but at least I can save up for one," Chase lamented as he started to get his register ready for the day.

That was her cue to get started on the trays. Melanie put her phone back in her pocket and looked at the directions for the fish trays. Seven fish per tray, no more, no less. Everything was measured out to make sure none of the dolphins were overfed. Melanie saw the tiny sardines staring up at her with their glassy eyes and looked away. It was as if they were all giving her the eye. She was pretty sure those eyes would haunt her in her sleep if she didn't get a handle on this real fast. Melanie was going to have to focus on the tails instead.

The smell was overpowering. She had never figured this into

the pros and cons of working in a tiny shack with the summer sun pounding down on it. Sure, it was air-conditioned, but it was going to be pungent by the end of the day regardless. The Arizona sun had a way of overpowering everything else. This was definitely going to be disgusting, but to get to where she wanted to be, she had to start somewhere. Melanie gave in and was about to pick up some of the fish when Chase handed her gloves.

"Trust me. You'll want these."

Melanie took the gloves from his hands and felt another wave of self-consciousness fall over her when his fingers touched hers. She cleared her throat before she uttered another word. "Thanks."

"Well, time to get to it. Don't worry. It will go faster than you think."

Well, that was a good thing, right? She turned to the trays and got to work. One fish, two…soon she was up to the hundreds as she filled one tray after the other, and that was before any of the people even started to line up for fish. Melanie carried tray after tray over to the counter as she saw the lines multiply with each session. In between feeding times, they had to stock the fridge with more fish, but at least that meant they could leave the small booth. Every time the feeding times opened up, they were swarmed with people.

By the time their shift was over, Melanie was more than ready to leave the booth behind her. Even so, she had still had a blast working with Chase. He had an upbeat air about him that made transitioning into her summer job more fun than she had thought it would be. Melanie tried to keep up with the crowds, but eventually, he had to help her fill trays. She was thankful for his help, even though it made her feel like she didn't know how to do her job well enough.

"Is it always that bad?" Melanie asked him.

"Some days are even worse."

"Sorry you had to help me." Melanie looked away when his eyes met hers.

"Are you kidding me? We're a team here, Melanie. We make it work together."

"Mel."

"What?"

"You can call me Mel. That's what my friends call me." Had she just implied they were friends? Sure, dig the hole deeper, Melanie. That's all she needed.

"Okay. Mel. You did better than I did my first day. Aaron about shoved me to the side to do half my work for me. He never let me forget it, either."

"Sounds like a jerk."

"He was, but he's moved on finally. Seniors…they think they know everything."

"I wouldn't know. I haven't met any yet. My sister Amber is seventeen. She's going to be a senior this year too."

"Amber Parker? I think I've seen her around. We've been in a few classes together. She's pretty quiet, really."

"Who? Amber?" Melanie snorted. She never saw her sister as the quiet sort. Amber was certainly not going to be quiet about this. When she found out she had a crush on one of her classmates, Amber would not let her live it down.

"Yeah. Then again, you can't hold a candle to Olivia Johnston. That girl never shuts up. She and her friends are like a pack of hyenas." Chase rolled his eyes and shuddered.

So, he wasn't into popular girls. Not that it meant she had a chance at all. Was she even vying for one after just a few hours working with him? Melanie was in unchartered waters for sure.

"I'll take your word for it."

"So, you work tomorrow too?" Chase asked her as he closed up the register. The dolphin experience was closing for the day, so all they had to do now was make sure it was cleaned up and ready for the next shift tomorrow.

"Yeah. You?" Was it too much to hope she worked every shift with him?

"Bright and early." He pulled out his phone and opened up his contacts. "What's your number?"

What? Was he asking her for her number? Melanie took the phone from his hand and entered her digits. "There."

"Thanks. This way, if we ever need to switch shifts, we can text each other."

Oh. That's what he wanted it for? Melanie felt a little deflated. She had been hoping he wanted it for other reasons. She tried to play it cool. "Good idea."

"Looks like we're done here." He nodded to the back door. "Time to call it a day."

"Yep. See you tomorrow."

As Melanie left the tiny shack, she couldn't help thinking tomorrow would not come soon enough.

CHAPTER 4

Two weeks later, Melanie was starting to feel like she had worked at the aquarium half of her life. The hours would have bled into each other if she didn't have Chase to break up the monotony. So far, she had worked every shift with him, something her friend Hannah had teased her mercilessly about. Hannah was a friend from the cancer support group she had started attending the moment she had been diagnosed with leukemia. It was a safe haven for kids like Melanie, who were trying to navigate everyday life with the cloud of cancer hanging over their heads. A tentative remission was something that she and Hannah had in common. NED, was what came before an official remission label, though. Having no evidence of disease was what every kid and parent hoped for.

Melanie read through the messages that Hannah had sent her last night. Today their friend Lori was heading back to the hospital. Melanie was trying to pretend that everything was going to be all right, but deep down, she knew something was wrong this time. The treatment had not done its job right now, but that didn't mean they wouldn't figure something out. They had to, right? Melanie wasn't ready to lose another friend. Their group had eight kids in it when Melanie had joined them. Over the past three years, it had dwindled in size. One of them had graduated from the group, moving into her adulthood with an ease that Melanie appreciated. John was now in college and had very little time for the group. Two of the other kids had lost their battle over the past two years. Melanie tried not to think about it, but it was inevitable.

Picking up the framed photo on her dresser, she ran her fingers over the edge. To say this didn't scare her would be an outright lie. Lori had been NED the longest. She had been so close to complete remission. It was just another reminder that life was limited and that they needed to leave their mark on it where they could. Nothing was forever, but some names lived on for infinity. Benjamin Franklin, Thomas Jefferson, Rosa Parks, Albert Einstein, Gandhi—all names that were part of history. Melanie wasn't sure she would ever be one of them, but she refused to think her time on this world was meaningless. If so, what was the point of fighting so hard?

Melanie set the picture down and tried to shake off the cloud that hung over her. Lori was going to be fine. She had to be. She texted Hannah and asked her to let her know what she heard. Hannah's parents were close to Lori's, which meant Hannah would learn more about Lori's situation before anyone else. Afterward, she sent Lori a quick message with a silly cat image. Cats had become their staple years ago, from the silly hang in there poster they had seen at the hospital. Melanie knew it would not heal her cancer, but if it at least made her smile, then her mission was accomplished. It was sometimes the little things that got them through.

Walking over to her mirror, Melanie ran a brush through her wet hair. She picked up one of her scrunchies and quickly pulled it back into a ponytail, which was the most efficient hairdo while working inside the booth. At least that way, none of the fish got in her hair, although there were times that she could swear it had, for the smell seemed to follow her around everywhere she went. So did Nite, who was looking for a free bite. River would sniff her, but was not as glued to her side, thankfully. While it was probably one of the grossest things she had ever done, Melanie was resigned to doing the best job she could. Today, she could certainly use the distraction.

At least she had lucked out in her hours and got to work with Chase most of the time. He was much nicer than she thought he would be for someone who looked like the captain of the baseball team or something. He was pretty down to earth and easy to talk to. She liked that about him. Well, she liked a lot about him if she were honest with herself. Melanie was still trying to figure out what to do with those feelings. This was not something she had ever considered before, as her world had revolved around doctors' visits and hospital cafeteria food for far too long. No one needed to know she was feeling just a little boy crazy right now, although she was pretty sure Amber would not hold that against her. Amber actually knew a few of Chase's friends, some of which she was interested in herself. Amber had not picked up on the embarrassing crush that was forming, but Melanie knew it was only a matter of time.

Straightening her uniform, Melanie nodded to herself in the mirror before she turned around and left her room. She walked down the stairs and headed into the living room, where she plopped down on the couch next to Kimmie. Amber was sitting in the chair next to the couch, and the two of them were watching some kind of baking challenge show. Kimmie was on a cooking fix lately. The nine-year-old was obsessed with learning different recipes and hacks for making desserts even tastier. Melanie would not be surprised if that kid ended up being the next Top Chef someday.

For now, though, Kimmie was resigned to baking with Grandma Mimi, because none of the adults trusted the kid to make something on her own. Not that Melanie blamed them. Kimmie was the daredevil in the family, the one person who would often leap before looking to make sure her landing was clear. One time, Kimmie had tried to boil some eggs but had become distracted from it. Before they knew it, the kitchen was filled with the sound of exploding eggs when the water had evaporated entirely from the pot. It had taken hours to clean the egg off the ceiling.

When the commercial break came on, Kimmie turned to her and wrinkled her nose in disgust. "Eew! You still smell like fish. Yuck! Didn't you shower last night too? It's only been a few days, but it's like your pores ooze Eau' de Poisson."

"Whatever. It doesn't bother me." Melanie shrugged off her words. Her head tilted down slightly to see if her sister was right. Melanie did not want to go to work smelling like fish. What if Chase could smell it? Maybe she should spray on some of her sister's perfume. Then again, that might make the fish smell worse. Mixing fruit and fish together was probably not the best idea.

"Not even when you get to work with Chase Makenzie," Amber teased her.

"Ooooh! Who's that?" Kimmie folded her hands together and pushed them down so she could cradle her head dramatically. She batted her eyes and made the big lip pouty face that a lot of girls did on their social media accounts. She looked like she was making fish lips or something.

"He's just a guy I work with." Melanie picked up a pillow from the couch and reached over to bonk first Kimmie, then

Amber. Kimmie shrieked in outrage and fell onto her back so she could start kicking her with her feet. She would have deflected the kicks with the pillow, but Amber had already yanked it out of her hand.

"Kimmie, enough!" Melanie held her hands up. She tilted her head at Amber and sent her a glare. "And we're just friends, by the way."

Amber let out a small snort of laughter. "Uh-huh. Sure. I see the way your face lights up whenever his name is mentioned."

Melanie felt her face start to flame up like a log covered in lighter fluid. Was she right? She couldn't be right, could she? Melanie felt like sinking into the ground and hiding out there for the rest of eternity. "It does not."

"What's wrong with her?" Kimmie looked at her as if she had grown a horn.

"She's crushing."

Amber dodged the other pillow that Melanie threw at her. River yelped as it landed against him. Then he grabbed the pillow in his teeth and started to shake it with a slow rumble in his chest.

"Crushing?" Kimmie's eyes narrowed on Melanie. "Ewww! You like a boy?!"

"I do not!"

"She does! Look, her face is turning red now!" Kimmie was enjoying this, even though the little rug rat didn't know what she was talking about. "Mel and Chase sitting in a tree...K-I-S-S—Ouch! What did you do that for?"

Melanie retracted the fingers she had used to pinch her sister on the arm. "Because you're being annoying!"

"Am not!" Kimmie stuck out her tongue and blew her a raspberry.

"Are so!" Melanie rolled her eyes at her sister.

Kimmie hopped up from the chair and farted in her face. "How's that for annoying?"

"Dude, no more crop dusting!" Melanie held her nose and waved away the wafting stench.

"Seriously, Kimmie? Ugh...that's disgusting! And you thought that fish smell was bad."

"Sorry, not sorry," Kimmie taunted them, cocking her butt like she was ready to go again. River turned to look at her, and his nose started to sniff the air. He put his head down on the floor and covered it with a paw with a slight whine.

"Careful, you're going to knock River out with that noxious odor," warned Amber.

"Am not! That's Mel! It's all those fish guts in her hair," taunted Kimmie.

"Ugh! They are not in my hair!" Or were they? Melanie was instantly worried that she had missed something on the back of her hair. Her hand rose to smooth over her hair, and her sister cackled at her.

"Made you look!" Kimmie almost fell over; she was laughing so hard.

Melanie fought the urge to feel irritated with her. The thing was, Kimmie's crazy antics were just what Melanie needed this morning. It made it a lot easier to shake off the worry that threatened to take over her. Instead of retaliating, Melanie just shook her head at Kimmie. "Just you wait. I'll find a way to get you back when you least expect it."

"Ooooh! I'm so worried." Kimmie rolled her eyes as she plopped back down on the couch.

"I just might have to help her," Amber added.

"You'll have to sleep with one eye open," warned Melanie.

"One eye open? You can't sleep with one eye open. Your eye

would dry out," Kimmie pointed out.

"She's got a point, Mel. Maybe you should just hide something slimy in her bed before she gets into it."

"Ugh! I'll just sleep under it."

"But then, where will the monster sleep?" Melanie teased her.

"Monster, sh-monster. There's no such thing." Kimmie crossed her arms over her chest, clearly not falling for their empty threats. "Besides, River will keep me safe, won't you, boy?"

River gave her a lazy glance but refused to get up. He was in cat-dog mode now. Unless they got the red laser pointer out, he would be there for the rest of the morning. His tail swished across the floor with an ease that had taken years to acquire.

Melanie was about to tease Kimmie more when a slight tickle irritated her throat. As she tried to fight it, a large coughing spasm shook her. It was almost as if she had swallowed spit down the wrong hole. Melanie had a few coughing spasms here and there, but this one lasted longer than others, and she almost felt like she hacked a lung up into the crook of her arm. When she turned to look at her sisters, the smile had dropped from Amber's face.

"You all right, Mel?" The concern was etched on Amber's face. Amber had seen her in her highs and lows, been at her side through every moment of her cancer. She was like a miniature mom, where Melanie was concerned.

"It's just allergies. And don't tell Mom. She'll just worry." That was what Mom did best these days. Worry. Always. Not that Melanie could blame her. Melanie had given her more than enough to worry about in one lifetime. She certainly did not want to add to it.

Melanie did not miss the look that passed between her sisters. To say they were not an average family like everyone else was an understatement. They had all lived through some pretty bad times over the past five years. It had taken its toll on all of them. She knew they were worried too. Of course, they were. Melanie was a little concerned too, but she could not give in to the fear that a relapse was right around the corner. Nor would she tell her sisters that Lori was back in the hospital. It would just set them into a hyper vigilant mode. Melanie was just starting to feel like a normal teenager.

"Mel...." Kimmie's bottom lip wobbled slightly. "You okay?"

"I'm fine. I promise. Besides, the last labs were fine—just a little heightened. If I feel worse, I'll tell her. I promise."

"Okay, but if you start hacking up a lung, I'm telling her anyway." Amber crossed her arms over her chest as if to punctuate how serious she was.

Melanie held her hand out and waved her words away. "You won't have to. I'm sure she'd notice."

Kimmie sneezed, and a slight panic filled her face. Amber rolled her eyes and tossed the pillow at her. "Relax, dweeb. Cancer's not contagious."

"I know that...," Kimmie mumbled as she looked down to the floor.

"Whatever." Melanie rolled her eyes and tried not to be irritated with them. "I don't have it anyway."

At that moment, their mother strolled through the room in her usual get-to-work rush. When she saw the three of them sitting at odd angles, her eyes focused on them with an almost laser precision. "Am I missing something?"

The three of them answered her unanimously. "No!"

Linda became even more suspicious. "You sure about that?"

Melanie gave her sisters a quiet glare that she knew they would interpret as an order to be quiet. "Yes. We're all fine. Are you ready to head in?"

Her mother's mouth turned into a half-smile, even though it looked as if she were ready to press it further. "Sure."

Melanie pushed up from the couch and followed her mother, who was already standing at the door. When Melanie made it to the door, she turned around to her sisters and waited to make sure they were watching. She split her fingers and pointed to her eyes, then turned to point her fingers at them. It was a warning that she had her eyes on them, and they'd better not squeal.

Melanie did not want to go back to the doctor over a stupid cough. That was not on her list of things to do any time soon. For now, all she wanted to do was lose herself in her work and forget the fear that had already implanted itself inside her long ago.

CHAPTER 5

As soon as they made it to the aquarium, all her worries melted away. Every day she worked was like that. Melanie loved being there, even if she hated smelling like nasty fish at the end of the day. The fact that she got to stare at Chase whenever he wasn't looking was a bonus, as long as he didn't notice. Melanie wasn't sure she wouldn't know what to do if he did notice. Dig a hole to China? Run as fast as her legs could carry her? Neither one of them were viable options. That would only make it even more uncomfortable. Besides, if she tried to run, Melanie would probably trip over her feet in the process. That would make an embarrassing situation completely unlivable.

"It's too early to clock in. You want to follow me on my rounds?" Linda suggested.

"Sure."

It wasn't like Melanie had anything better to do. Chase wouldn't be there until right before their shift anyway, so hanging out with him wasn't an option, even though she wished it was. Instead, she would help her mom get a jump start on the inventory she took every week. It was the part of her job that was the worst because they were always out of something crucial due to ill planning on the owner's part. That man liked to cut any corner possible. Melanie had heard all about it when her mother complained to Grandma Mimi. Those were times when she was supposed to be sleeping, but chose to creep into the hallway and listen to the adult conversation downstairs. Melanie couldn't help it. Sometimes hearing her mom's voice helped her fall asleep, but usually only if it wasn't covered in concern for her health. Listening to her issues from work was infinitely more gratifying, not because she wanted her mom to hate work, but because it made her feel like her life was normal. Adults hated their work sometimes, too, just like kids hated homework. How human.

"We're checking the bathrooms first. You know how busy it can get."

"Yep."

Some days the cleaning staff forget to fill up the toilet paper dispensers. That was not a good situation to walk into at all, especially if she was the one that needed to use the restroom. Melanie had learned a long time ago to make sure there was toilet paper in the stall before she even used the restroom. It was a lesson that every girl learned at some point in time.

As they walked to the employee restrooms, Melanie saw one of the dolphins swimming alone in the isolation tank, which was kept away from the public. It was a female dolphin, one that had been brought to the aquarium the week Melanie had started. This was the first time Melanie had a chance to see her closer. The dolphin was in a private viewing tank for the trainers, one that Melanie rarely had access to. The only reason she could see her now was because her mother had brought her back here with her. From what Melanie understood, she had been taken from the wild and held in captivity at one of the other aquariums. It was clear to Melanie why the dolphin had not lasted long, as it darted back and forth, searching for any way out. When it came close enough to smash its nose on the glass, it turned at just the last moment.

"Is she okay?" Melanie was already worried about the dolphin. This was not the right place for it.

"The dolphin? I suppose. They all do this at first." Linda stood beside her for a moment.

"Sure seems cruel to put her by herself," Melanie frowned. Melanie could not imagine what it must feel like to be so isolated. Even when she was at her worst, she had her family surrounding her. At times she almost wished she had more space, but Melanie was still thankful for them.

"It's safer that way, though. Gives them time to make sure the dolphins are healthy enough to join the others."

"I get that, but she just looks so miserable," Melanie sighed thoughtfully.

Walking over to the tank, she put her hand against the glass. Part of her wished she could hop inside and comfort the dolphin, but she knew that was not a wise idea. This dolphin was not born in captivity, she was wild and would probably see her as a threat. There was no telling what a wild animal would do. She wasn't even sure she would blame it. From what she understood, the way dolphins were captured in the yearly dolphin drives was traumatizing, and even deadly to some of them. One day they were swimming away in the ocean with no care in the world; the next, the hunters used their fears against them, corralling them in their terror before they were thrown over the side of their boats. Some were sold for food, others to private collectors and aquariums that were only interested in exploiting them. Melanie felt sick to know that The Oasis was one of those places, but there was very little she could do about it except hope that this dolphin made it out okay in the end.

Melanie was reasonably sure that the rest of the dolphins at The Oasis had never known any other life than living at an aquarium. None of them had been born here, but all of them had come from other aquariums that had an actual breeding facility to manage pregnancies. All of the dolphins here were female, and it would probably always remain that way. It was far easier to purchase a new dolphin than do the care necessary to birth one at the aquarium. The trainers that were here loved the animals. That was a certainty. Unfortunately, their thoughts were only listened to by the management, who could never really count on the owners to listen to their concerns. All they could do was care for them the best that they were allowed to. While no rules were broken, Melanie still was concerned about the animals' welfare.

"Poor thing. What are they calling her?" Melanie turned to her mom.

"Sandy." Her mom glanced down at her checklist again.

"That's a horrible name. It doesn't fit her at all."

Melanie crossed her arms in front of her as she watched the dolphin float to the top of the water to get a breath of air through her blowhole. She had always thought it fascinating that some marine life could breathe above water, especially considering there was no way Melanie could live under the water without equipment. They were remarkable creatures.

Even though Linda was incredibly busy, she stopped to listen to her daughter. "What would you call her, Mel?"

"I don't know. I have to get to know her first." A loud peeling sound interrupted her. She glared at the timer on her backpack and grumbled. "Not again."

"Time for—" Linda started to say.

"Mom! I know! Gahhh!" Why did her mother always treat her like a child? She had not stopped taking medicine since she was diagnosed years ago. Melanie just hoped she would not be on this disgusting stuff for the rest of her life. Most of them were to keep the cancer at bay. Some were vitamins to keep her strength up. Most times, there were too many to count, so much so that she often felt like a walking pharmacy.

Unzipping her bag, she pulled out the offensive container that held her daily medicine. When they had received her last blood work, there had been a slight anomaly. Dr. Strand had ordered more tests, which Melanie was still trying to forget. CT scans were never her favorite, but at least she got to watch a movie while she was trapped inside the cylinder. The bone marrow aspiration was still something she would never get used to. She shivered just thinking about the needle sucking marrow from her bones. It was the after-effects that were the worst since she was always asleep when they took it. After all the tests came back, her levels were slightly elevated—not enough for Dr. Strand to believe the cancer was back, but enough for her to up the dose on some of her medicine.

Medicine. She hated all of it. If she never had to swallow another bitter pill, Melanie would be ecstatic. Unfortunately, those days were nowhere near the present. She had no choice but to suck it up and take her medicine. Sitting down on the ground, she placed it next to her on the cement and pulled out a bottle of water. Melanie scrunched her nose shut as she swallowed the first round of pills. If she did not breathe when she swallowed, the taste was more bearable. Gulping down a few glugs of water, she closed her eyes and willed the pills to do their job once and for all, before pulling the others out. She repeated the process and put her head on her knees.

"I know this is hard, Mel, but we're almost there, honey." Her mom forced a smile, but the fact that tears now shone on the rims of her eyes communicated her true feelings.

"Right."

Melanie looked away from her before her own sadness was reflected on her face. It was hard to have a body riddled with an invisible disease. Melanie was regularly taking medicine that made her feel like her body was a puppet to some unknown master. Even now, when her life was supposed to be getting back to normal, her strings were still being pulled this way and that. And there was no guarantee that it would keep it at bay forever. Just look at Lori. Melanie closed her eyes and willed her thoughts not to turn back to Hannah's messages. Part of her wished Hannah had never told her, but that was only a small part. Melanie knew that the two of them would be there for her in a heartbeat, no questions asked. She would do the same for them. Maybe later, she could ask her mom to schedule a trip to visit Lori. At the very least, Melanie would plan a video chat with her soon.

Melanie wished she could turn back the clock to the time when cancer had not existed in her life. Everything had been so much easier then. Her life had become nothing but single moments of happiness, and usually, the worst part was dealing with the cancer, but that was not always the hard part. Pretending to be strong, when Melanie felt like she was just a moment from giving up…that was the worst. There had been days when Melanie doubted her own strength, but she could not let anyone else see that. Even at nine, she had known that it was her resolve to live that kept all their pieces together. Everyone had tried to put on a brave face, but at times their sorrow cut through the surface, and Melanie had been the one to broadcast a sunny smile to them when her insides felt like they were on fire. Melanie gave them hope because she could not bear to see them so broken.

Those days were far behind her—at least that was what she

tried to tell herself. The one thing she could not do was give in to her doubts. Even now, she told herself that Lori was going to be all right. They all were. There was no other choice for them. Fight or die wasn't a chant they had ever taken on. Fight and live was the only one they had.

Melanie turned to look at her mom and plastered a bright smile on her face. "All gone."

Her mother gave her a slow smile and nodded to the bathrooms ahead of her. "I need to check the bathrooms."

"No problem. I'm just going to stay here if that's okay. My shift doesn't start for a while." Melanie wanted to be alone for just a moment. All she wanted was a little time to shake the thoughts from her head before her mother had a chance to catch on.

Melanie continued to stare into the isolation tank. The dolphin was zipping back and forth at a slower rate than most of the other dolphins.

"You poor thing." Melanie put her hand on the glass and sighed. "It's like being trapped in a tiny bubble when you've had a whole world to explore."

As if it heard her words, the dolphin stopped right before her hand and appeared to be looking directly at Melanie.

"Hello, there. Sandy, is it?"

The dolphin tilted her head as if she were listening intently to her every word. Melanie looked into the eye closest to her and almost felt like she could see into her soul.

"You're not a Sandy, not like these other dolphins. You're not used to the sandy shores or the desert heat around here. You're more like an island, aren't you, girl?"

The dolphin bobbed in the water slightly before rising to the surface where Melanie could barely see her. Then the dolphin dove back into the water and swam near the glass next to her.

Her actions were almost a language in itself. Did she agree with Melanie?

"An island, eh? Blue waters, palm trees? Have you ever been to Hawaii? You remind me of a Kona. I think that's what I'll call you."

Kona watched as if she truly understood what Melanie was saying to her. Melanie moved from one side of the tank to the other, and Kona followed her. She jumped up and down, and Kona mimicked her. Melanie giggled aloud at her antics, and Kona sang a sweet song to her.

"You're amazing, girl!"

Melanie nearly jumped out of her skin when Mr. Marcus interrupted her.

"Good morning, Mel. You're here early."

Melanie tried to take a deep breath to still her racing heart but ended up coughing slightly. "I came with my mom. She wanted to get a head start on the inventory."

Mr. Marcus grinned at her. "She beat me here again. Are you watching Sandy?"

"She's beautiful. My mom said she's been depressed, though." Melanie probably should not bring that up, but she could seem to help herself. Melanie wanted to know everything about the dolphin.

"She's having a little trouble adapting. We're hoping it will turn around for her soon."

At least he looked concerned. Melanie knew that he was not the enemy here. From what her mother had told her before, Mr. Marcus was a huge animal advocate who did what he could from the sidelines to help the animals that they housed in the aquarium. Melanie wished there was more they could do to keep the owner from making such irresponsible choices, but as long as no rules were broken, he could pretty much get away with anything.

"Well, I should probably see if there's anything I can do to help my mom."

Melanie walked over to retrieve her bag. As she did, Kona followed her every movement. The dolphin stopped just short of where the glass wall met the cement. Her eyes were watching Melanie intently all the while.

"Hold on, Mel. Do that again," Mr. Marcus interrupted her.

"What did I do?"

Mr. Marcus shook his finger, then pointed to the other end of the tank. "Just...just walk to the other side of the tank."

"O-kay." Melanie did as he asked, even though she was not quite sure why.

Mr. Marcus watched as Melanie moved past the tank. Kona followed her every step of the way. "Well, I'll be. Let me get Julia."

Melanie stopped short, now alarmed. Had she done something wrong? When she spoke, she nearly squeaked. "What? Why?"

"Nothing to worry about, Mel. She just needs to see this."

Melanie waited there, and as she did, her stomach started to churn furiously. By the time Julia returned with Mr. Marcus, Melanie had thought she was going to puke. It wasn't like she had made the dolphin do anything. All she did was talk to her. Kicking the floor absently with her foot, Melanie wondered what would happen next, and if they would be dragging Chase along too. That would be incredibly embarrassing. Please let him be anywhere but here right now.

When Mr. Marcus returned, he smiled at her. "Melanie, show Julia."

"What? This?" Melanie moved across the glass, and Kona

followed her once again. The dolphin's sweet cherubic face seemed to light up as she swam near Melanie.

"Wow. I think she likes you." Julia's voice was surprised.

"Remarkable. I wonder what she would do if you introduced the two of them topside," Mr. Marcus suggested.

Julia debated that for a moment. "That could be worth trying."

Melanie glanced at Mr. Marcus. Was he being serious? "Really?"

Mr. Marcus shrugged his shoulders. "I don't see why not."

"Come with me, Melanie." Julia waved her closer with her hand.

"Wait, I just need to check in with my mom."

Melanie raced into the bathroom and found her mom checking the supplies in the bathroom closet.

"Mom, Julia wants me to help her with something. Is that okay?"

Linda gave her daughter a half-smile. "I suppose. As long as you're not in the way, and you don't miss your shift."

"Awesome! Thanks, Mom!" Melanie raced over to the stall and slid across the wet floor and almost upended herself. Reaching for the door, she steadied herself and giggled. When she regained her balance, she threw her arms around her mom's neck.

"Watch out! They just finished the floors!" Linda warned her.

"Love you, Mom!"

"I love you too, kiddo." Linda hugged her tight. "Now, shoo you. Go on now. Have some fun!"

CHAPTER 6

Melanie followed Julia, feeling a little excited for the first time in months. She had no idea what they were about to do, not really. Her stomach felt like a thousand butterflies were ready to burst free. Was this really happening? Was Julia going to take her topside where the trainers worked one on one with the dolphins? "Where are we going?"

"To the pool, where Sandy can see you from above the water." Julia was already in one of the park wetsuits and had pulled her blonde hair in a ponytail behind her head. She had the air of someone ready to hop in the pool with the animals at any given moment. "We should probably put you in different clothes, though. I'd hate for you to get your work clothes wet."

"Am I getting in the water?" Melanie felt a nervous excitement floating inside her. She had always wanted to swim with the dolphins, but something told her that this was probably not the right moment for that, not with the way the wild dolphin had been acting lately.

"No. But you might get wet, and if you don't have a change of clothes, you'll be smelling like tank water for the rest of the day. I'm sure we have some shorts and a shirt in your size."

"Thanks. Where's Chase?" Melanie didn't know why she

opened her mouth to ask. She had assumed he would be here at the aquarium if his mom was already here.

"He's doing a few errands right now. He'll be here in a bit."

"Wait, you let him drive?" Melanie almost clasped her hand over her mouth. She did not mean to make it sound like she was crazy for letting him take her car. It has just been a running joke between the two of them lately.

"Crazy, right? But it saves me a trip later. Here we are." Julia led Melanie into the locker room, where the trainers changed. She pulled out some clothes from a pile near the door and handed them to her. "There are a few changing rooms right there."

Melanie nodded to Julia before racing to the first open changing room. Quickly changing into the clothes she'd been given, Melanie then folded her own into a small pile that she shoved into her backpack. Melanie tucked her shirt in the shorts and double-checked her shoelaces. Taking a deep breath, she tried to calm her racing heart. This was probably going to be her favorite day in all the history of days. While it had a bumpy start, Melanie was pretty sure it was going to be epic very soon.

Glancing in the mirror, Melanie was surprised to find a pink flush on her face. Lately, every time she looked in the mirror, she looked pale. She tried not to let that get to her because the fear inside her was almost too much to handle most days. Her mother tried to reassure her that it was her body dealing with the medication while it found its new normal. This was true, but part of it was the fact that she had spent very little time out in the sun. Even this summer, she would be stuck in the shade all the time. Melanie was pretty sure her mother liked it that way. Linda was adamant about preventing any form of cancer now and had even taken to buy more organic food to keep all the chemicals away. That had been a lot to adjust to, but in the end, they would all be healthier for it, so Melanie couldn't complain.

Melanie sighed as she remembered the times when she had done other things. Dancing, gymnastics. They had both been part of her childhood until she no longer felt like she was able to keep up with them. Not to mention the toll it had taken on her mother's bank account. After paying for all her extra medications and doctor's visits, it had become a financial strain. Sure, some programs covered her treatments while in the hospital, but other bills crept up on them from the cracks, making it hard for them to stay afloat.

Melanie closed her eyes and reminded herself that this was not the time to dwell on those things. This was going to be a good day, one that would last in her memories forever. It could be the beginning of something amazing. When she opened her eyes, all she had on her mind was the dolphin that she was about to meet.

Melanie opened the door and gave Julia a shy smile. "I'm ready...I think."

"Great. So, what I was thinking was we would just have you sit close to the island and see if Sandy will come up to you. Sound good, Melanie?"

"Sure, Julia." She could not wait to see Kona up close.

Melanie did not have to tell anyone else the name she had chosen for the dolphin. Kona would never be a Sandy to her. The dolphin had never belonged in the desert heat. None of these animals did, but that did not seem to stop the owner from buying more and more of them. Nor did it stop the people from buying the tickets to come to see them. Supply and demand caused people to make decisions that were uneducated and misguided.

Melanie followed Julia through the stairwell leading to the pools where Kona swam in her isolation tank. As they climbed the last step, Melanie could see the tiny waves rippling over the small concrete island where the trainers waited for the dolphins. Nervous excitement raced through her stomach like a hundred butterflies flapping their wings all at the same time.

"Wow! I've never seen any of them this close before."

Julia smiled at her. "It's a thing of beauty, right?"

Julia pointed to the other dolphin tank across the way. There were a handful of dolphins moving around the tank. "What we really want to do is get this girl in with the others. That would be the best scenario possible."

Right. Best for who, though? If they were truly worried about what was best for Kona, the dolphin would never have been captured in the first place. Sure, the aquarium was not the one responsible for how she came here, but the fact that they were a willing participant was just as much a problem. Without a market for live capture dolphins, the people responsible for stealing them from the ocean would not have a reason to take them. As angry as it made her, Melanie kept her words to herself. Her opinion would not be popular here, and she did not want to do more damage than good. Julia was one of the trainers that wore her heart on her sleeve. She'd have to be blind not to see how much Julia loved them all.

Melanie glanced down at the water and wondered just what Julia had in mind. "So, what do you want me to do?"

Julia pointed to the back corner of the island where the water just barely touched. "Well, just go sit as far back on the island as possible."

Melanie walked over to the small cement bar, taking care not to slip on the wet surface. Putting her hands down behind her, she eased herself down to the ground. "Just sit?"

"Yep." Julia stayed at the side of the pool, where she could keep an eye on her.

"Okay…I'm sitting. Now what?"

"We wait." Julia marked something down on her clipboard.

"Wait? Okay…for what?"

Melanie could not help thinking that Julia was a little half-cracked. Sit down? That was it? It was not nearly as exciting as Melanie had thought it would be. She would have had more fun watching the dolphin from down below. Not to mention that she would have to work her shift in a little while. There was no way Melanie could stay here forever. Chase would never forgive her if he got stuck working the fish hut by himself.

"For her to come to you. So far, Sandy has not come up to anyone. She seems to be afraid of us." Julia's eyes were on the water.

"Well, do you know how she was captured?" Melanie knew she was taken from the wild, but she had no idea what had happened. She imagined the worst, though, for the people who hunted dolphins often used means that were terrifying and disarming. Melanie had read about the dolphin drive hunters in Taiji, Japan, who herded the dolphins together each year. Some were used for meat, while others were live captures sold to aquariums and random collectors. Only a small portion were released back into the wild. All of it seemed terrifying to Melanie. She could not imagine surviving that kind of trauma. It made Melanie sad to think this could have been what happened to Kona.

"We were told she was a live capture, but not much else." Julia looked uncomfortable with her question. She should be, though, right?

"Shouldn't you know where she came from and how she came here?" Melanie could not stop the words before they left her mouth.

"Yes. We normally do, but the new owner is still learning the ropes apparently. We know the others were born in captivity, but this one here, she was captured and transported here." Julia's face was filled with a sadness that Melanie understood. The trainer cared deeply about all these animals.

"Well, if you knew how they brought her, you would be able to figure out why she's afraid. The more we know about her past, the easier this would be." Melanie imagined the worst-case scenario, a dolphin captured from fishermen who were trying to capture tuna. Dolphins often got caught in nets like that. Kona was probably afraid of people because of it. Melanie did not blame her. Humans could be cruel. And if she was part of an actual dolphin hunt, it was probably even more traumatic than they could ever know for sure.

"I agree. We're doing the best we can to keep her happy here," Julia tried to explain.

"I under.... What was that?" A small splash of water shot at her, and Melanie turned around to look in the water.

"That was Sandy. She popped up and down." Julia smiled excitedly. "She doesn't like to come to the surface."

"Oh, right."

Melanie kept her eyes peeled on the water and mentally willed the dolphin to come back up. She sat there for a few minutes, so focused; she forgot to blink. Her eyes started to well up with annoying drops, which reminded her to let her eyelids do their job.

"Come on, girl." Melanie put her hand over to the side and tapped the water. She was not sure why she thought to do it. It just felt right.

Kona's face popped up about six feet away from her. The dolphin sang a sweet chatter that made Melanie's heart feel light.

Melanie turned to Julia. "Did you hear that?"

"I sure did. Sandy likes you. Tap the water again. She seemed to like that."

"Okay. Come here, girl. Come on, Kona." The dolphin seemed to smile as she inched a little closer.

"What did you call her?" Julia asked her.

"Oh, sorry. I didn't mean to, but Sandy just doesn't fit her. She's like an island alone in the water. So, I called her Kona."

"Kona...I like that." Julie smiled at Melanie. "I'll talk to the others and see if we can get them on board with that. Especially since she seems to respond to it."

"Really?! That's so awesome!" Melanie would have jumped up, but at that moment, Kona went back into the water. "Oh, no! Did I scare her?"

"I don't think so." Julia stepped over to the side and looked down into the tank.

Before Melanie knew it, Kona popped up next to her. She would have scooted further back, but her back was already touching the back of the pool. Melanie tried to slow the beating of her heart. She reminded herself that Kona was afraid too.

Smiling softly, she tapped the water lightly. "Hello, girl."

Kona tapped the water with her fin, mimicking Melanie's motion. Melanie turned to look at Julia, who seemed quite surprised at the turn of events. "What do I do now?"

"Just keep doing what you're doing. We need her to get used to people without being afraid. Just sit there."

"Okay."

Melanie let out a small sigh, wondering how long she would sit here with Kona staring up at her. Surely the dolphin would tire of this, right? Not that Melanie would, but eventually she would have to head to her shift. Sliding fish onto trays was not going to be nearly as entertaining as playing with a dolphin, but it was a paycheck. Not to mention, Chase would be there too. She did not want to miss a shift with him if she could avoid it.

"Hello, Kona."

Melanie tapped the water, and Kona repeated her actions. Melanie did it again, but this time tapped too hard, making a slight splash. Kona stuck her snout in the water and flung water toward Melanie.

"Hey, now!" Melanie shrieked as Kona splashed again, this time hitting her with the small spray.

Melanie put her hand in the water and pushed just a small bit of water toward Kona. The dolphin ducked under the water and disappeared. "Oh, no. Should I not have done that?"

"You're fine, Melanie. Watch."

Julia must have known what was going to happen next, for Kona launched out of the water and arched across the air before diving back into the pool.

"Whoa! Did you see that? That was amazing!" Melanie was filled with awe. She had never seen a dolphin leap so close before. The dolphin rose up one more time and dove back in. Melanie was in dolphin heaven.

"I think she likes you, Melanie. This is the first time she's done that since she's been here. Someday you'll make a wonderful trainer."

Julia looked as if she wanted to retract her words as soon as they left her mouth. Melanie recognized that look. The pity, sorrow for a future that might not come. Julia knew about the cancer. Did Chase? She sure hoped not, because the moment people learned about it, they treated her differently. Chase had been the first person to treat her normal in forever. If he stopped, Melanie would be devastated. Melanie tried to shake off the sadness. She was always caught between wanting to believe that someday she would be all right, and somehow learning to live in the moment.

She waved away the depressing thoughts and focused on right here and now. "Do you think so?" Kona popped up to look at Melanie. The sixteen-year-old gazed down at her and tapped the water again. "What do you think, girl?"

Kona made a shrill dolphin noise, one that neither one of them would truly be able to translate, but Julia answered anyway. "I think she agrees."

Melanie sure hoped so. It would be a dream come true to work with dolphins for her career. For now, she would get as much experience as she could and hope it led her down that path.

She continued to work there with Kona until her shift was about to start. Heading to the stinky shack would not be her favorite part of the day, even if Chase would be there with her. That was okay, though. It was still a better start to her day than earlier. Melanie was going to focus on the positive and try to push her worries to the back of her mind, if only for the moment.

When Melanie made her way to the hut, Chase was already making sure the money in the drawer was correct. He turned to smile at her when he heard the door close. "Hey."

"You'll never guess what I got to do!" Melanie couldn't help herself. She was way too excited to keep it bottled up.

"What?" His eyebrow rose curiously.

"I got to help your mom with one of the dolphins." Melanie set her bag under the counter and went back to start putting trays together. She quickly put on a pair of gloves to keep the fish slime off her fingers before she pulled the fish out of the fridge.

"Which one?"

"The new one."

"Sandy?" His voice was filled with surprise.

"Yeah. I was just walking near the tank by the viewing area, and the dolphin kept following me. Mr. Marcus called your mom in to show her. They had me go the surface on the island to see if she would come to me." Melanie was already filling the trays as she talked. Living in a house with all girls demanded multitasking skills for sure. Sometimes they were all talking at once.

"And?"

"She responded. I know it was only a little thing, but I got her to splash water."

Melanie stopped what she was doing and looked over at Chase. She saw the admiration on his face.

"That's not a little thing at all. My mom has been so worried about her. What you did, even though it seems little, it was huge."

Chase dropped the money in the cash register drawer and closed it. He walked over the table and put on a pair of gloves to help her make up some of the trays. Melanie smiled at him, and for one moment, felt like a girl who did not have the weight of the world on her shoulders. It was nice to feel that way for a change.

"Thanks. It was good to see Kona happy."

"Who is Kona?" Chase asked her as he plopped a few fish on a tray.

"Oh, I mean, Sandy, unless they let Julia name her Kona. Sandy just doesn't fit her. I told Julia that Kona was a much better name because it reminds me of the beautiful waters around Hawaii."

"I like it. Look at you, future dolphin trainer. I'll be starting the program soon too."

"Does that mean you won't be here?" Melanie tried to hide her disappointment.

"Worried about working with Leon?" Chase teased her.

"No...." Let him think that, though. The alternative thought was no better. She simply did not want to miss seeing his smiling face every day.

"Well, don't worry. You'll be stuck with me. I need the money, and junior dolphin trainers are volunteer hours."

"Maybe she'll let me help then too." Melanie would sure love the chance.

"Anything is possible." Chased nodded to the register. "Time to open. You ready?"

Melanie looked at the trays they had already loaded and knew this was just the beginning. No matter, she'd crank them out as fast as she could. "Sure. Let's do this."

As Chase turned away, Melanie's mind was filled with daydreams of working with him and his mom. This was already turning into the best summer ever. Could it get even better? She certainly hoped so.

CHAPTER 7

By the time Melanie got home, she was barely able to contain herself. Sure, she was exhausted from work, but she was still way too excited about Kona to let that get to her. The moment the front door swung open, Melanie nearly raced through it.

"What's the rush?" Her mother teased her.

"I have to tell Amber!" Melanie gave her mom a look as if she should have already known why she was in a hurry.

"You do realize she's still at work, right?" Linda set her purse on the table by the door.

"So?" Melanie deflated slightly.

"Look, I know you're excited, but maybe you should slow down a little?" Her mother suggested.

"Mom!" Melanie plopped down on the couch and let out a slow groan. "Julia said I could work with Kona any time I have free time."

"I know, honey, but you're already doing so much. And you've got a lot on your shoulders right now."

"You talked to Lori's mom, didn't you?" She knew that look. Her mom was afraid. That same fear popped up every time one of her friends had a relapse. "She's going to be fine."

"I sure hope so." Linda looked away from her, and Melanie

started to wonder what was really going on.

"You know something," Melanie accused.

"Lori's not in great shape this time, Mel. There were so many mets."

Melanie hated that word. Mets. In the simplest terms, mets were cancer cells that broke away from where they were first found. When the cancer moved to other areas, it could be tough to treat. There was nothing simple about mets at all. Treatment became much more complicated once more of them started to appear. Lori's cancer had started in her lymph nodes. Lori had Non-Hodgkin's lymphoma and had been struggling with it since she was six. After all this time, they had all hoped Lori would never have to face it again. Life never worked out the way they wanted, though, did it? Whenever cancer was involved, it gave very little thought to what its carrier wanted. Like a parasite, it destroyed them all one cell at a time.

Melanie stared at her feet and tried to push those thoughts out of her mind. The problem was, whenever they started, it was like an avalanche of reality. It would always be in the back of her mind. Her cancer, acute lymphoblastic leukemia, would always be there, wouldn't it? It was there in her bone marrow, destroying her from the inside out. It was the same with Hannah. The two of them had been diagnosed around the same time. Hannah had become the closest thing she had to a best friend, even if it was from hundreds of miles away. She understood Melanie when no one else could.

"Can we just focus on today? Mom…please. I don't want to think about this."

Melanie took a deep breath and tried to push the cloud away from her. It was a constant battle, especially when she was not the only one who manufactured them. Her mother's face was so bleak that Melanie knew she was not going to stop thinking about all the times Melanie had been weak in the hospital; all the times cancer had tried to win. The thing was, it hadn't won. Not yet. And Melanie refused to let it.

"Sure, baby."

Melanie knew this was not the end of it. Not by a long shot. "You know, I'm the only one who has gotten Kona to show any interest."

"So, Julia told me. I like the name."

"It fits her much better than Sandy, that's for sure. She seems to like it too. You're not going to stop me from working with her, are you?"

"I suppose not. I just don't want you to overextend yourself, honey."

"At some point, you have to let me figure out my limits, Mom. I'm sixteen. I can handle more, you know." Melanie crossed her arms over her chest.

"And this wouldn't have anything to do with Chase Makenzie, would it?" Her mother's eyes twinkled slightly.

"Mom!" Melanie rolled her eyes, but she knew there was a blush rising up her cheeks.

"Do you have a crush on him?"

"What? Yuck...," she lied. It was awkward for her mom to be bringing this up. Moms weren't supposed to be in the middle of this at all. It was something she should talk about with her friends, like Hannah. Hannah was already telling her to push their relationship further. Hannah was more courageous than Melanie, sometimes. Melanie wouldn't even know where to start.

"What? It's natural to like someone. When I was your age...."

Melanie stuck her fingers in her ears and squeezed her eyes as tight as she could as if her mother's words would conjure up images in front of her. "Please!"

"He's a nice boy, Mel." Linda looked down at her fingernails. "He might be into you too."

Melanie removed her fingers from her ears and stared her mom down. "That's not funny, Mom."

"What's funny about it? I was talking to Julia, and—"

"Ugh. You are not supposed to do that! Mom!" What was she doing, matchmaking? Moms were not supposed to do that. Melanie almost wished she would go back to talking about Lori now. That was territory the two of them were familiar with.

"What? He talks about you a lot." She shrugged her shoulders and waved her hands around. "If you don't want to know about it, I guess I can just change the subject."

Did he think about her? Probably not as much as she thought about him. Chase was seventeen. What could he possibly want with her?

"You're lying."

Linda's eyes met her with a seriousness that almost cut Melanie to the core. "Have I ever lied to you?"

No. She hadn't. Not even when it would have been far kinder to do so when the cancer had first been diagnosed, her mom could have softened the blow and made up some other kind of explanation for what was going on, but Linda had been adamant about educating everyone about what was happening. She had made it clear that autonomy in treatment was essential. While Melanie had not made medical decisions for herself, her mother had made sure she understood the options and why certain choices were made.

"Well, we work together. That's all."

"Okay. But if something does happen, you know you can talk to me, right?"

"I thought you were against dating before thirty?" Melanie tilted her head and scrunched her lips together. Why was her mom suddenly changing her mind on some of these things?

"I'm okay with a relationship with boundaries."

Melanie groaned. Please don't let this be the talk. Melanie did not need to know any details about sex. She was certainly not planning on doing any experimenting any time soon. Melanie had other priorities.

"Mom...."

"It's important to think about your future. You know my rule."

"I know. Graduate high school, go to college, earn a degree, have a successful career, then maybe get married and have kids. I got it."

Mom had been ingraining that into their heads from the moment they first started kindergarten. Linda wanted her girls to be self-sufficient so that if the bottom fell out of their relationships, they could always support their children independently. While her parents were very much in love, it had not been enough to keep her father alive. When he died, her mother had to shoulder the financial responsibilities as well as all the emotional ones. Some days had been easier than others, but her mother had survived them all and had become a good role model for her children.

Her mom was right. Serious relationships had no place in high school. Too many mistakes could happen, mistakes that could affect the rest of her life. Melanie was just trying to live her life one day at a time. But her mom was right. She did have a thing for Chase, and even though she wanted to pretend she didn't, it was staring her in the face every time she worked with him. Was she right? Did he like her?

"Good girl."

"So, does that mean if he asks me out, you'll let me go?" Not that Melanie thought that would happen in reality. Was it a fantasy? Yes, definitely.

"Because I know his mother and that she has raised a good, moral son, yes. I would."

"Really?"

Why did Melanie feel like squealing? That was such an immature reaction. Then again, she didn't always have to be older than her age, did she? None of this mattered, though. Chase was not going to ask her out. That was not in the realm of things that could actually happen to her. Besides, she should focus more on Kona right now.

"Really." There were tears in her mom's eyes, a sadness that Melanie did not want to deconstruct, because inside she knew it was distinctly related to mortality. Everything had been from the moment Melanie had received her diagnosis. Every moment was painted with it, the highs and the lows. It was a reality that most people never knew. How nice for them.

"I need to take a shower." Melanie pretended to sniff her shirt, but in reality, she just wanted to get away from this discussion and pretend that it had never happened. For as much as she would love to think about what could happen in a normal person's life, Melanie knew it was too much to hope for. She needed to send a message to Lori, and that was something she had been dreading since the moment Hannah had told her about the relapse. She would take a shower to clear her head before attempting to write something.

After she was clean, Melanie sat on her bed with her legs crossed under her. She stared at the phone in her hand and tried to think of what to say to Lori. Words in messages never translated the way she wanted them to.

Melanie entered one simple word. *Hey.*

Three little dots formed on her screen as Lori was already typing in a response. *Hey.*

Hanging in there? Melanie typed back.

Trying to. At least the nurse is cute.

Oh? Melanie added a smiley face. *Do tell.*

His name is Jason. Looks like Dr. Eckland.

Melanie giggled despite herself. They had all joked about Dr. Eckland. At one point, they'd had a game to see who could get him to smile the most in one sitting. His teeth were brighter than freshly fallen snow. Melanie still wondered how he kept them that way. He was so kind to all of them. It was safe to say they were all a little crushed when he got married.

Pics or it didn't happen, Melanie messaged her.

Deal.

You okay? Melanie ripped the bandage off and waited to see what Lori would say.

Three more little dots before Lori's answer came back. It seemed almost like an eternity. *I've been better.*

Melanie felt tears start to form in her eyes. Lori had always been the most positive of all of them. Always a role model for courage, Lori had held them all together when they felt like falling apart. If something happened to her, Melanie wasn't sure how she would get through it. But what choice did she have?

Do you need anything? Can we come and see you?

You just want to see my nurse, Lori teased her.

Guilty as charged. Melanie sniffed as tears fell down her face. She didn't want to think about it, but she was afraid if she didn't see Lori soon, she might never see her again.

Have to go. Nurse Hottie is here to take my vitals.

Melanie set her phone down and grabbed her pillow. She burrowed her face into it and started to cry. The undertone was there. Even in a message, it could not be misunderstood. Lori was trying to be strong for others. It was the status quo for all cancer kids. But as a cancer kid, she could read the sadness behind it. The pretense was clear to her. Lori knew she was terminal, or she would never have said she'd been better. Her answer was always great but lined with sarcasm. Great for a pincushion, great for someone half chemo-baked. That's what they called the sickness that came along with every chemo treatment. Chemo-baked. It was just something the three of them had created, a code among friends dealing with one of the world's hardest challenges. Today, though, Lori had said there had been better days. It was code for "I'm not doing well. I might not make it." They had always told each other they would keep it real. Up until now, Melanie had appreciated it. Now, it scared the crap out of her. Melanie was not ready to lose anyone else.

Her phone dinged, and she looked down at it. Hannah wanted to see if she could go with her to see Lori this weekend. Melanie closed her eyes and took a deep breath before responding. *I'll ask. What day?*

Sunday.

Sundays were good. That was the day the aquarium was closed. She was reasonably sure her mom would take her, too, especially since Mom already knew what was going on with Lori. *I'll let you know.*

Melanie turned her phone off and threw herself back on the bed. Staring up at the ceiling, she wondered if her life would ever be predictable. Nothing in the future was guaranteed. Good times were often surrounded by bad, and sometimes the in between was all she had to keep herself going.

CHAPTER 8

The rest of the week was a mixture of excitement and dread. Melanie had only been able to work with Kona one other day, but Julia had promised her that she would have more opportunities soon. Melanie couldn't wait to spend more time with Kona, so that was the better part of her work. The part that sucked the life out of her day was knowing she was going to see Lori on Sunday. Her mom had agreed to go almost the moment the idea had come out of Melanie's mouth. Part of her had wished that her mom would have something else she wanted to do. The rest of her knew that this would be one of the last chances she had to see Lori, especially if none of her treatments helped.

Melanie did not like to think about it, because if she did, her own mortality would smack her in the face. Any time one of them had a relapse, it was like a wakeup call. Even this morning, Melanie had taken her temperature three times just to make sure it was normal. Then she had counted all her pills and made sure she was keeping the same schedule every day for taking them. Melanie could not afford to let anything sidetrack her from her life right now. For the first time in years, she had started to feel like a normal person. Melanie was not ready to give that up just yet.

This morning, Sunday, Melanie got up earlier than usual. She had promised her mother she would be up and ready to go by eight o'clock. Even though the Phoenix Children's Hospital was only twenty minutes from their house, her mom wanted to get there as soon as possible since she had other plans that afternoon. Melanie was almost glad that they were doing it the first thing in the morning. That would give her the rest of the day to process her visit so her every thought the next day would not be plagued with it. To say she would just forget it was a bald-faced lie. Melanie would be thinking about it a lot over the next week, but she worked tomorrow, and Julia had already promised her that she could work with Kona. Chase, too, because he was starting his summer training program working under his mother.

Melanie was glad she would be working with Chase. He made the days pass faster than she ever thought possible. Whenever the lines were overrun, and the heat was sweltering, his sense of humor carried them through their shift. One time he had even picked up one of the larger sardines and started to pretend it had come to life and was trying to make a run for it or swim for it. He was becoming more than just a crush. Chase was becoming a friend, which was something she had not realized how much she needed.

Part of her wanted to tell him about Lori, but she was afraid it would open far too many questions. He was the first friend she'd had that had no idea about her leukemia. It was something she did not want to have to share with him. Melanie was afraid if he knew about her cancer, he would treat her differently. It was a pattern she was used to. She would make a new friend and think that maybe for once she could have a normal friendship like other people her age. That only lasted until one of the other kids spilled the beans, or until she had to go through another treatment that made her miss school again. Right now, things were good. Sure, she'd had to change her meds up a little. That kind of came with the territory, and it wasn't the first time this had happened.

"So, you're going soon?" Amber poked her head into the living room. Melanie was surprised to see her awake. Amber always slept in on the weekend. Her shifts were usually later in the day.

"Yeah, I think so. What are you doing up so early?"

"I just wanted to make sure you were okay."

"Mom told you?"

Melanie hadn't had a chance to tell Amber about what was going on with Lori. For one, Amber was working so many hours she fell asleep as soon as her head hit the pillow. The other reason was that Melanie couldn't quite put what she was feeling into words. To vocalize, it made it that much more real.

"I'm sorry, Mel." Amber plopped down on the couch next to her, nearly sending Nite toppling to the floor from the arm. The black cat hung onto the arm with her nails and gave a vocal protest with a meow that sounded like she was gargling hot rocks. Leave it to the cat to bring some humor into any situation, because now the dog was trying to mimic her meows, with pitiful whines that only irritated the cat more as she climbed back to her perch. Nite gave Amber the evil eye and hissed when she tried to pet her.

"Fine. Be that way, grouchy butt."

Any other day Melanie would be rolling on the floor laughing at Nite and River, but even the dynamic duo could not bring her spirits up just yet. Maybe later. Right now, she was focused on breathing. That was the hardest part right now. Any second she would start hyperventilating. Hospitals were not her happy place, that was for sure.

"What time do you work?" Melanie picked a safe topic.

"Noon to eight."

"Wow...that's a long time." Melanie was limited to four-hour shifts right now. That was long enough for her. "You going to make it?"

"I'll be all right. You?"

Amber's eyes searched her own, and Melanie felt her walls start to topple slightly. Her eyes darted away. Melanie did not want to get into it. "I will do what I always do. Survive."

"I'll be home later if you want to talk."

"Thanks, Amber." Right now, there was no telling what Melanie would feel like talking about later. Maybe she'd pretend to be asleep, so she didn't have to talk about it. That was the problem with sharing a room with her sister—she couldn't hide much from her. Amber always seemed to know when Melanie was upset, even when she wanted to hide it from the rest of the world desperately. At least Amber kept most of it to herself.

"What are you two doing up?" Kimmie scrunched her nose up at them. "Is this some early morning book club or something?"

"Book club?" Amber shook her head. "Who told you about those?"

"Grandma Mimi has one." Kimmie nodded to the book on the coffee table. "That's the book she's supposed to read, but I've never seen her even open it."

"That's because you don't actually read books for book club." Amber picked up the book and rotated it in her hand to read the back.

"If they don't read the books, then what is the point of a book club?" Kimmie challenged her.

"It's just somewhere adults go to hang out," Amber explained.

"But what do they do there?"

"No one really knows, actually," Melanie could not help

adding. "It's like some adult secret society."

"Sounds sketchy to me. Maybe we should talk Grandma Mimi out of it." Kimmie plopped down in the beanbag chair and crossed her legs under her.

"Good idea. You can do that while Mom and I are out," suggested Melanie.

"Where are you two going?" Kimmie didn't even skip a beat.

"Kimmie!" chided Amber. Her eyebrows rose as if to say it wasn't something they should be talking about.

"Oh…right. Never mind." Kimmie tapped her fingers on her leg. "Do you want to take Simon with you?"

Simon was Kimmie's favorite teddy bear. He had spent a fair amount of time in the hospital with Melanie. Kimmie had wanted him to protect her from all the germs. It was a sweet gesture.

Melanie sighed softly to herself as she tried to keep from crying. "No, thanks. I'll be all right."

"For Lori. Maybe he can make her better the way he did you."

"Oh, Bug, that's so sweet. You keep him. You never know when you will need him."

Melanie cleared her throat as she started to choke up. What Melanie did not say was she might need him again sometime too. That was one thing she did not want to admit, but the reality was life would be unpredictable for a while.

Footsteps sounded in the hallway, which was an indicator of her mother's arrival. When she peered into the living room, Linda cleared her throat. "I'm almost afraid to ask."

"What?" Amber held her palms up.

"You're never up this early together at the same time." Linda looked from one to the other. "Am I in the right house?"

"Mom! You live here, silly!" Kimmie rolled her eyes and twirled her finger near her head as if to say their mother was losing her mind.

"Miracles do happen," Grandma Mimi said from behind her. "You guys better get a move on. It sounds like you have a pretty full day."

"So, will you. We'll be back after lunch, Mom."

"No problem. I'll get Amber to work, and then Kimmie and I will hang out."

"Oooh. What are we going to do?" Kimmie was immediately intrigued.

"I don't know yet, but we'll figure it out after I've had some coffee."

Grandma Mimi looked like she could use a cup. She had worked until late last night after picking up an extra shift. Melanie felt bad because she could have probably worked today if she wanted to, but now she was forced to stay here with Kimmie. They could have taken her with them—Kimmie was certainly old enough this time. Then again, this was something that she would probably not understand.

"Are you ready to go?" Her mom asked her.

Melanie looked around at the prying eyes around her. She did not want to admit that she wasn't ready at all. Inside she knew that her time with her friend was limited. Melanie would never be prepared to say goodbye. Nor would she want someone to say that to her if she were in the hospital the way Lori was. Melanie would have to think of some way to keep the mood light because it was hard enough for Lori to keep her spirits up right now. Melanie knew that struggle. It was the face of the brave soldier, the one that every kid wore in the face of such adversity.

"Mel?" Her mom was looking at her with concern.

"What? Oh, yeah. I'm ready."

Mel got up slowly from the couch, ignoring the glances

everyone seemed to share. She shook off the melancholy and tried to hang onto her happy thoughts, like working with Kona. And then there was the thought of sharing that same time with Chase. Any time she got to spend with him was time well spent. Her mom was right; she did have a major crush on him, one that only seemed to grow the more she got to know him.

"Good. Megan said Lori is excited to see you and Hannah. Let's get a move on, kiddo."

Melanie grabbed her small backpack and headed to the door. She had put a few odds and ends in there for Lori and Hannah both. Every once in a while, she would see a knickknack here or there that reminded her of her friends. For Hannah, it was any kind of bee because her grandparents tended beehives, and they had become one of Hannah's favorite things. They weren't Melanie's things, as she didn't care for insects, but she had learned more than her fair share about them, for Hannah was so well-versed and wanted to save the bees. For Lori, it was butterflies. Lori loved the complexity of the designs throughout many butterflies. When she was at the hospital, they hung butterflies all over the room. Melanie had made several butterflies to tape to the walls and windows, using every bright color she could find. If the hospital walls were all Lori would see for the rest of her life, Melanie wanted to make sure they were filled with love and light, for Lori to know how much they all cared about her.

Those weren't the only things in her bag. Melanie had to bring all her medications with her too. She would not get a free pass from them. They were always there, and probably always would be. She'd take them from here to eternity if it meant the cancer would stay away. She still had a lot of life to live and planned to make the best of it. Even though nothing was a guarantee, Melanie refused to think she was here on this world to just muddle her way through some hard times. Where were the happy times? Where was the pot of gold at the end of the rainbow? And how come she could never make it where the rainbow touched the ground? Wasn't she worthy of its light? Weren't they all? When she was younger, it had been one of her dreams to chase the rainbows. When her father was alive, they had hopped in the car and tried to find where the light touched the ground. They were never able to find it.

That felt a lot like a metaphor for her life, chasing a light she could never hold on to—first her father, then the cancer. Melanie probably shouldn't complain, though. She was still fighting, still strong, and her family would never give up the fight with her. Her mother had the patience of a saint when it came to all her ups and downs. Like right now, her mother had dropped everything to be with her today. Linda Parker was staring at a potential future in the face with Melanie, one that neither one of them wanted to visit, but she was going to be there with her daughter nonetheless. That took strength, love, and courage to face. Melanie would never be able to put her real thoughts and feelings into actual words. Instead, she gave her mom a tentative smile as they got in the car.

"Thank you, Mom."

Linda smiled at Melanie. "Of course, Mel. I know how important this is."

The ride there was short, but her thoughts made it feel like an eternity. By the time they got out of the car, she was having trouble pretending everything was status quo. As they made their way across the parking lot, her heart started to pound so loudly it felt like a roar in her ears. Her mom must have sensed the fear, for she reached for Melanie's hand. While she felt a little old to be holding her mom's hand, Melanie took it for the lifeline it was. If anyone understood what it was like to walk back into the Phoenix Children's Hospital, it was her mother. They had spent a fair amount of time there in the past, and it had almost become a second home. While the staff always did their best to make it feel like home, there was no way to truly make it as cozy and safe as a real home. No one wanted to be in the hospital that long.

"It's going to be all right, Mel," her mom reassured her.

"I know." She didn't know that, though. How could it be?

When they got in the elevator, Melanie closed her eyes. Elevators were not her favorite thing. They were even worse when she was strapped to a gurney traveling from one scan to another. Not that wheelchairs were all that much better.

By the time they made it to the right floor, Melanie was able to breathe again. Before they could enter the level, they had to sanitize their hands and put on masks, which was what they did as they signed in at the desk. The attendant handed them their visitor passes and opened the door for them. They walked quietly down the hallway, and she saw her old room on the way. She tried not to think about it, but it was hard not to. It was a walk down memory lane that she had not wanted to take. None of them ever did, for as many smiles and laughter as the staff tried to manufacture for the kids, there was only so much they could do to keep the kids from the reality of their situations.

When they found Lori's room, she saw that Hannah was already there. While the hospital usually had a limited number of visitors, there were times when they made an exception. This was one of those times. The only one they didn't break was the age. Melanie remembered when Kimmie had been too young to come to her floor. Her sister had been heartbroken. That's when she had insisted that her mom take her bear in her place — that, and a huge bouquet of balloons. Melanie smiled despite herself. Kimmie might be annoying sometimes, but at the heart of it, she was one of Melanie's favorite people.

"Mel!" Hannah jumped up from the side of Lori's bed and threw her arms around her. Her arms held her so tight that Melanie almost had trouble breathing.

Melanie finally stepped back to look at her. Tall and lanky, the African American teenager looked as if she was finally getting back to good health. Hannah had been sick a lot in the last year and had lost a fair amount of weight. Her hair had finally started to grow into short tight curls, which were very flattering to her face — well, the parts that weren't covered in the pale blue medical mask.

"You look amazing, Hannah!"

"Thanks! You look good too. Looks like you're getting more sun this year."

"Yeah. A little. I mean, I stand behind the counter a lot, but a fair amount still filters in."

Melanie walked further into the room and took in the space around her. Hundreds of butterflies were hanging from the ceiling, something Melanie was sure the nurses had helped with even though it was something that might get them in trouble in other hospitals. They bent over backward here to make life more engaging for the kids in the cancer ward. That was probably the only reason Melanie wasn't shaking right now. The moment she had stepped into Lori's room, she no longer felt like she was in a hospital, even though several wires and tubes were coming down from different parts of Lori's body. There were a few Melanie had never seen before, but she was not about to ask what they were.

"Mel!" Lori's voice was a little hoarse and low, but Melanie could still hear her.

"Lori."

Melanie turned to see her mother talking with Lori's mom in the hallway. The adults must have decided to give them some time alone. Melanie was happy about it. Sometimes the parents only made things more awkward.

"Have a seat, girls." Lori patted both sides of her bed.

Melanie saw the ghostly white skin and the shadows that were under Lori's eyes. She looked so frail in the middle of the bed. Her head was covered in a pink butterfly cap that seemed to sparkle in the light whenever she moved her head. It suited Lori.

Taking her backpack down from her shoulders, Melanie sat down on the edge of the bed. "I've got stuff for both of you."

"You didn't have to." Lori held her hand up.

"Psst. It's not about you, Lori," teased Hannah. "You didn't have to get thrown into the hospital to get us to come to visit."

Lori gave Hannah a feeble smile. "It worked, didn't it?"

Melanie snorted. "Always the drama queen."

"You know it." Lori smoothed the covers around her.

Melanie pulled out the small gifts she had wrapped in colorful tissue paper. She handed one to each of her friends and waited for them to open them. "It's not much, just stuff I've been saving up for the next time we got together."

When Lori saw the butterfly creations, her eyes started to water up, and she reached for Melanie's hand. "Thank you, Mel. I love them."

"It was nothing." Melanie felt a tear start to form in her eye and tried to will it away.

"It was everything. Your friendship, both of you, it means the world to me. I just wanted you to know that."

"We do." Melanie squeezed her hand.

"Girl! These are amazing!" Hannah was holding up the bee

earrings.

"I wasn't sure if you'd wear them or not."

"Have you met me?" Hannah tilted her head at her.

Melanie looked at the quilt that Lori was wrapped up in. She didn't know what words to speak next. "I...."

"Yeah...," Hannah added.

"It's going to be okay, you guys." Lori's voice was calm, but there was a shakiness underneath it. Lori was terrified.

"You don't have to pretend with us, Lori." Hannah put her present on the table next to her. "We always said we'd keep it real."

"Hannah's right. Don't sugar coat. Tell us."

Lori closed her eyes and looked as if she were trying to find the right words. "It's bad. They say maybe a few weeks, a month if I'm lucky. I have to tell you. I'm not feeling lucky."

"I'm sorry," Melanie whispered.

"Don't be. I'm not done fighting, neither are you, do you hear me?" Lori reached for both their hands. "Whatever happens to me, this is not an excuse for you to give up. Do you hear me?"

"Yes," Melanie mumbled.

Her eyes met Hannah's, and she saw the turmoil raging inside her. Every time was just like this. They never knew how long they had. Time was always fleeting—that's why it was easier to be in denial than face the disease that had taken over their lives so long ago. Melanie had to fight to remind herself that she was still okay, that her cancer was under control. It was a mantra that only got easier to believe when she was far away from the beeping machines and labyrinth of wires that came with every hospital visit.

The girls spent a little more time just trying to pretend everything was all right, speaking of things that no one would remember later. Less than two hours had passed before Lori was falling asleep. Melanie could have stayed there with Hannah, but truth be told, neither one of them wanted to speak to each other. They were both anxious to get away from there and return to their lives, where they could pretend that cancer was a figment of their imaginations, if only for an hour or two.

CHAPTER 9

When Melanie woke up the next morning, she almost didn't want to get out of bed. Her night had been filled with tossing and turning as her stomach turned on her. Seeing Lori that way had shaken her up. Pulling the covers over her head, she just wanted to ignore the sunlight drifting through the curtains. That was hard to do, considering the alarm clock kept going off.

"Mel!" Amber groaned. "Would you get up already?"

Throwing the covers back, Melanie let out a loud sigh. "Why does the morning have to come so early?"

"It's the same time every day." Amber put her arm over her head and tried to block out the light. "Would you be quiet so I can go back to sleep?"

"Lucky," grumbled Melanie as she pushed off her bed. Tiptoeing around the room, she gathered her things for her shower, even though getting ready was the last thing she wanted to do right now. She didn't have a choice, though. If she wanted to work with Kona today, Melanie had to go to work.

Kona. Melanie knew that the dolphin would make it easier to forget the depressing thoughts that followed every waking moment. Melanie had a way of losing herself in every moment she spent with Kona. Maybe it was because the dolphin needed to feel safe, the way Melanie did. She understood what it was like to be trapped in circumstances beyond her control. While Melanie had a support system to help navigate through those moments, Kona did not have the same trust built up with the trainers at the aquarium. Melanie wasn't sure why Kona had connected with her so easily. Maybe Kona recognized the same things in her. They often said dolphins were extremely intelligent. Did Kona know how hard it was for Melanie to put one foot in front of the other every single day? Sure, Melanie held her head up high, living her life from moment to moment. On the outside, she would always seem brave and not resigned to her fate, but that was the mask she wore. Sometimes she did feel confident and ready to tackle the world, but today, all she wanted to do was crawl back in bed and pretend the rest of the world no longer existed.

Her thoughts turned to Lori, and Melanie realized how pissed Lori would be. If Lori had known visiting her would make Melanie fall into a deep spiral, she would have refused to see her. Melanie would have felt the same way had she been in Lori's place. Closing her eyes, Melanie reminded herself that she was living, she was safe, and her world had not ended. She had a whole life ahead of her, one that Lori would want her to take part in, no matter what happened to her. The mantra they all held fast to echoed in her head as she looked down at the picture of Melanie standing next to Lori's bed. Never give up, ever. Fight until there is no longer a reason to fight. There was always a reason to fight.

Melanie resigned herself to working through her emotions quickly. Today, she would put them past her and try to enjoy life. It was what Lori would want. It was what they all wanted.

She got ready as quickly as possible and headed downstairs to have some breakfast. When she got into the kitchen, Melanie was surprised to find Kimmie standing on a step stool next to the counter. Kimmie's arms were going all over the place as the nine-year-old stirred over a bowl furiously. Melanie could not help but wonder what in the world she was up to.

"Good morning."

"Ah!" Kimmie jumped in surprise and almost upended the bowl in the process. The wooden spoon she was holding was not as lucky. It went flying through the air with a speed that was almost impressive, but not nearly as remarkable as the way River snapped it up in his mouth. Nite gave the whole scene before her a bored glance as she continued to lick her front paws like they were Sunday brunch or something.

"What are you doing?" Melanie was almost afraid to find out.

"Making muffins." Kimmie's eyes darted to the phone on the counter suspiciously.

"Are you recording yourself?"

"I might be...I might not be. It depends on who you're asking." Kimmie's voice raised a pitch as she reached down to push the button on the phone.

"I'm asking you, half-pint." Melanie's lips started to turn up at the corners despite the urge to continue frowning at her sister.

"Okay. So maybe I was trying to film myself baking so I could enter the junior baking championship." Kimmie suddenly deflated. "Which you ruined by scaring the heck out of me."

"Language...," Melanie warned her. Their mother was pretty strict about which words they could or could not use.

"I didn't say it," grumbled Kimmie.

"Close enough. And why didn't you ask first?"

"Because I have to be ten. I mean...." Kimmie clapped her hand over her mouth.

"So, let me get this straight. You were going to enter a contest, lie about your age, and planned to keep it all from Mom?" Melanie had to admire the audacity of her kid sister. She certainly had goals—misguided ones, but goals nonetheless.

"Can I plead the eighth?" Kimmie's head dropped slightly, and her shoulders rose.

"It's the fifth...and no, you can't do that. Besides, you haven't done anything wrong yet. There's always next year, Bug."

"I know," Kimmie mumbled.

"You could start a kid's video channel. Lots of people do. But I would make sure you talk to Mom first."

"That's not a bad idea. And I bet Amber can help me. She's always doing those stupid makeup videos that no one ever watches."

"That's not true, Kimmie. She's got a lot of followers." It was true. Amber was pretty good at angles and lighting, which made her videos pop. The only thing Melanie hated was that her sister often turned their room into a filming studio on a whim. Melanie never knew when she was walking into some kind of photoshoot.

"Don't let her hear you. She'll start making more of them." Kimmie shivered in revulsion. "Ugh...all that makeup. I'm surprised her face isn't covered in craters. Isn't that stuff bad for your skin?"

"It's called bathing. You should try it more often," Melanie teased her as she pulled the wooden spoon away from River.

"Hey! I'm not the one who smells like dead fish." Kimmie pinched her nose and stuck out her tongue as if she were gagging on some invisible stench.

Melanie rolled her eyes. "Whatever. You going to bake those or not?"

"Will you help me?"

"Sure."

Melanie reached into the closest cabinet. Pulling out the muffin tins, she then placed them on the counter and went to look for some cupcake papers.

Over the next hour, they finished up the muffins, which to Melanie's surprise were actually more than edible. She couldn't help thinking the kid might have a knack for this kind of thing, not that she was going to tell Kimmie that. Her sister already had enough crazy ideas in that head of hers. It was good that Kimmie had the desire to branch out to something more fulfilling than mud pies and rock pizzas. These were a great improvement, and Melanie didn't have to pretend to eat them.

"Well, what is this smell?" Grandma Mimi called as she entered through the kitchen.

"Orange and cranberry muffins. I even cut up all the oranges myself, and threw in some of the marmalade we had in the fridge." Kimmie beamed up at their grandma.

"They look delicious."

"They are," Melanie added. "Kimmie must have gotten all your skills in the kitchen."

Grandma Mimi beamed at Kimmie. "Well, I've still got a lot to teach you. Maybe we'll work on some puffed pastries later."

"Ooooh! Can we?" Kimmie clapped her hands together.

"Well, good morning." Linda Parker saw the scene in front of her as she walked into the kitchen. "Are we having a party?"

"I made muffins," Kimmie proclaimed as she took one of the muffins and raced over to their mother.

"With a little guidance," added Melanie so that her mom wouldn't freak out over Kimmie baking something by herself.

"This is good. Now, I just need one more and some coffee; then we can get out the door." Linda walked over to the fresh pot of coffee and poured herself a large mug. When she turned to look at Melanie, her face was covered in ill-concealed worry. "You ready, Mel?"

"Yep. I can't wait to get to work. Today I get to work with Kona and Chase. It's his first day as a junior trainer. If I play my cards right, Julia might let me be one too."

"Sounds like fun. Just don't overdo it, all right?" The worry in her voice was easy to hear. Her mom had probably had the same trouble sleeping that she had. Melanie didn't blame her. It had been hard for her mom to see Lori like that. It only amplified her own fears for Melanie's health. How could it not?

"Promise." She didn't intend to keep it, because Melanie was tired of limiting herself. Would she go crazy? No, but she planned to do everything any normal kid would do in her situation.

"Let's go then."

Thankfully, her mother did not say a word about Lori. She wasn't sure what she would have done if the topic had been brought up. Melanie just wanted to separate herself from those thoughts while she was at work, at the very least.

When they made their way into the parking lot, Melanie almost bolted from the car. Before she did, Melanie saw her mother looking at her. "Don't worry, Mom. I'm fine. And yes, I'll take my medicine."

"Good. You can help Julia until your shift starts."

"Really? Awesome!" Melanie was actually surprised that her mom was being so lenient. Melanie wondered what had gotten into her. Rather than second guess it, though, Melanie sprung into action. She made record time across the park to the trainer's locker room, where she found Julia was already making her plan for the day.

"Morning, Mel," greeted Julia.

The door to the changing room opened, and Chase stepped out of it, already dressed in his junior trainer gear. "Hey, Mel."

"Hi, Chase. I didn't know you were going to start so early."

"You might as well get dressed too," Julia suggested. She reached down into the pile of clothes that were on the table behind her. "Welcome to the team, Junior Trainer."

"Wait....what?" Melanie looked from Julia to Chase in disbelief.

Julia nodded to her son. "It was his idea."

"Really?" Melanie threw her arms around his neck and hugged him. Then she realized her mistake and stepped back from him. His grin told her that he had not minded, but even so, her face now felt like she had eaten a handful of hot peppers.

"I'm surprised he kept it a secret so long. Your mom too." Julia nodded to the door. "I'm going to check a few things out there. Come on out when you're done."

"Right." Melanie watched her leave then looked up at Chase, who was still grinning. "Why didn't you tell me?"

"I wanted to surprise you."

"Why?" What did it matter why? Chase was probably just being nice to her. That's all this was.

"Because you deserve it. You'll make a great trainer."

"Oh." Melanie was hoping he had another reason, even though she liked the fact that he thought she would be a good trainer.

"And because it's another excuse to spend time with you," he added. His hand reached for hers, and she had a strange feeling in the pit of her stomach.

"What?" Melanie clasped her other hand at her side and tried to find the words that would settle the fluttering heartbeat in her chest. Was her hand suddenly clammy? Did he notice? "You know you don't need an excuse, right?"

"Good." He nodded to the changing room. "You should get changed."

Melanie didn't want to let go of his hand, but she knew she would have to. "I'll be right out,"

"Okay. I'm going to go help my mom out front."

Chase was giving her privacy, and she was happy about it because her mind was now racing. First, she got to be a junior trainer with a woman she highly respected. And then...she wasn't even sure what that was. Did he like her that way? He did hold her hand, but did that really mean he wanted to be more than friends? Melanie had never been in this position before, so it was not all that clear to her. The only thing she could do was play it by ear until it was spelled out for her.

As she changed, she wondered if her mother had been right. Did he have a crush on her? He was two years older and gorgeous. Why would he have a crush on her? Melanie looked at herself in the mirror. She wasn't ugly, just normal. Her sister Amber was the pretty one. That might be because she wore a layer or two of makeup, but still, Amber was beautiful, and his age. That thought made her stomach turn. She had to keep him away from her. What if he fell for her sister? Would Amber go out with him? No...probably not. She knew that Melanie liked him and had been teasing her for some time. Amber would be more likely to talk him into dating Melanie than scooping him up for herself. Amber was her ride or die...her protector and her partner in crime most of the time.

"Well, time to see what happens next," she told herself. If she weren't careful, she'd break out into a full-blown pep talk. That would be embarrassing, especially if Chase could hear her talking to herself.

When she came out of the locker room, she found Julia and Chase were waiting for her outside. Melanie smiled at them. "So, what's first? And don't we have a shift in a few hours?"

"We do, but Mom thought we could get an hour in at least." Chase shrugged his shoulders.

"And then when you're done, you can come back." Julia reached down to pick up one of the buckets. "Can you two get these?"

"Sure." Chase reached down to pick one up first. Melanie followed suit.

"What are we going to do?" Melanie was overly curious at this point.

"Sea lion duty," answered Julia. When she saw Melanie's deflated face, she continued. "We'll work with Kona after your shift."

"That way we have more time with her," Chase added.

"Okay."

Melanie could not believe how fast the time moved. They fed the sea lions and then had to turn around and get ready for their shift. Chase hadn't said anything else to her, which made her start to think she had imagined his previous words. She did have an active imagination. It was entirely plausible.

It wasn't until after they had finished their shift at the fish hut that Chase said anything else. "So, what are you doing on the Fourth?"

Melanie scrunched her lips together as she thought about what her family might be doing that day, besides working at the aquarium. That was only a week away at this point. That was how fast the summer was flying. As far as she knew, they would be doing the same thing they always did. They would drive across town and park along the side of the road so they could watch the fireworks without the huge crowds.

"Probably checking out the fireworks with my family. Why?"

"We're having a barbecue. My mom said it would be okay if I invited you. You can see the fireworks from my roof."

"Your roof? Are you nuts?" Melanie was overplaying this— she could tell how high pitched her voice was. Was he asking her out?

Chase grinned at her. "Best view in the town. You can see fireworks from every angle."

"Sounds like fun. I'll ask my mom." Melanie was sure her mother would let her go if she begged her enough.

"Good."

"Good." When her eyes met his, she felt the same warm feeling inside her. "Is this a...?"

"Date?" Chase fidgeted slightly, almost making her feel like she had misread it until he smiled at her. "I mean, yes. If you want it to be, that is."

"Are you asking me out?" Why was she such a blithering idiot?

"Yes, this is me asking you out." His grin disappeared, and he had a slightly nervous look on his face.

"I'd love to." She would make sure to give her mom her puppy dog eyes and remind her of how hard she had been working all summer.

"All done here?" Chase looked as if he were desperate to change the topic.

Had this been as embarrassing for him as it felt to her? Good, but a tad unusual and awkward. Was it like this every time? She sure hoped not. Melanie was pretty sure the ground had been about ready to swallow her whole earlier. She tried to shake her nerves off, but they were laced with excitement that she couldn't quite shake. Melanie could not wait to tell her sister. Amber was going to lose her mind!

Melanie blinked and told herself that Chase had just asked her a question. It would be weird not to answer. "Yep. Let's go clock out so we can get to the tank." Melanie followed Chase out of the booth and waited as he made sure the door was locked. "So, what do you think we'll do today?"

"I dunno. Maybe more of the same?" Chase shrugged his shoulders.

"I hope we get to work on the rings." Melanie liked tossing the rings to Kona to see how fast the dolphin could retrieve them. It was second to splashing the dolphin with water.

"She seems to like them, almost as much as she likes soaking you," Chase teased her.

"Hey, I don't mind getting drenched. Besides, you nearly fell in the water last time, if I remember correctly."

Chase raised his hands in the air. "Hey, I caught myself at the last second."

Melanie shook her head at him. He nudged her with his elbow, and she rolled her eyes. "Whatever. If you say so."

"What time does your mom get off work today?"

"Later. I was planning on sticking around here until she was done."

"Do you want to hang out with me?" Chase looked almost hopeful.

Her alarm beeped, and Melanie looked down at her bag. "Yeah, sure. Hold on. I have to do something real quick."

Why did reality have to slap her in the face? She had almost forgotten to take her medicine at all. Her mom would have her hide if she forgot to take it. As much as it irritated her, she knew that the medication was keeping her cancer at bay. Melanie had so much to live for. It was not time to let it come back. Hannah was going to have a cow when Melanie told her about Chase. All she had to do now was convince her mom to let her hang out with him. Then again, that might not be too hard. Hadn't she already given her the green light on that? Still, better safe than sorry. She'd make sure to check in with her mom later.

When she was in the bathroom, she quickly swallowed her medicine. If every Monday were like this one, it would soon become her favorite day of the week. Melanie could not wait to see what else lay in store for her. Her heart was beating erratically in her chest as she thought about seeing Chase later when they were done working. Would it be awkward? It had been fine until he expressed his interest in her. Now she was feeling even more self-conscious. She decided to do the only thing she could do—make the best of it and pray that she didn't make a fool of herself. Why did most of life feel that way?

CHAPTER 10

When Melanie finally came out of the changing room, she was ready to face the rest of her day. The fact that she would be spending the majority of it with Chase made her feel a little warm and fuzzy. Was she supposed to feel this goofy and light headed? Was that normal? Did he have the same mixed up feelings inside, or had he had a girlfriend before? Was that what he really wanted her to be? Melanie had never considered that option previously. Not really. Having a crush on someone was different than actually having them be interested back. This was unchartered territory.

"Hey," Chase greeted her.

"Hey." Yeah, it was awkward already. It was going to take some time to get used to. The dynamic between them would change. Nothing would ever be the same, but then again, that was the status quo for her life. Everything was always changing when she least expected it like Lori. None of them had expected her to get sick again. Part of her wondered if Lori had known for a while, but had chosen not to tell them. Maybe she hadn't wanted them to worry. Too late. Melanie was well past worried at this point.

And she was nervous. Excited. Sad. Happy. Angry. Part of

her felt as if she was swinging on a pendulum, riding the highs and lows with no real idea of when it would just even out. Fat chance of that, though. It was the same ride that she'd been on forever. Except now, she got to throw a new curve into it. Chase. That grin. Those eyes. The fact that he liked the same things she did. He was just as interested in helping Kona as she was. Chase would probably be more ready to listen to her go on and on about Kona than her sisters would.

Julia smiled at them, and by the way she glanced at Melanie, she knew he must have told her. Melanie wasn't sure what to feel about that.

"So, Junior Trainers, it's time to get started."

"Kona?" Melanie was more than hopeful. All she needed to make her day complete was to spend time with her favorite girl. Kona had become so important to her. Every time she helped the dolphin get a little closer to feeling comfortable made her feel better, if only for a short time. What Melanie wanted more than anything was for the dolphin to be released back into the ocean where she belonged. The moments she spent with her were not enough to carry Kona to a fulfilled life at the aquarium.

When they made their way up to the island, Kona was already watching for her. Melanie smiled despite herself. She reached over and patted the water to call her up. "Hello, girl."

Kona chattered at them before coming over to the island. She was getting much better at that. The tap of the water worked well since it produced sound waves in the water. The dolphin could sense her position using echolocation. Kona sat at the top of the pool watching them with her jaws open. Her teeth made her look like she was grinning up at her. Maybe it was her imagination, but dolphins always seemed to be smiling to her. A trick of the light perhaps, but Melanie found it charming anyway.

"Well, look at you." Melanie reached down and splashed water into Kona's mouth. The dolphin snapped her mouth open and closed as if trying to catch it. Melanie giggled despite herself. When Kona flicked the water with her fin, it shot toward both her and Chase, but he was the only one who got soaked.

"Hey!" Chase shook his head. "I see who she likes. She barely even got you."

"She's got good aim," teased Melanie.

"Says you," he grumbled, but he had a grin on his face.

"Throw her some fish." Julia nodded to the bucket beside them. Usually, it was Julia who fed her the fish, so her request caught Melanie off guard. Julia noticed and gave her a reassuring smile. "It's okay. One of the first things any trainer does is get the dolphin used to taking fish from them. It builds their trust."

Melanie reached into the bucket for a fish, then tossed it into Kona's mouth. The dolphin devoured it easily and looked at her as if she were ready for more. She waited for Chase to follow the same orders. Kona did not seem to mind who was feeding her the fish, which was a good sign.

From there, they took turns throwing rings out to Kona. For the first time, Melanie saw Julia get in the water with Kona. She just floated near the side of the tank while they continued to play with Kona. The idea was to get her used to having someone in the tank, in case Julia needed to work with her in the water. It was also to test Kona's tolerance to Julia's presence. So far, Kona was not too freaked out by her. Maybe that was because they were still distracting her.

After an hour and a half, Julia told them their time was up. She still had other things to do, so they went back to the locker room to get their things. Melanie grabbed her stuff and changed as quickly as possible. When she was done, she texted her mom to make sure it was okay for her to spend the rest of the afternoon with Chase. Her mom just told her to stay out of trouble and keep her nose down, like she usually did. Even so, Melanie was pretty sure she was going to hear more from her later. More than likely, her mom would tell her she told her so. They would also need to talk about the fact that Mom had kept Melanie's move to a junior trainer from Melanie. While she knew it was supposed to be a surprise, part of her felt like she should have known all along. She was not in the mood for any more curveballs in her life, even if they were good ones.

When she left the changing room, she found Chase sitting on one of the benches. Why did she have to feel nervous all of a sudden? He was the same old Chase, wasn't he? While she had only known him for a few weeks, certainly one conversation did not change him into something else, unless that something else was a two-syllable word. One did not simply become boyfriend and girlfriend just by deciding to hang out with someone. There was more to it than that. At least she thought there was. This was new territory that she hadn't expected to find herself in so soon. Sure, some girls had already dated in middle school, but not her.

"Want to go watch one of the shows?" Chase suggested.

"Sure, if you don't mind sitting next to fish girl." Melanie pulled her shirt away from her and shuddered. "I didn't bring any clothes."

"You and me both." Chase waved his hand in front of him. "Smell those fumes."

Melanie giggled. This was the grossest conversation in the world, but it made her feel better. "Well, I wasn't going to say anything...."

"Ah, well, it could be worse."

"How's that?" Melanie's eyebrows rose curiously.

"I don't know honestly, but it could." Chase nodded to the sign ahead. "Dolphins?"

"Dolphins," agreed Melanie. She'd seen the show so many times she nearly had every word memorized. The script rarely changed. They needed to get a new writer.

"Shall we?" Chase held his hand out to her, and she nearly stopped in her tracks.

Hand holding? Were they already up to that? Wow, color her surprised. Melanie wrapped her fingers around his and gave him a shy smile. "We shall."

"This way, my lady," he teased her.

Melanie blushed slightly, all the while pretending not to be affected by his pretend chivalry. Chase was everything any girl could want in a boyfriend—cute, polite, funny, nice, and smart. He was also extremely focused on saving up for his car. From what he had told her recently, he would be there by the end of the summer. Nothing fancy really, just a puddle hopper that would get him from one place to the other. Melanie wondered if her mom would let her go out in the car with him. Wasn't that a typical teenage thing? Probably best not to push her luck just yet, especially considering Amber had never even been on a date yet.

Oh man, was she ever going to be jealous. Melanie would probably never hear the end of it, but it wasn't her fault that Amber had not found a boyfriend yet. She'd had plenty of opportunities, but Amber was picky. Melanie still wasn't sure what she was looking for in a potential boyfriend, for it changed from one moment to the next. Melanie had never bothered to make a list. She had simply met a boy that made her heart flutter in her chest the moment she saw him. Did that mean she would be with him forever? Forever was never a guarantee. Melanie knew better than to wish for something like that. Right now, she would settle for holding his hand and spending time with him.

As they made their way into the show arena, Chase let go of her hand so that they could walk across the metal bleachers. When they sat down, his hand reached for hers, and she smiled at him. "I've never watched a show like this before."

"I thought you'd have seen it a hundred times by now," he teased her.

"No…that's not what I meant. I mean…with someone else. Like this."

He squeezed her hand. "Me either."

"I kinda like it," Melanie said before she could second guess herself.

"Me too."

Did that mean he'd never had a girlfriend before? That made her feel a little better. That meant they were both in foreign territory together.

Melanie turned to watch the trainers getting ready for the show, afraid that if she looked at him too much that she would start blushing all over again. She quickly changed the subject. "Do you think someday that will be us?"

"Working a dolphin show?" Chase shrugged his shoulders. "Who knows?"

"I think I'd rather find a way to help the dolphins. Not exploit them."

"I hear you. It weighs on you. My mom sometimes can't sleep; she worries so much about the animals here."

"Your mom is the exception. A lot of the people here are just working for their paycheck. I know your mom cares. It's clear in everything she does. I've always admired her." Melanie knew that sounded cheesy, but it was the truth.

"Me too. I wouldn't mind working out in the field studying

the migration and health of whale pods, even."

"Whales, huh?" Melanie was surprised. "Why aren't you helping one of the other trainers?"

"Because if I did, I wouldn't get to spend the time with you." That charming grin showed the dimples at the corners of his mouth. He could probably get away with a robbery if he just flashed those things.

"I see. I thought it was because you liked dolphins." Melanie felt a little uncomfortable.

"It's both, really, but I do find the whales fascinating too, from a distance, of course."

"Yeah, you can only get so close to those guys." Especially orcas, she almost added. Everyone knew that they were killer whales and dangerous to other animals, including humans. There had been plenty of horrific accidents when an orca had attacked its trainer. Times were certainly changing. If only they would change so that dolphins were no longer allowed in captivity. As much as she had loved watching them for so long, Melanie knew that these animals were not meant to be kept in their tiny tanks. Even those that were born into captivity deserved much better.

"Truth." Chase shook his head as the first few lines of the show started. "They really need to switch that up."

"I was just thinking the same thing."

"Great minds." Chase winced when some lady in front of them turned to shush them. "Sorry."

Melanie bit back a giggle and used her other hand to zip her lips shut. The two of them stopped talking so everyone else could enjoy the show. Not that it bothered her. It was nice just to sit there holding his hand; it was simple and easy. There was no pressure to do anything but exist in the moment, and it made her feel at peace for the first time in forever.

The afternoon faded away faster than she would have liked, but that was what happened when she was having fun. She said goodbye to Chase before she had to report back to her mom. It had been awkward at first, for Melanie did not know how to say goodbye to a boy she was almost sort of dating. They had simply parted ways the way they usually did, which was a little awkward considering they had held hands for so long. There was no hug, no kiss; just a see you later with the promise of something more when she was ready for it. Neither one of them was pushing the limits, which was something Melanie was more than thankful for right now.

When Melanie made her way to her mother's office, she saw her looking over a file on her desk. "Hi, Mom."

"Someone's in a good mood," her mother teased her.

"I am?" Did she look any different? Melanie felt like the same person she always was. Maybe her outlook was a little lighter. Then again, anything was lighter compared to yesterday.

"Yeah. I haven't seen you smile this much since we brought River home from the shelter. Did you have fun?"

"Yes. This was the best day ever. I can't believe Julia wants me to be a junior trainer already. Did you twist her arm or something?"

"No. Not at all. She thought it would be a good idea considering how much rapport you already have with Kona. I think she's right. You're a natural, Mel."

Had it been anyone else, Melanie would have faded under her praise, but coming from her mother, it made her feel like she was the queen of the world. Mom had a way of making her feel like anything was possible. It was something that had been perfected over the years, as they both dealt with the ups and downs that came with her leukemia. Melanie sat down in the

115

seat across from her desk.

"And how was Chase?"

"Sweet." Melanie looked down at her hands and remembered how long he had held them. She smiled and looked up at her mom. "You were right."

"I told you. You do know my rules," her mom reminded her.

"Yes, Mom. I'm only sixteen. I don't have any serious plans." Hand holding was the right pace for her anyway. Why did everyone assume that every teen had to be interested in pushing the limit with their relationships? Not every teen was ready to be a full-blown adult. Besides, Melanie believed in saving some things for much later in life. There was plenty of time to be an adult later. At her age, she was barely able to make her own choices, much less be responsible for anyone else.

"Good. Just remember, no boy has the right to pressure you into anything that makes you feel uncomfortable. Do you understand?"

"Mom! It's Chase. He's not exactly a player."

At least she didn't think he was. From what Amber had told her, he kept mostly to a small crowd of teens at the high school. He was quiet in the classroom, always doodling on his notebook as he paid attention in class. Polite to his teachers, and always ready to help someone out if they needed help with their work. Chase was like an angel compared to some of the other guys, according to Amber. That made Melanie feel a lot safer with him, not to mention that he made her feel normal in a world that was often tilted off its axis.

"I know, but it still needs to be said. No one has the right to treat you with disrespect."

Melanie nodded. Her mom was right. Melanie believed in treating others the way she wanted to be treated. The world could benefit from The Golden Rule a little more often. If only that extended to the way animals were treated. Melanie would never understand why humans were so bent on dominating the creatures that walked upon this earth. She tried to push those thoughts aside, but having spent time with the traumatized dolphin earlier only drove that point home.

"So, any plans?" Her mom prodded.

"Julia already asked you, didn't she?" Melanie sighed. It was clear that the two of them had pushed for their kids to come together. While she should be irritated with her mom, Melanie was not. "Can I spend the Fourth of July with Chase?"

"I think that would be all right."

"Thanks, Mom." Melanie knew that her sisters would be upset with her for leaving them alone on that day, but she would try not to think of it. There had only been one Fourth of July that she had been absent from, and that was only because she had been sick in the hospital.

"You're welcome. You deserve to be happy, Mel."

Did she deserve it more than anyone else? She didn't think so. Everyone deserved to have some kind of happiness. Melanie didn't feel like she was in a special category just because her life had been so limited over the past few years. If nothing else, her cancer had taught her that life was what she made of it. Melanie was choosing to make the best of it. So far, she was more than succeeding. She had a lot to be thankful for, more so than ever.

CHAPTER 11

Melanie had started to count the days until the Fourth. Sure, she got to see Chase a few more times that week, but the Fourth felt like their first official date. Even though it was at his house, Melanie felt as if she were heading to the movies with him or something. It didn't bother her that his mother would be around because Melanie actually enjoyed spending time with her. Julia was a lot like her own mother. Melanie could tell how much she cared about Chase. As a single parent, he had been her entire world since he was born. Maybe that was why the two mothers had instigated this relationship. They both had a lot of respect for each other.

"So, are you going to do your face?" Amber was lying on her stomach with her head propped up on her hands as she stared at Melanie from her bed.

"No. Why would I do that? It would only melt off. Besides, what's wrong with my face?" Melanie didn't like to wear makeup. It made her face feel cakey. Besides, not every girl wanted to hide behind it. Melanie liked the natural glow on her face, probably more because she had seen a deathly pallor on it far too often. She did not ever want to look pale and pasty ever again.

"I was just offering if you wanted." Amber shrugged her

shoulders. "I still can't believe Mom is letting you date him."

"Why? Is something wrong with him?" She narrowed her eyes on her sister. Did she know something Melanie didn't?

"No, not at all. Chase is harmless. I just always thought I would be the first one to date."

"Me too," agreed Melanie. "So, what's stopping you?"

"I guess I'm too goal-oriented to waste my time."

By goal-oriented, what Amber really meant was she was focused on her job and building her social media. One day, Amber hoped to have a large enough following to support herself with it. YouTube stars made a lot of money because they used the followers to market to advertisers that paid for exposure. All Amber had to do was do what she did every day and grow her audience. She was close to views that would bring in a small amount of money. It was a good thing their mom was already on board. Social media could be a very dangerous place, which was why Linda Parker monitored their exposure to it.

"I thought I was too, but I never imagined I would have a guy like Chase in my life."

"Have you kissed?" Amber was not playing any games. She threw it right out there like it was nothing.

"No. Not yet." But she thought she might want to. She had barely even hugged him yet. Both of them were a little timid in their interactions with each other. Not to mention, they were pretty busy working and volunteering to focus on a real relationship. What they had was simple and new, and Melanie was not in a hurry to put it to the test.

"It will happen," Amber assured her.

"Have you ever kissed a boy before?" The words slipped out before Melanie could retract them.

"Yes."

"What?" Melanie's eyes narrowed on her sister. "When?"

"Eighth grade. It was stupid, really. He dared me to do it."

"What was it like?"

"Kissing a slimy fish." Amber shuddered as she recalled it.

"Ew." Melanie now imagined all the dead fish they filled the trays with every day. The thought of putting her mouth on any one of those made her feel sick to her stomach.

"But then there was Leo." Amber seemed to sigh dreamily.

"Who is Leo?" Melanie did not remember her talking about him ever.

"Freshman year. He was a sophomore. We were in the same math class."

Melanie realized that different ages were grouped into the courses at the high school. Not all subjects, just the ones where instruction needed to be differentiated. Her sister excelled in math, which often put her in classes with older students. "Excuse me? How come you never told me?"

Amber looked at her fingers, guiltily. "I didn't want to take away from...."

"Me." Melanie suddenly felt deflated. Her cancer had kept her sister from telling her something that had been epic. She thought they were closer than that. "I'm sorry, Amber."

"For what?"

"Not being there for you." Melanie sighed and fidgeted with the edge of her frayed jean shorts.

"You had a lot on your plate." Amber waved away her concern.

"So! I'm always here for you. Please don't hold out on me."

"I just didn't want you to feel bad because I was...."

"Living?" Melanie filled in the blanks when her sister paused. She saw the look of guilt flash on her face and wanted to soothe it away. "Look, Amber. No matter what happens to me, you will have an amazing life. You do not have to hide things from me. Besides, who do you think I'm going to tell when I have my first kiss?"

"It better be me." Amber gave her a "You know what's up" glance.

"It will be. And what happened to Leo?" Melanie was now honing in on the details her sister had left out.

"He moved at winter break. We tried to text each other, but long-distance never really works out. Besides, we weren't official." Amber paused. "That doesn't mean you should go around kissing random people. I mean...I thought we were a thing. And well, I think he thought I was just a way to pass the time between classes."

"Oh...that sucks on so many levels. I think we're a couple. I don't know that we've defined it."

"Trust me, you are. I've seen some of those texts. No guy sends heart emojis if he's not feeling you."

"True." Melanie blushed slightly. "He's sweet."

"Yes, he is. So, you're going to watch the fireworks together?"

"Yeah. I know it's always been our thing." Melanie felt a little guilty for not being with her family tonight, but she was too excited to let it bring her completely down.

"It's okay. I would have done the same thing, honestly. Make sure you put in a good word for me."

"Still eying, Trent?" Melanie remembered Amber talking about him the most. He was one of Chase's best friends, not that Melanie had met any of them. They had only been dating for a week, but she had already heard about most of his friends while she had been working with him this summer. Apparently, they thought they were daredevils. Thank goodness Chase did not feel the need to try to jump his bike over parked cars. Sometimes boys were just plain idiots.

"Sorta." Amber looked up at the ceiling and shrugged her shoulders. "At least he's not boring."

"Neither is Chase." Melanie didn't know if her sister was calling him boring or not, but to Melanie, he was just right. They had the same interests and wanted the same future working with marine life—albeit the particular marine life was in question, but still, they seemed to be on the same path.

"True. I didn't mean he was. It's just there are quite a few boys in my school who think they are God's gift to all girls. I don't know why they think that or why the girls fawn all over them. It makes no sense." Amber shook her head and sighed. "Sometimes, I feel way older than my age."

"Girl, same." Melanie agreed with her, but her words came from a different place altogether. She had already dealt with enough trials in her life to make someone run screaming, and yet Melanie met every challenge head-on. She would continue to do so as long as she was able. As long as luck was on her side, she would ride the wave, living the life she had in front of her the way Lori would want her to. Melanie hadn't told her about Chase yet, because she didn't want to rub it in her face. She knew Lori would be happy for her, but it seemed too much like a slap in her face. Melanie wished she could save her from the darkness that had wrapped around her.

Even though Lori was still fighting, the end was closer every day. She barely had the energy to read her texts, so her mom was reading them to her and would type in her replies. The drugs were not working. The only thing they seemed to be doing was making her feel worse. It made Melanie feel so helpless. There was no rhyme or reason as to why one kid got better, and the other fell behind again. No one ever knew when it would happen. That was why it was essential to continue to live her life to the fullest. Melanie refused to give in to the cancer that hung over her head. Especially now, when everything was going so well for her.

"So, when are you going?"

"Soon. Mom said I could go around lunch and hang out until after the fireworks."

"As long as you're home for curfew, right?"

"Julia's going to drive me home." Their moms had already worked out all those details. Melanie couldn't figure out if it were a good thing they knew each other so well or not. Only time would tell.

"Nice. Mom won't let you ride with Chase yet?"

"Not yet. Maybe in a few months when he's had more experience. By then, he might even have his own car."

"That's always possible. Just don't let him drive like an idiot," her sister cautioned her.

"I wouldn't." Melanie wasn't going to let some stupid random act take her out if she could control it. She had certainly not fought so hard to lose her life to something stupid, like texting and driving. No message was ever that important.

Amber got up and started to set some of her makeup on her desk. Melanie could tell she had something turning in her head. "Going to make a video?"

"I might as well, especially if I'll have the room to myself."

"Have fun! I think I'll go downstairs." Even though there was still an hour before she had to leave, Melanie was starting to feel antsy.

"Okay. And Mel?"

"Yeah?"

"Have fun."

"I will."

Melanie walked down the stairs and turned on the TV and watched it for the next hour. Kimmie was over at her friend's house right now, as she had spent the night there. She would probably come home after lunch. So for now, Melanie could watch whatever she wanted. Melanie got lost in a cheesy sitcom while she wasted time.

When her mom finally came down, Melanie was ready to go. Her mom said very little to her, which Melanie appreciated. She was in her head too much as it was, and didn't need her mom to make her any more nervous. This was a date outside the aquarium, maybe not as real as going to the movies, but Melanie was excited nonetheless.

As the car pulled into the drive, Melanie took in the house before her. It was a small brick ranch with a two-car garage attached. The fact that it was an average size house reminded her of how typical his family was. With it just being the two of them, they didn't need the space that Melanie's family did. The Parkers lived in a two-story house that had four bedrooms to accommodate the three children, Mom, and their grandmother. Melanie and Amber had shared their room for as long as she could remember, but it wasn't a hardship since the two of them had the largest room in the house.

When the screen door swung open, Melanie saw Chase peek his head outside. Hundreds of butterflies fluttered inside her stomach, making her nervousness equal to the excitement that rose inside her. Melanie unbuckled her seatbelt and reached for the bag at her feet.

"You got everything, Mel?" Her mom asked her.

"Yep. Got my meds, my swimsuit, my cellphone." Melanie knew her mom was asking if she had brought her meds, but she decided not to hold that against her. She was just being a mom.

"Do you need me to come inside?" Was that a hopeful look on her mom's face?

Melanie decided not to crush her need to check in with Julia. "Up to you, Mom."

"I'll just come say a quick hello to Julia. Then I'll head home."

Melanie shrugged her shoulders. "Whatever."

Melanie got out of the car and closed the door behind her. As she walked up to the front door, she saw her mom following behind her from the corner of her eyes. When she got closer to Chase, she nodded back to her. "Mom just wants to say hi to your mom. Not like she won't see her at work tomorrow or anything."

Chase grinned at the hidden meaning. "The more, the merrier. We have some family coming soon. My grandparents, my uncle, and his wife."

Melanie was already well prepared for that. He had told her it was a family get together, so it wasn't that much of a surprise. All their extended family was scattered across the country, so family get-togethers were a rare occurrence. Melanie just hoped she didn't stick out like a sore thumb.

"Come on in." Chase ushered Melanie inside, then greeted her mother. "Hello, Mrs. Parker. Come on in. My mom's in the kitchen."

Melanie followed him into the kitchen and tried not to fidget when she saw his mom cutting up fruit on the counter. She was trying to think of what she should call Julia in this setting. At work, she called her Julia, but this was a different situation.

She decided to use the manners that her mother had given her. "Hello, Mrs. Makenzie."

"It's just Julia." Julia smiled at her and then turned to see her mom there too. "Hello, Linda. Glad you could bring her by."

"Of course. You have a lovely home."

"Thank you. It's probably only this clean twice a year."

"Sounds about right. That's the life of a working mom with growing kids, though."

"Isn't it, though? And trying to get them to keep on top of it is like herding cattle." Julia set the knife down and wiped her hands on a towel.

"Hey! I resent that remark," complained Chase.

"Really? There's only one of you, and yet somehow, six towels are always on the floor."

"It's the cats. They're always pulling them down." Chase nodded to the orange tabby cats that were perched near the glass patio door.

"Uh-huh. Likely story. Did they take a shower with them and get the floor wet too?"

"I plead the fifth," grumbled Chase.

"Do you need any help?" Melanie offered.

"Aren't you sweet? If the two of you could make sure all the pool floats are operational, that would be great. I'm almost done here anyway."

"Okay." Melanie turned to see her mom looking at her with pride. "See you tonight, Mom?"

"You bet. You guys have fun. I'm just going to chat with Julia for a few mins, and then I'm heading back home to hang out with the rest of the family."

"See ya!" Melanie reached over and kissed her mom on the cheek, which made her mom smile brighter. If it had been any other people around her, Melanie might not have let down her guard, but she did not care if Chase thought she was weird for having a strong relationship with her mother. Mom had been through hell and back with her. Melanie was not about to forget that any time soon.

"Bye, baby."

"The pool floats are out here." Chase gestured to the glass door. He walked closer to it and shooed the cats away. They glared at him before they moved out of the way.

"Do they ever go outside?"

"Sometimes, but we've had coyotes come into the yard over the years, so we tend to keep them inside as much as possible."

"Coyotes?" Melanie gave him a dubious look.

"Well, we do have a larger yard, and it backs up to a lot of open space."

"I see what you mean." Melanie almost whistled. While the pool wasn't all that huge, the yard was at least half an acre, which was a big size for the real estate in the area. "Wow, you must spend a lot of time here."

"When we're not at the aquarium. That's where the bulk of Mom's tax returns have gone."

Melanie couldn't help but think it must be nice to have something else to spend money on besides doctor's visits and medication. Not that they had a large yard themselves, but she could dare to dream. She could see herself spending a lot of time here with him. "It's nice."

As she looked around her, she almost felt like she was in the middle of an oasis. The moment she stepped onto the patio, she was shaded by the pagoda that was constructed over it. To the left was a built-in grilling area that almost looked like an outdoor kitchen. On her right was a large patio table with cushioned chairs that looked almost new. The patio under her had large rectangular cement blocks that were lined with about two inches of gravel rocks on each side. This wasn't atypical for a backyard in Arizona. What she was actually surprised by was the small patches of landscaped grass around the yard. How in the world did they keep it so green in this desert heat? They didn't have grass in her yard. Mom said it was less maintenance to keep the graveled look. Not that it mattered to the girls at all, because it was too small to play in anyways.

The pool was not humongous, but its lima bean shape had enough room for a small group of people. Melanie wondered if Chase had learned to swim in this very pool. Melanie had learned at the local parks and recreation with her sister Amber. Small floats were sitting in the pool already, probably kept off the ground to keep the heat from the cement from melting them. It was going to be a hot one today. If it stayed under a hundred, it would be a miracle, good thing they were used to the heat. Although they would still have to watch their exposure, too much heat was a bad thing.

"So, which floats need aired up?" Melanie asked him.

"None of them. Mom was just getting us out the door so that they could talk about us."

"Oh." Melanie nibbled on her bottom lip. "What do you think they're talking about?"

"What parents talk about when their kids start dating." He smiled at her, and Melanie felt as if the sky was filled with double rainbows.

"True. Or maybe they're talking about the aquarium." It could be that, couldn't it? They did work together. Melanie half-hoped that were the case. She didn't want to be under her mother's scrutiny. There was no telling what her mom was talking to Julia about.

"Maybe. I heard there was a problem with one of the seals yesterday."

"Which one?"

128

"Sammie."

"Figures. He's a character, isn't he?" Melanie had seen him trying to chase the birds off his island one time. It wasn't that he was a bully. He just liked to play a little more than the birds did.

"He is."

The screen door opened, and an older couple came out, decked in Americana from head to toe. The moment they saw Chase, the older woman made a bee-line for him. "Chase, honey. How are you?"

"Good, Grandma." He stepped forward for a mandatory hug, and rather than stiffen, he threw his arms around her. It was clear how much his family meant to him. When he stepped back, he turned to face Melanie. "This is my girlfriend, Melanie."

"So it is. You're right; she is a looker."

Melanie's mouth nearly dropped to the floor. Did he talk about her? Not only that, but he had also referred to her as his girlfriend to his grandmother.

Melanie stepped forward and gave her a shy smile as she offered her hand to her. "Nice to meet you, Mrs. Makenzie."

"Oh, honey, no. It's nice to meet you. And it's Grandma." The woman waved her hand away and wrapped her arms around her.

Melanie looked over at Chase with a mild sense of panic. His grin told her he knew that his grandmother was going to bear hug her. Melanie had no course of action but to sink into the hug. She closed her eyes and smelled roses that reminded her of her own grandma, who was at home holding the fort down right now.

"He hardly ever stops talking about you." Grandma patted her on the back before she released her.

Melanie's eyebrows rose curiously. "Oh, he doesn't?"

"This is Grandpa John." Chase nodded to the man who was

watching the interaction with a merry twinkle in his eyes.

"Nice to meet you, dear. Don't worry; she's the hugger. I tend to be the lazy waver." He held his hand up as he waved a slight greeting. "Louise, don't scare the poor girl off."

The nerves she had manufactured earlier started to disappear as the conversation turned from her to what they did at the aquarium. Before long, they were all talking about a common topic that took the heat off of her. When his aunt and uncle arrived, it was pretty much a rinse and repeat. Melanie felt at home with all of them, which was a relief. The day passed faster than she would have liked from eating to swimming to playing cards with his family. Melanie was almost sad to see them go, but they didn't have plans to stay for the fireworks.

When dusk started to fall, Chase set a ladder up against the back of his house. Melanie gave him a worried glance, even though he had secured it properly. "You weren't serious about watching the fireworks on the roof, were you?"

"It's perfectly safe. I've been climbing up here since I was five," he assured her.

"What if I'm afraid of heights?" She challenged him.

"Are you?"

"No. But...." She heard him snort with laughter.

"Then what's the problem?"

"Nothing. It's just I've never sat on a roof before." Melanie looked up at the sloped roof and wondered how in the world he expected her to climb up it. It looked steep from here, but maybe she just imagined it.

"Just give it a try. I promise you won't be disappointed."

"What about your mom?"

"She's going to watch the local show on TV tonight."

"Oh. Okay. You go first." Melanie nodded to the ladder. She

was not about to go first. No way, no how.

"No problem." He reached down to the ground and picked up the thick woven blankets he had set there earlier.

"What are those for?" Melanie wondered if he planned on sliding down the roof on them. That did not seem like a good idea.

"The roof gets hot," he explained.

Chase tossed the blankets over his shoulder and started to climb the ladder. It shook just a little but was sturdier than she thought it would be. When he got to the top, he climbed onto the ledge and disappeared for a moment to toss the blankets somewhere she could not see just yet. Then his head popped over the side. "Are you coming?"

"Sure." Melanie wished her voice sounded more confident. She wasn't a risk-taker, really, but she didn't think he would purposefully lead her onto the roof if he thought it would be a bad idea. Besides, his mom was on board with it too, so how bad could it be? Melanie took one step at a time, and while she thought the ladder would tremble under her, it was actually quite sturdy. When she got up to the top, Melanie slid her knees onto the roof briefly, not realizing how hot it would be.

"Here." Chase offered his hand to her and helped her to her feet. She was almost unprepared for his strength as her body slid way too close to his. He wrapped his arms around her and hugged her close to him. Even though she was far above the ground, she had never felt so safe as she did wrapped up in his arms. She closed her eyes and breathed in slowly, smelling the sunblock and chlorine that were like a cologne only she would appreciate.

"Let's sit." Chase gestured to the blankets.

"How much longer?" She asked him as she climbed the slight angle of the roof to sit on the closest blanket.

"Not long. You can see they are already starting to test them. So perfect timing."

Melanie watched the sky and saw the first few bursts of bright lights exploding across the sky. Like tiny umbrellas, they dazzled her from afar. Even from here, she could hear them explode before they rained their colors down on the world below. This was the perfect view.

"It's so beautiful," she whispered in awe.

"Yes, it is."

Melanie turned to find him staring at her instead of the display before them, and her heart seemed to melt like a slab of butter on a summer-soaked sidewalk. As he moved his face closer to hers, Melanie almost forgot how to breathe. His hand touched the side of her cheek right before his lips touched hers, and she nearly sank into them. Closing her eyes, Melanie tried to capture this moment forever in her mind.

It was a gentle kiss, soft and sweet like the soft breeze that filtered across the roof. When it was over, he wrapped his arm around her shoulder, and she sank against him. This was truly the beginning of a romance that she hoped would last much longer than the summer. For the first time in forever, Melanie forgot about the shadows in her past. Her world was covered in a rainbow of colors inside and out as she watched the rest of the lights swirl in the sky. No matter what, she would hold onto this moment for the rest of her life.

CHAPTER 12

When Melanie awoke the next day, the nostalgia of the night before still surrounded her. It was almost like she was living a fairytale life with her very own Prince Charming. She knew that what she felt for Chase was growing much faster than she'd thought it would. From crush to first love, Melanie was already head over heels for him. If anyone had told her this would have happened to her, she would never have believed them, but here it was. Her worries seem to slip away for the first time in forever.

That was until her phone started to blow up with messages. Melanie leaned over to the nightstand and picked up her cell phone. Hannah had been texting her since five o'clock in the morning. Melanie had been too asleep to hear the small dings. She was surprised that Amber had slept through them too. Melanie thumbed through them and saw the direness inside them.

Lori. Her parents had withdrawn care. She was going to live out her final days with her family in the comfort of her own home. Her heart sunk to the pit of her stomach. Guilt rose in its place. Here she was feeling happier than she had in a long time, while her friend was dying. Melanie closed her eyes and tried to remind herself that it was okay to live, to believe in something bigger than herself. Tears pooled in her eyes, and a burning sensation filled the back of her throat as the anger rose inside her.

Hope. They all held out for it, but for Lori, it was well past its expiration. Melanie had the urge to throw something just to see it smash against the wall, or to rip the curtains down and watch the rod come crashing to the floor. She reached for her pillow and shoved it hard against her face as the sobs she had been holding back, wracked her body painfully. Before she knew it, Melanie could no longer hide the anguish that welled up inside. She tried to stifle it into her pillow well enough to keep it hidden from the rest of the world. No one would understand how she felt.

Amber sat up in bed and saw her crumpled over the pillow. "Mel? What's wrong?"

Melanie could not put it into words. She held up her phone as Amber rushed over to her. While her sister read the messages, a light dawned on her face. Amber wrapped her arms around Melanie and held her while she cried. This wasn't the end for Lori. She hadn't died yet, but it was just around the corner, and Melanie wasn't ready for it. How could she be? Melanie had spent so much time wrapping herself up in a confident bubble, trying to ignore the reality most people with cancer faced every single day. The good, the bad, the ins and outs, they all slapped her in the face like a cold washrag.

"It's not fair," Melanie forced out through sniffles. "She was so close."

"Mel, she's still here."

"She is, but it won't be long." Melanie had understood the undercurrent in the texts more than her sister ever would. Cancer kids had a bond; no one could decipher. Their language was one of perseverance, determination, and often heartbreak. Their parents came close to deciphering it, but unless they were members of the club, they would never truly understand it.

"Mel, I'm so sorry." Amber hugged her tight.

The whole outburst must have caught her mother's attention, for the door opened slowly. Linda saw her daughters huddled together on Melanie's bed and walked over to them. The bed sank under her weight as she shooed Amber away. "I've got this, Amber."

"Okay." Amber released her almost reluctantly and moved from the bed.

Melanie saw her sister's face as she walked out of the room. Helplessness, fear, and something else she couldn't quite decipher was written across it. When her mom slid her arms around her, she felt a little bit of the cloud slide away. Melanie let herself cry for the day that was yet to come, the day that she would have to watch her friend's family say goodbye to her that one last time without wondering whether or not she or Hannah might be next. Every time one of them died, the fear of relapse entered her mind. Melanie didn't want to think about it, but it was there like a haunting whisper that would never stop. It washed over her like a flood.

"Would you like me to call you in sick today, Mel?" Her mom offered.

Melanie tried to slow her breathing and let herself think about what she needed to do to feel all right. Today, she would not be able to think about anything but Lori, but if she stayed home, she wouldn't be to spend time with Chase. Then again, if he saw her like this, he would probably wonder what was wrong. Melanie didn't have the words to explain it to him right now.

"Yes. Can I please stay home?"

"Sure, baby. I'll move one of the runners to the hut. It will be fine," her mom assured her.

"Thanks, Mom."

"Just hang in there, Mel. You're going to be okay."

She hoped so. Right now, nothing felt okay. Melanie watched her mom leave the room and closed her eyes. What was she going to tell Chase? Headache? Stomach ache? Family emergency? The truth? Would he understand, or did she underestimate him? There was only one way to find out.

Hey. That was simple enough. She didn't want him to think he had done something wrong. Would he think she was avoiding him? Melanie had to make it clear that she wasn't.

Morning.

I'm not feeling well today. Maybe that was a poor choice of words. She might want to rethink it. It was too late now, though.

Everything all right?

Yes. No. I got bad news. A friend of mine is dying. That about summed it up without her even needing to mention cancer. It also made it clear that it wasn't anything he had done at all. Part of her wished he were here now. Melanie felt safe in the circle of his arms, like nothing in the world could touch her. If only it worked that way.

Do you need anything?

Time. Which was why she was taking today off. She would regroup, reach out to Hannah, maybe even make a video message for Lori to watch later. More than anything, she would come to terms with what was about to happen. Death. Melanie prayed that Lori's comfort care would at least be able to minimize the pain.

I'm here if you need me. Would he really be? What if her cancer came back too? Would she be able to let him be there for that? Or would it chase him off? That thought terrified her.

Thank you. I should be back for my next shift on Wednesday. Tell your mom I'm sorry. Melanie felt bad that she wouldn't be there for Kona today. The dolphin had started to look for her whenever Julia got near the tank now. It was good that Kona was adapting a little, but there was still a long way to go.

Don't worry about it. I'll keep Kona happy until you're back. Chase's assurance made her feel a little better. He knew her heart was conflicted. How she didn't know, but he seemed to know her better than most people, and in a short time too.

Thanks, Chase. What would I do without you? Her summer would have been boring, that's for sure. If it weren't for Lori's crisis, this would be the best summer of her life.

Stay on the ground without risking your neck.

Melanie giggled despite herself. Yes, she had been terrified to climb up on the roof, but once she had gotten to the top, she realized it was not as scary as she thought it would be. It had definitely been worth it. Her first kiss was almost like a fairytale. He had certainly planned it well if that was what he had intended to do when they got up there. Melanie would carry that memory with her for the rest of her life.

I'd risk my neck with you any day of the week.

Same. Take care, Mel. Here if you need me.

Thank you.

She wanted to add "I love you," but that seemed like it might be too soon to say. Just because they'd kissed did not mean she could assume she was the love of his life. Nor did she want to be the one to say it first. Part of her didn't want him to say it at all, because it seemed to her that everyone she loved seemed to leave her one way or the other. Her father, her friends. Who would be next? Grandma Mimi? Her mother? Melanie squeezed her eyes shut and told herself not to go there. Those thoughts were destructive.

Picking up her phone, she texted Hannah back, thanking her

for letting her know. Melanie had planned to tell her all about her date with Chase, but now it seemed so unimportant. Pulling the covers over her head, Melanie sank back into the mattress. Happiness was way too fleeting. It never seemed permanent.

As the day continued, Melanie received random texts from Chase. He was worried about her. It was sweet, especially when he sent her pictures of Kona's smiling face with the words *Smile, someone loves you.*

Melanie smiled despite the melancholy she felt. *Thank you, Chase. I needed that.*

Thought so.

I'll be okay. And Melanie meant it. She knew somewhere she would find the strength to get past this. All she had to do was get over the fears that echoed inside. That was easier said than done, but Melanie could do it.

Good. Cause Kona loves you too.

Wait, was he saying he loved her before? Melanie closed her eyes and conjured the images from the night before. The explosion of light, the touch of his lips on hers, the cool breeze that made her snuggle up against him. Rainbows and light swirled inside her as she realized that she could only take on so much of Lori's pain. It was his declaration that made her realize that this was the life that Lori would want her to be living. If Melanie let Lori's illness impair her own happiness, Lori would never forgive her. Did that mean that Melanie had to ignore the sad feelings inside? No. She should acknowledge them for what they were: grief. Grief was natural in this situation. It would ebb and flow around her as Lori's final days came to pass, but the people who loved her would help pick up the weight and lift her spirits.

I love you too. Was it normal to feel head over heels like this? She felt like a goofy teen who had suddenly forgotten how to speak or walk while chewing gum. Any moment she was about to stick her foot in her mouth or trip over her shoelaces. She was sure to make a fool of herself eventually, but that was something she could survive.

Time for water drills. I'll text you later.

You better.

And he did for the next two days at different intervals. He left enough time in between each one to make her wonder when he would text her next. When he texted her a picture of his cats posed in precarious positions, Melanie almost lost it. She was glad his sense of humor kept her spirits high. It made it easier for her to remind herself that she was all right and would continue to be all right.

Melanie spent her time trying to come to terms with Lori's cancer while she had the chance. She was determined to go back to work on Wednesday and get back to her normal life. Melanie sent text messages to Lori's parents every day to let them know how much she loved Lori. She sent every butterfly picture she could find in text messages, finding ones that were unique. Hannah and she both had tried to find species that Lori might never have seen before, as the only thing she had ever wanted was to be able to find different species in the wild. They had all thought Lori would have time to do so, but life didn't always work out the way they planned. Especially not when cancer seemed to be behind the wheel.

Time wasn't infinite. It was evident with every single one of her friends that had died. Her mortality stared her down, and Melanie could feel it. The cancer inside her was like a ticking time bomb, ready to explode onto the scene at a moment's notice. Melanie didn't want to admit her fear to anyone else. It was hard enough to see it in her mother's posture whenever she walked in the door. Linda was getting the same updates that Melanie was. The outlook was bleak, but they all gathered around Lori from near and far, sending her prayers wrapped in enough love to send her off when it was her time to go. They would not visit her again, because this time was for her family to come to terms with the end.

Melanie banded together with Hannah to keep focused on the future instead of being trapped in the miserable present. They were keeping a constant vigil with each other to make sure their spirits didn't get too low. Melanie had confided in her about Chase, even when she didn't feel like confiding in her sister. Hannah was more than excited for her and told her to hang onto her happiness. Lori would not want her to focus on the sad. Melanie knew she was right, but it was a hard road to walk, knowing someone you loved was not going to survive. How could she stay happy while Lori was losing everything? Because Lori had lived her life to the fullest, even up to the last treatments. Lori hadn't let her illness limit her. While she didn't get to travel around the world to find her butterflies, Lori's voice had been influential in the cancer community as she told the world about her experiences. The seventeen-year-old had been blogging for years now, with every up and down, every twist and turn, as she tried to educate others.

When she took her last breath on this earth, Lori would still be remembered. Even in seventeen years, she had made her mark. That was what Melanie wanted. To have a life that was put to good use while she was able to live it. Did that mean she wouldn't break down every time she lost another friend? No. But for each one that didn't survive, there were at least two that did. There was hope, and Melanie would remember to look for it in every living moment. She would not let anyone forget it.

CHAPTER 13

Wednesday came and went, and Melanie got back to living her life. Chase asked for her to share only what she was willing to about Lori. She told him about Lori's cancer without telling him about her own. Melanie was afraid that if he knew the truth, it would be too much for him to handle. She should know. Melanie had lived with it for years now, and she barely had a handle on it. How could she expect him to? So, instead of telling him, she pretended that the only thing she was worried about was losing Lori, when deep inside, she was afraid she would lose herself too. That was something he would never understand.

When Melanie woke up that morning, she was exhausted. Having worked the day before, she chalked it up to just overdoing it a little. She had stayed to help with Kona for a few hours, then spent the majority of the evening with Chase and Julia. Melanie had fallen asleep almost as soon as her head hit the pillow, which was a rare occurrence. Usually, she had to find a way to fall asleep, like reading a book or listening to music. It wasn't even like she went to bed late. It was around seven when she went to bed.

Melanie tried to wipe the sleep from her eyes, but it felt like a permanent feature. Her phone vibrated on the nightstand, and she wanted to shove it to the floor. Melanie was not ready to be up yet, but she had already slept too long. She pushed up in bed and reached for the phone. Twenty messages since six? It was only seven now. Melanie scrolled through them, and a knot formed in the pit of her stomach. She had known this day was coming, but even so, nothing could have prepared her for it. Tears fell down her face despite her strong will to keep them at bay.

"Mel?" It was like Amber had a beacon for her distress. "What is it?"

"Lori...." Melanie couldn't say the final word that would clear it up.

Amber did not need her to say another word. She leapt from her bed and wrapped her arms around her shoulders. Melanie sank against her as the tears flooded her face. Her sobs wracked her body with a force she did not expect. Melanie clung to her sister's arms, trying to find a way to make sense of it all. There wasn't a way, not where the cancer was concerned. It was a senseless disease that reared its ugly head whenever it wanted to with no rhyme or reason, and while the medical field had made leaps and bounds to eradicate the disease, there was still so much more to be done.

"It's okay, Mel. I'm here." Amber soothed her as she hugged her tighter.

Melanie cried until no more tears would come out of her eyes. And even then, the sobs continued. She cried for Lori, for the life that had been cut way too short, and for the hope that had withered like a dried-up dandelion in the cracks of a sidewalk on a hot summer day. She cried for Hannah, who had been even closer to Lori than she had. Hannah would be more than devastated by Lori's death. And then she cried for herself, for the tiny girl who had lost her childhood way too early to an invisible disease that dictated her entire life. The fear that raced inside her almost paralyzed her. Every time one of them relapsed, they all relapsed inside themselves, hiding among the fear they tried to keep hidden from the outside world.

Fear? She was well past the fear. Paranoia sliced through her like a wicked blade that left only invisible scars.

"Do you want me to tell Mom?"

"No." Melanie wiped her eyes. She just wanted to get through today and pretend none of it had happened.

"But, Mel —"

"I'm okay. I just need to get ready for work." Melanie brushed her words off, ignoring the concerned look on her face.

"Mel —"

"She probably already knows, Amber. Besides, I have work to get to, and that's just what I'm going to do."

It wasn't like Melanie was trying to pretend that it never happened. She was simply moving forward with her life the way Lori would want her to. Besides, Kona needed her. The past few weeks had brought her even closer to Melanie, and she refused to give up that progress because Lori had died. Melanie could deal with her death later. Right now, she needed to think about the living.

"Okay." Amber was reluctant to give in to her.

"I'm going to be all right. I'm just going to take a shower." Melanie gave her a feeble smile that she hoped would put her sister at ease as she pushed away from the bed. Gathering her work clothes, she headed into the bathroom to get ready for the day. She stayed in the shower until all the puffiness under her eyes had disappeared. By the time she was finished getting dressed, no one would have ever guessed that she'd had a crying session.

No one except Amber, who was barely able to keep herself together. Amber hadn't known Lori well, but her death was a reminder to her sister that Melanie would always be trying to outrun the same fate. Melanie wished she could comfort her and let her know that she was all right, but deep down inside, Melanie was afraid something was wrong. She prayed that wasn't the case, but prayers were not always answered. Melanie struggled to maintain her faith in a world that seemed ready to tear it down every single day.

When her mom came downstairs, worry was etched across the wrinkles on her forehead. "Mel?"

"I'm all right. Can we go to work now?" Melanie knew her mom would know about Lori. It was stupid to pretend otherwise.

"Are you sure you want to work today?"

"Mom! Yes. Please, can we go already?"

Melanie heard the touchy volume to her voice, but she couldn't help herself. Why couldn't anyone understand that she didn't want to talk about it? She wasn't there to absolve them from their own feelings about Lori. She could barely handle her own. Melanie was tired of being everyone's smiling emoji. At any moment, her smile would crack and show the struggling child beneath, the one who wanted to stay in bed, snuggling the world's largest teddy bear while she begged the sandman to wake her up from the dream he had slipped into her head. This was no dream, though. It was a nightmare she could not wake up from.

"If you're all right."

All right? Far from it, but Melanie was not about to admit that any time soon. Melanie grabbed her backpack from the closet and swung it over her shoulders. "I'm ready. Let's go."

Thankfully, her mother was quiet on the way to the aquarium.

Even so, it left Melanie to her own thoughts. She tried to distract herself with her phone, but the messages just popped up. Hannah was having a hard time with Lori's death, and Melanie had no idea what to text her back. Nothing she said would truly help her. She settled for the only words that made sense. *The world is filled with less light.*

It was the truth. Every time one of them passed, a little more light fizzled. They all banded around each other with their battle cries to never give up, but sometimes they simply could not outrun the fight.

Yes, it is.

I'm working today, hoping to shake the blues away.

Are you sure that's wise?

Yes. I need to.

Be careful.

Be kind, Melanie wrote her back. She knew Hannah's mood would be up and down all day. Hannah would want to rage at the world, but in the end, the only one who ended up hurt would be Hannah. Her friend would probably overeat, then get sick. Sometimes too much food did not interact well with all the medications they took. Hannah would likely fall into her old patterns where she had the ultimate debate—to eat or not to eat. Either one could be damaging unless she were self-aware. Usually, Melanie was up to keeping her on task from afar. Today was not one of those days. As soon as she reached the aquarium, Melanie planned to check out from the whole situation.

And that was exactly what she did. When she saw Chase at the hut, she greeted him the way she usually did, with a smile she had manufactured for years to mask the pain inside her. "Morning."

"Good morning, sunshine." He smiled brightly at her, and

she soaked it up.

His carefree nature carried them through the entire shift. Melanie was able to pretend that she was the same old girl he had always known, even though inside she felt like part of her had died. A few times during her shift, she felt the heat almost take her breath away, but she hid it the best that she could, chalking it up to waking up tired and dealing with news no one wanted. She continued to push through, holding out for the moment she could get to her work with Kona.

"Can you believe it went so fast?" Chase asked her as they passed the fish hut on to the next shift.

"Yeah." She gave him a half-smile.

"You all right?" He asked her.

"Fine. Just tired. I don't think I slept well last night," she lied. Melanie didn't want to talk about Lori with him. Not just yet. She knew he wouldn't quite understand. This went far deeper than just losing a friend to cancer. It was like she was losing herself in the process, for her fears gripped her from every angle.

"Me either. Must be something in the air. You ready to work with our girl?"

"Always." That was the truth. There were two things Melanie thought of every night when she went to sleep—working with Kona, and having a boyfriend who was as wonderful as Chase. Sometimes she had to pinch herself. Melanie had never dreamed life would bring her this amount of happiness amidst the fear and sorrow that were trapped inside.

After they changed, the two of them made their way to Kona. Neither one of them held hands, but that was because they had made the pact that their relationship should only exist outside work hours. It was the responsible thing to do, even if Melanie hated the distance it put between them during their time on the clock. That was the way it had to be.

"Well, hello, you two. Looks like you're ready," Julia commended them. "Do you have plans today?"

"Mel and I were going to hang out here until it was time to go home."

"Sounds good. No dinner plans?"

"Not tonight," Melanie answered her. They hadn't made any plans. Besides, Melanie wanted to head home after work. Then she would allow herself to feel the emotions she had bottled up all day.

"Gotcha. Pizza for two then." Julia nodded to the buckets near the island. "I've got the fish ready. Let's get started, shall we?"

Melanie climbed up the ladder and stepped out onto the island. Chase followed her, settling down a few feet from her. They each had a bucket of fish to reward Kona with as she completed the tasks they gave her. From there, the three of them took turns calling Kona to them as they threw toys out for her. Melanie lost herself in the moment, taking joy from seeing Kona's trust as she came even closer to Chase. Their assumption was that Kona had been captured by men, which made it harder for her to trust him. Seeing her get close to him felt a little like a miracle. Then again, he was pretty sweet if she did say so herself. He had not been what she'd expected him to be, but he had ended up being everything she found herself needing. Seeing his smile made her feel like the darkness was not nearly as close to swallowing her up as she thought.

After a while, the sun started to hit Melanie hard. Sweat poured down her face in tiny rivers that she didn't seem able to wipe away fast enough. To say that Arizona was hot in the summer was an understatement. The heat had been known to melt the tires straight off the cars. It was not like Melanie was not used to that, but for some reason, it took more out of her today. Even though Kona had done a good job at soaking her shirt, Melanie almost wished she could be in the water with her. She squinted her eyes when she started to see small dots in the air around her. A slow dizziness took over, which made her clench her fists together.

"I think I need a minute."

Concerned, Julia rushed to her side. "You all right there, Melanie? You look pale."

Melanie gave her a weak smile. "Probably just overheated. Really, I'm fine. Just need some water."

"I'll go get some," offered Chase. He moved from the island with concern etched on his face.

She hated to see that worry, but there was nothing she could do about it. Her mind told her to keep going, but her body was apparently putting on the brakes. She had been at this crossroads before, where her body would simply not comply with her commands. Melanie tried to hold onto her explanation that it was just the heat that was beating down on her. Deep down inside, she worried it was something else. That fear would never give her any peace.

"Maybe we should stop for the day." Julia put a hand on her shoulder. "Do you want me to get your mom?"

"No, please don't. She'll only start to worry. I'm just hot. Maybe I didn't eat enough for lunch." Melanie looked for any excuse that would work. She knew the first thing that would pop into her mother's head. To be honest, her mind was already spinning the same wheels. Something was off. Melanie knew it, but she wanted to pretend that everything was okay, because today was not the day to find out her worst nightmare was back to haunt her. Not after losing Lori. It just couldn't be.

Chase was already back with an ice-cold bottle of water. He must have run, for he was completely out of breath. "Here, Mel. This should help."

Melanie took the bottle and nodded to him. Unscrewing the cap, she took a long drink. "Thanks."

Julia shook her head, worry still etched her features. "I still think we should tell your mom." Julia was not going to let this go.

Melanie sighed as she prepared herself for the mental game that was about to come. She knew it was the right thing, but part of her wanted to just hold it off a little longer. Melanie took another big drink of water and let it slide down her throat. It helped a little, but she knew it was not going to be enough. As she stood up, a wave of dizziness made her sway on her feet.

"Fine. I think I might need some help."

What happened next was a blur. Melanie remembered her mother coming to her at the tank. The next thing she knew, they were both headed home where her mother could keep an eye on her. Melanie hated that her mom had to take time off from work, but she was glad at the same time. Sometimes a girl just wanted her mother. Chase had sent her a string of texts to check in with him later. He was worried too.

Now she was lying down on her bed in the room that she shared with her sister. The white four-poster had called her name the minute she crept into the room. Sleep would not come, though. She was not foolish enough to think it would. Her head was swimming with so many thoughts that she could not keep up. She sent a random text to Chase to let him know she was just overheated and would see him later. The truth would have been harder to say. She wasn't okay. Melanie would probably never feel that way.

Melanie stared at the blue walls lined with pictures of dolphins. It reminded her that she was missing her time with Kona. That irritated her to no end, but there was no help for it. She had planned for her day to end much better than it had started, but there was no help for it now. Maybe she should have stayed home today, but going to work had distracted her from her thoughts far better than staying between these four walls, walls that she was afraid would start closing in on her at any moment.

The meow of the cat near her foot made her smile. "I love you too, Nite."

Melanie leaned over and stroked the black cat's fur absently. The cat had been her sounding board through it all. Nite always seemed to know when she needed a friend. Right now, her thoughts were filled with what-ifs that she wanted to shove deep down inside. She looked over at the white desk across from her, where her sister had sat so many times when Melanie was sick. Amber would straddle the chair and prop her elbows up on the back and listen to her for hours on end. She had confided many things to her sister in this room, things even her mother would never know. Amber had been her rock, and today her absence made this all harder to deal with. Melanie almost wished Amber was not working today. Her sister understood her better than anyone else.

A knock sounded on the door before her mother entered the room. She reached down to feel Melanie's forehead with a worried look on her face. Her mom sat down on the edge of her bed and appeared to be looking for the right words. "Have you been taking your meds on time?"

"Yes!" Melanie let out an irritated sigh. "I just got overheated.

I'm fine."

"I think we should make an appointment."

Of course, she did. That was what she always said any time Melanie looked the least bit sick. Melanie knew she meant well, but some days it made her wish she could shake away the panic that always came with it. Deep inside, though, Melanie was a little worried too. "If it means you'll let me sleep, then do it."

At that moment, Amber came into the room and tossed her things on her desk. Melanie almost felt as if she were saved by the bell. Amber turned and saw the sour look on her face. "Well, someone's grumpy."

When Amber fell onto her bed, her mother chided her. "Shoes, Amber!"

Amber groaned aloud. "Ugh! But I don't think I can take them off." Amber tried to lift her feet, but they fell with a heavy thud against the bed frame. "They feel like bowling balls. I'm going to have to cut them off."

Linda shook her head at her as she started to walk from the room. She leaned back in for one second. "No work tomorrow, young lady."

"Fine!" Melanie rolled her eyes, then turned back to her sister. "Rough day?"

"If my feet could talk, they'd be barking."

Melanie giggled at her sister. "I'm imagining toes the size of hotdogs."

"Ugh! No more hotdogs. We sold a couple of hundred today. I hate it when they do the dollar sale." Amber gestured to the door. "So, what's up with her?"

Melanie sighed. "I wasn't feeling well."

Amber nibbled on her bottom lip as she scrutinized her sister's appearance. "Now that you mention it, you do look a little pale. Maybe you need more sun."

"I just need some sleep. I'll be fine in the morning."

Melanie yawned and snuggled into her blankets. Nite protested the movement by hopping to the floor with a loud yowl. Melanie was glad that her sister did not bring up Lori. Then again, she feigned sleep long before she could.

CHAPTER 14

For two days, Melanie stayed in bed, not really wanting to do anything. Thankfully, her mother had been able to get a replacement for her hours. Melanie had told Chase that it was just a summer bug. She was afraid to tell him what was really going on or what they feared. For less than two months, she had been able to pretend that she was an average teen. Melanie had been treated like everyone else. No one treated her like a fragile piece of china that would break at any moment. She had a feeling it would never be like that again.

On the third day, they had received information about Lori's life celebration. In lieu of a funeral with a massive amount of people, they would be having a private interment. They asked that instead of the public attending, her extended family and friends join them for a celebration of Lori's life. It was a request that Lori had made before she passed. She did not want people looking back on her life with sadness, but to look at the wonderful ways she had lived every moment. Lori wanted there to be music and laughter everywhere, which was not that surprising. Lori had been the most uplifting person Melanie had ever met. Her spirit would never be forgotten, and her story lived on as her blog continued to get hits. Lori had written her last blog, her final farewell, that she had asked her parents to post the day after she died. Melanie had read it yesterday and tried to take it for the cheerful farewell that Lori had intended it to be. Lori's words had only made Melanie even more lost in her misery, as she wondered if she would follow in her footsteps before long.

The fear was hard to lasso once it took root. Yes, she was a fighter, but even warriors had their doubts from time to time when they faced their giants. Every minute she was awake was filled with dread that she was having trouble concealing from her family. So Melanie spent her days in her room, snuggled deep under the covers, hiding out from the rest of the world. That only made her mother worry more, which she could not help. Melanie was doing the best she could.

By the time day four rolled around, Melanie found herself sitting in the exam room again, getting blood drawn. She did not have long to wait, for the doctor wasn't playing around with the results. With a rush, she was back by the next Monday, and while she should have been happy that they got her in so quickly, Melanie knew the odds were not in her favor. Instead of the exam room she had been in earlier, she now found herself sitting beside her mother in Dr. Strand's private office.

Melanie crossed her right leg over her left and leaned as far back in her chair as she could, knowing it would irritate her mother, but right now, she did not care. "I can't believe I missed work for this."

"Melanie—" her mother started to correct her behavior.

"I haven't seen Chase in almost a week." Melanie let out an irritated sigh. It wasn't Chase she wanted to see, though. It was Kona. Helping the dolphin let her push her insecurities away. Melanie felt like a different person altogether.

Melanie didn't care, though. She was feeling better now. All

Melanie wanted to do was get back to work where she could spend her days with Chase. Well, except for the fact that he would probably have a ton of questions. She wasn't prepared to give him real answers yet. Melanie was too afraid of the wall that would build between them if she did.

Dr. Strand waved her hand in front of her and offered Melanie a consoling smile. "I'm sorry to hear that. It's hard to miss out at times. Sometimes we have no choice, though."

"It's bad, isn't it?" Melanie felt her stomach start to churn. She had been here before, a time she never wanted to return to. If Melanie could will it away, she would have already done so, but her body was a traitor that she could not convert to her side. Her nails bit into the sides of her arm as she tried to keep the panic at bay, a silent defense mechanism no one else noticed.

"Your white blood cell count is elevated. There was a slight abnormality with the last test. Your scans show a slow progression." Dr. Strand crossed her fingers together.

Melanie watched as Dr. Strand attempted a reassuring smile that had worked on her nine-year-old self, but sixteen-year-old Melanie had been down this road. This was about to be a pep talk that probably made other people feel like they could take on the world. It was just that Melanie did not have time for this. She had too much going on right now to hear the noise that was about to come out of their mouths. It started with her mother's fear and would end with the doctor explaining all the steps they would have to take again.

"So, she's no longer NED?"

Melanie saw the panic on her mother's face and reached over to hold her hand. As hard as it was for Melanie to focus on her own battle, the anguish on her mother's face broke her heart. Melanie had never wanted to see her worry this way again. She had already put her through a lifetime of suffering. Her resolve to stick to her guns and ignore the discussion in front of her withered on the spot. Melanie smiled at her mom reassuringly and saw her mom lift her chin as if to remind herself to take strength where she could.

"It's going to be all right, Mom." It didn't feel all right, though. Melanie had felt it creeping up on her but had chosen to ignore the voice inside. She had been so desperate to keep it at bay, but in doing so, Melanie had only put herself at risk.

Dr. Strand shook her head sadly. "No, she's not."

Melanie thought of all the things she wanted in life, things that had seemed so attainable just a few weeks ago. She realized that it would be harder to achieve them, but she refused to think she had to give up. Kona needed her. And there was Chase. At least, she still hoped there would be Chase. She knew that she would not be able to work anymore—not for a while, at least. Would her illness make him run? Would he shut down and push her out of his life the way everyone else had? He had been the first person ever to treat her as if she was special, and not because of the invisible illness that no one else could see.

Would it be easy to fight again? No. It never was, but the fight was worth every single struggle if it meant she could be free from the illness that tried to run her life. And this time, it was not just about her. The work she had done with Kona so far had started to change the dolphin's life. Melanie could not give up on her now. Kona needed her. Even if it became too much for Chase to handle, she did not care. She refused to give up her work with Kona. He would have to figure out how to deal with her, one way or the other.

"So, what's the plan?"

A determined look crossed her face. This was the time to

buckle down and push through. Melanie was not going to sit back and let the world pass her by. Not if she could fight. She was reminded of Lori and how she had fought with every inch of her being to beat her Non-Hodgkins lymphoma. Even though the end had not been the one she had chosen, Lori had lived every day she had to the fullest. Melanie had promised her that she would go on living, and that was what she planned to do.

"Same as before. Hit it with everything we've got." Dr. Strand nodded to her.

"It was so rough on her the last time." The fear was evident in her mother's voice.

"I'll be fine. When can we start?" Melanie knew she was going to have to be the strong one here. Her mother had been worried about this moment since she first had no evidence of disease on her scans. The fear was driving her mom right now. Melanie had to make sure it did not consume her too. Melanie was on a mission, one that required her to dig deeper.

"We need to run a few more tests, so we have the correct treatment nailed down, but I would say within the next week."

"Good." Melanie sat up in her chair and mentally prepared herself for the tests that would surely follow.

"Good?" Linda Parker looked at her daughter as if she'd lost her mind.

"I don't have time to waste, Mom. Kona needs me." Melanie clenched her fists together in determination.

"Kona?" Dr. Strand's eyebrows rose curiously.

"A dolphin...and honestly, Mel, the dolphin can wait. You need to get healthy."

Melanie pulled out her phone and showed Dr. Strand a picture of her sitting on the island. Kona was in the water next to her. "I'm helping her adjust to her life."

"You are not the only one responsible for her well-being, Mel. Julia can take care of her. And she has Chase too." Linda Parker gripped the side of her seat.

As if seeing the underlying current between them, Dr. Strand held up her hand. "With the right precautions, I don't see why you can't spend some time with her here and there."

"See, Mom? We can make it work." Melanie nodded to the doctor in front of her. If she could just get her mother to understand how vital Kona was to her. Melanie had seen her go from a depressed creature to one who was starting to thrive. There was still so much work to do with her, though. Melanie was not kidding herself. She knew that Julia could handle it, but it gave her a sense of purpose to be included. The fact that Chase was there too only made her want to fight even harder. She only hoped this wouldn't be too much for him to handle. In the back of her mind, she was already figuring out how to deal with a life that did not include him as her boyfriend. But as long as she still had Kona, Melanie knew she would make it.

"Honestly, Mel. Let's just get through the first few weeks, okay?" The fear that had been there moments before was now hidden past the nervous smile her mother forced on her face.

"Wise words there. We'll have a game plan started as soon as possible. How does that sound?" Dr. Strand added.

"Good." Linda Parker nodded as if that was helping her come to terms with the information in front of her.

"If you say so." Melanie shrugged it off. What else could she do right now? She knew there would be more tests before the end of their visit, and while she was not looking forward to it, it was a means to an end. Melanie would do whatever it took to fight the cancer that plagued her body. There was no other option. She had tackled it head-on when she was nine, and while it had been

158

a scary thing for a child to go through, there was still a kind of innocence back then. Now, she was just a teen who wanted to live a healthy life and have normal dreams. She refused to think about it now. Melanie would only focus on the future, no matter how hard that would be to do.

***

That very same day, Chase was sitting on the little island where he had spent so many days before with Melanie. His feet dangled in the water as he gazed into the tank. "Look at her, Mom. She's looking everywhere for Mel. Has her mother told you anything? I'm starting to worry about her."

Julie sat down next to her son. She searched for the words to explain what was going on with Melanie right now. "I'm afraid Mel's pretty sick."

"She looked a little pale the other day. She said she had a stomach bug."

Julia sighed softly. "I'm afraid it's a little worse than the flu."

"What do you mean?" His eyes scanned her face for more details.

Julia brushed his hair back from his eyes. "Mel has leukemia."

His face paled at her words. "Cancer?"

"Yes. Linda called me a little while ago to tell me that she's not sure when Melanie can return, or if she can return at all. Linda is a mess with all this."

"Why didn't she tell me? How long has she had it?"

"Melanie was diagnosed when she was nine, Chase."

"Nine?" His face dropped. "And that's why she was so upset about Lori?"

"Lori?" Julia looked perplexed.

"One of Mel's friends." Chase looked down at his feet. "She had cancer too. I can't even imagine."

"Me either. I don't know what I would do if anything happened to you." Julia's eyes filled with tears.

"Can I see her?"

"I don't know if that's wise right now, Chase. She's dealing with a lot, and this is a lot for you to take in." Julia put a hand on his shoulder.

"I love her, Mom. That doesn't change just because she's sick."

"Chase, I'm just worried you might get hurt if —"

"I refuse to live my life afraid that the people I love will leave me. Just because Dad left you, doesn't mean I have to lose her too." Chase jerked away from her touch.

"Chase Adam Makenzie! Take that back." Julia's eyes were filling with tears.

"I didn't mean it, Mom. I just...." His face was pale and filled with an anguish that he had trouble vocalizing.

"It's going to be okay, Chase." Julia pulled him into her arms and held him tight. She rubbed his back and soothed the angst that seemed to rage inside him. Chase was not one to give in to his emotions, but as she held him, he started to cry.

"I don't want to lose her."

"Shh...it's going to be okay. I'll take you to see her when Linda gives the all-clear, I promise."

He stepped back from her hug and sniffed slightly. "I know you think I'm naïve that we're young, but Melanie is special."

"She is," agreed Julia. "It's going to be rough on her, you know, being away from here. We have no idea what Melanie will have to go through."

Chase nodded to her, taking in her words as he bent down to retrieve some of the rings on the island. Chase leaned over to toss a ring to Kona, then stood back up as he watched her chase after it. "Don't worry, girl. Melanie will be back soon."

When he did not sound convinced, Julia put her arm across his shoulders and hugged him tightly. "She's a fighter, Chase."

"How do you know?" Chase grumbled.

"Because, so is Kona. Those two are so much alike." Julia nodded to the dolphin, who started to sing when she heard her name.

"That's true. Maybe I'll text her later."

"I'm sure she'd like that, Chase."

"What do I say?" Chase wondered aloud.

"That you are here for her. Tell her about Kona if she wants an update. Remember, let her lead the conversation. That's the best thing you can do. Let her know you care."

"I can do that." Chase squared his shoulders as if taking on a new responsibility.

"Yes, you can." Julia ruffled his hair, and he pulled away.

"Mom! The hair?" Chase shook his head at her.

"Right." Julia snorted and rolled her eyes. "Teenagers!"

"Mothers!" Chase shot back at her and laughed when she gave him a pained glance.

Chase leaned down and tossed another ring into the water. Kona retrieved it and brought it back to him. He patted her on the snout and praised her. "Good girl, Kona."

When she turned to look for Melanie, he splashed some water at her to get her attention. "Don't worry. She'll be back soon."

CHAPTER 15

As the day wore on into the next, Melanie was starting to feel like the walls were crashing down around her. Her fears had been confirmed, and while she had hoped she was wrong, deep down that voice that told her something was wrong had been strong. Sometimes it was hard to decipher the truth from the fear, for the fear was always there no matter how hard she tried to keep it at bay. Now that the leukemia had started to rear its ugly head, Melanie was left trying to figure out how to keep focused on the road ahead. She hadn't even told Chase yet. Melanie had no idea how he would react, nor did she have the energy to figure it out. Not after this morning.

Earlier that morning, her mom had taken her to Lori's celebration of life. Melanie had to pretend during all of it that everything was okay. She wasn't ready to tell any of the others that the cancer had returned. It didn't seem like the right time or place. Throughout the morning, she listened to all the happy memories that Lori had shared with others, all the while, trying not to pretend that this very thing could happen to her. Cancer did not differentiate between its victims. It wasn't until the very end that Melanie started to find the room to breathe.

At the end of the celebration, Lori's family opened five large white boxes. The moment they did, hundreds of butterflies flew into the air. Tears filled her eyes as she watched them fly all around them. It was as if Lori's spirit filled the space surrounding them. When one of them landed on Melanie, she closed her eyes and made a wish before it flew away. As the butterflies flitted out of sight, Melanie felt like she could breathe for the first time in days. Now that she had said goodbye to Lori, she felt like she could focus on herself and do what she needed to do to get through it all.

Her mother said very little to her before she took her home. The truth was if she had Melanie would have just tuned her out. Her mom seemed to recognize her need for solitude. When she dropped her off at home, she squeezed her hand before Melanie got out of the car. Melanie knew that her mom had to go to work. She was actually glad to see her go. Her mom needed to get back to life, to focus on something else. And Melanie just needed time to let it all sink in.

For the next few hours, Melanie tuned out the world. She felt a wet nose nudge up against her as she sat curled up on the couch. River whined when she ignored him and would not let up until she scratched behind his ears. "What's wrong, boy? Nite kick you out of the tree again?"

His chocolate eyes scanned her face as if he were trying to understand what she was saying. His mouth opened and closed with a small puff of air, leaving him with the quietest of whines. When Melanie dropped her hand in her lap and looked away, River put his head down on her leg.

"Go away, River," she whispered, but he refused to. Instead, River did something he didn't normally do. He leapt onto the couch and curled up behind her legs. The Labrador retriever put his paws on her feet and propped his head up on top of them.

Melanie hated to admit it, but that small gesture made her feel safe for the first time that day. It was almost as if the dog's empathy was on master level. Animals were smart like that sometimes.

Much smarter than people, because Kimmie had still not caught on to why Melanie wasn't in such a great mood. Melanie didn't have the energy to explain it to her. Even now, Kimmie burst into the room like an atomic bomb ready to explode. "What's wrong with you?"

"Leave her alone, Kimmie," cautioned Grandma Mimi.

"Someone die?" Kimmie teased her.

"Yes," Melanie answered

"What? Who?"

"Lori."

Melanie waited for understanding to dawn on her face. She hadn't told Kimmie about Lori. Maybe she should have, but it had been hard to talk about, and while the others could have told her, they had been dealing with how Melanie felt. No one had told Kimmie about her relapse either.

Kimmie sat down on the chair next to the couch and looked down at the floor. "I'm sorry, Mel."

"It's okay, Bug." Melanie sighed as she realized that the next part would be hers too. "Kimmie...I need to tell you something—"

"Mel, you don't have to be the one to tell her," Grandma Mimi interrupted her. Melanie could hear the emotion in her voice, telling her that her grandmother was having trouble dealing with it too.

"Give us a minute, will you?" Melanie requested. She saw her grandma start to refuse, but Melanie held her ground. "Please."

"I'll be in the kitchen."

Melanie waited until their grandmother was out of sight before she started to talk. "Look, Bug. Do you remember when I

164

was sick?"

"Yes. And no. I mean, I was a little kid then, you know."

Little kid? Melanie fought the urge to laugh at her sister. At nine, she was still a little kid. Then again, at nine, Melanie had thought she was a kid too but had to deal with things that aged her well before her time. Maybe Kimmie felt the same way, even if she hadn't gotten to experience most of the hospital stuff. Kimmie would probably remember the way Melanie was at home during her recovery and not surrounded by wires. This was going to be a lot harder this time around for her sister.

"Yes, you were." Melanie tried to think of the best way to tell her kid sister that her cancer was back. There was probably a good way to do it, but Melanie couldn't seem to find it. "Look, Bug, I'm sick."

"You have a cold? Can I get you some orange juice?"

"As much as I love orange juice, it's not going to help." Melanie saw the fear on her sister's face and wished she could save her from it. This was the part her mom was better at probably, but Melanie knew it would be best if Kimmie knew she could still talk to her. And Melanie needed to be able to say it out loud. "My cancer is back."

"No, it can't be. You beat it," Kimmie denied. Melanie loved her for it too. That denial was something Melanie could relate to.

"I did, but sometimes it's not permanent."

"Are you going to die like Lori?" Kimmie's eyes seemed so small in her face as worry instantly swallowed up every other emotion.

"I don't know, Kimmie." Melanie gave her a sad smile. "I'm going to try not to."

"Good." Kimmie's chin jutted out, and her lips trembled slightly. Tears started to cloud her eyes as if they were trying to push their way out, but Kimmie was fighting to be strong. "I'm sorry I was so mean to you. I'm sorry, your friend died."

"Kimmie…." Melanie opened her arms and gestured for her to come closer. Her sister leaned over and hugged her tighter than she ever had, and Melanie let her. "You haven't done anything wrong. Being mean doesn't cause cancer, by the way. Besides, you give only as good as you get. I'm not always nice to you either, you know."

"Yes, but I'm a spoiled b-b-b-brat," she said in between her cries, which were now small sobs that were being absorbed against Melanie's shoulder. River raised his head and started to howl slightly as he commiserated with her.

"Oh-oh-oh. Now, now. Let it out, Bug." Melanie held her tight and rubbed her back with small circles the way their mom had always rubbed hers. When Kimmie finally pulled away, her tears were still lining her face. Melanie reached over and wiped them free. "No more tears, Kimmie. We've got this, you hear me? We're going to fight this with everything we have, okay?"

"Okay."

"Now, why don't you take River outside to play? He's been inside most of the day, and I bet he'd like to watch you ride your scooter."

"Will you come too?"

Melanie tried to think of the best way to say no, but Kimmie's need outweighed her own. Kimmie had been like this a lot when she was sick before. Her sister would soon enter the stage where she would not let Melanie out of her sight. For now, Melanie gave in to her. It would be good to get some fresh air anyway. "Sure."

Melanie spent the next hour watching her sister burn off the energy she wished she had. They were just about to go inside when a car pulled into the drive. As she looked closer, Melanie

166

saw it was Julia's car. Part of her wanted to go inside and hide, but what good would that do? Melanie had not answered any of Chase's texts. He probably thought she was angry with him. That was far from the truth. She just didn't know how to tell him about what was going on. To say she had a lot on her plate was putting it lightly.

When Chase stepped out of the car, he reached down to pick something up. As he started to walk up the drive, he carried a bouquet of sunflowers and a large plush dolphin. "Hey."

Melanie stood up from the porch and walked closer to him. What did she say to him? She had been trying to form the words for the past few days, but none of them made sense. "Chase...I—"

"Wait." He handed over the dolphin and the flowers and started to dig in his pocket.

"What are you doing?" Melanie was confused when he pulled out a piece of paper.

"I wrote it down so I would get it right." His hands shook as he read to her. "No matter how long the road is, I'm going to walk it with you. When it gets too hard to bear, you can lean on me. If you feel like giving up, I'll hold your hand. You are not alone."

"You know...." Melanie turned away from him and tried not to let this beautiful moment be ruined by the doubt and fears inside her.

"My mom told me." He stepped closer to her, so close she could feel him behind her.

"I.... Chase, I'm sorry." She turned to him with tears already falling down her face.

He wrapped his arms around her and held her so tight he almost crushed the flowers. "You have nothing to be sorry about."

"I should have told you earlier." Melanie pushed away from

him, trying to find enough air to breathe so that her next words could make their way out of her mouth. "You were the first person who treated me like I was normal. I just didn't want that to end."

"You are normal, Mel."

"It may seem that way, but everything is so complicated. It wasn't fair to do that to you." Melanie sniffed and held the gifts in front of her. "You deserve so much more."

"You don't have to push me away. I won't go." His face was filled with a determined light.

"I'm a mess, Chase. I have so much baggage. I don't even know where to start."

"I'm not afraid of a mess. And I have strong shoulders. I can carry the weight." His thumb wiped away one of her tears.

"Why do you have to be so amazing?" Melanie tried to resist the pull she felt toward him. It would be a kindness for him to be without her worries and fears.

"I blame my mother for that." His grin was as bright as the sun, and it made her feel hope for the first time in the last few days.

"I'll make sure to thank her." Melanie sighed as she laid her head down on his shoulder. "Thank you, Chase."

"For what?"

"For being you." She felt him kiss the top of her forehead and fought the urge to start crying all over again. He had no idea how bad it could get. Melanie should probably warn him, but right now, she didn't have the strength to change this moment. It was everything she needed it to be.

"Eww...are you two going to kiss?" Kimmie asked from the doorway.

"Kimmie!" Melanie felt a blush slide up her face.

"Is that the one you keep writing about?" Kimmie teased her.

"I do not." Melanie was going to hurt that kid.

"Do too. I know where you keep your journal," Kimmie added.

"Oh, really? So what does she write about me?" Chase stepped away and headed toward the door that Kimmie was keeping open.

"Come on in. I'll tell you all about it. But you'll owe me."

"Kimberly Lynn! You better shut your trap."

Melanie chased after them. She knew she should feel irritated with Kimmie, but deep down, she wasn't because it had distracted them from the moment. Melanie was actually thankful for her timing. It had gotten way too serious there for a moment.

CHAPTER 16

Time ticked by slowly some days, dragging her along with it, kicking and screaming on the inside. No one would know the way she felt inside. The summer faded into fall, and while Melanie wasn't able to work at the aquarium, Chase had not disappeared from her life. He visited her when he was able, but now that school had started, he had less time for her. Melanie tried not to dwell on it, for her energy was better spent trying to fight the cancer that had retaken her hostage. It took a lot of mental energy not to give up, and to hold on to the hope that this would be the last time cancer touched her life.

Melanie wasn't able to go back to school the way she had planned to. Instead, she had been kept at home to give her the best chance at recovery. Kimmie had not wanted to leave her at home. Melanie remembered how she had nearly kicked and screamed her way out the front door on her first day of school. That kid had a set of lungs on her. Melanie had to talk her down and promise she would be there waiting for her when she got home from school. Kimmie was terrified of losing her but was starting to come to terms with it all.

Thankfully, this was not their first rodeo where homeschooling was concerned. Melanie was old enough to do most of the work herself, and when she needed help, either her mother or grandmother was around to help. Her mom worked as early as possible so she could be home for afternoon appointments when it was necessary. Mr. Marcus had been more than reasonable with time-off requests. Even so, Melanie saw that her mother was starting to look overworked. She wished she could help her mom, but the only thing Melanie could do was try to get better.

Try. Like it was that easy. None of this was easy. Each day Melanie took the meds that made her feel like her whole world was unraveling. Every radiation treatment made her want to curl up in a ball for weeks. Melanie was barely holding it together. Without her family supporting her, she didn't know if she would have had the strength to make it through. Even though Chase was here and there, she never shared the worst with him. They were her burdens to carry, things he would not truly understand, nor should he have to. Sometimes she tried to pull away from him, to let him find his way without her, but he refused to take the hint. Chase was more stubborn than Melanie had given him credit for.

Life continued to move one day after another, as if this was just the status quo. It was like clockwork at the Parker residence. Mom worked early. The girls went to school while Melanie stayed home with Grandma Mimi. When her mother was home, her grandmother worked at the hotel in the evening. Grandma Mimi was part of housekeeping but had switched to do the laundry and cleaning the common areas until Melanie was better. They were all lucky that Grandma Mimi was able to help as much as she did. Their family unit would not be the same without her.

Everyone sacrificed a little bit at a time, which made Melanie feel guilty. Her illness had sidetracked everyone else's lives yet again. Melanie felt so helpless, and yet amidst all the sadness that swirled inside her, Melanie refused to let go of the hope that had been ingrained in her from day one. Hannah always reminded her that she was not allowed to give up, ever. Melanie held onto those words each day, knowing that her friend was right. It was the hardest fight of her life, but Melanie was determined to win it again.

She had so many things to be thankful for—family, friends, doctors, insurance. This Melanie knew, but there were days that she had to pull herself out of the dark pit she had sunk into. On those days, Chase seemed to know, for he sent her texts to check on her. Sometimes he sent pictures of Kona because he knew how much Melanie missed her. For months she had been away from The Oasis. All she wanted to do was get back there and help Kona again. The dolphin was struggling without her. Even though Chase tried to tell her everything was okay, she could see in the pictures and videos that Kona had slid backward into depression again. Melanie felt like she was letting Kona down, but that wasn't something she could change. If only she could speed up her recovery and get back to a normal life again.

Even Amber treated her differently this time. Before her sister had been her rock, this time, Melanie could sense the fear inside her. Did she look that bad? Raising her hand, she adjusted the cap she wore around her hair and wiped some of the sweat from her head. The peach fuzz from her shaved head almost tickled her fingers. Melanie had her sister shave it off one night because she knew it would fall out eventually anyway. Her mother had not been too happy about it, but what could she do? What was done was done. In one way, it was Melanie taking back control over some part of her body. She could not control how her insides felt when she took her medicine, but she could cut her hair off before it fell out a clump at a time.

Melanie stared at the wood grain in the chair she sat in, wondering how to make sure her body would do what it needed to do to heal. If only it were that easy to just will the cancer away. She spent a lot of time trying to do just that when she was not journaling about Kona. Over the past few months, Kona was making a few gains here and there, but her state of mind had been low. Chase recorded some of the progress for her to watch, and the two of them would video chat when he was too busy to come over. Even though she tried to push him away, he was like a mountain and completely immovable. It only made her love him more. He was the lifeline she did not expect to have. Chase understood her need to be there with Kona, so he had done his best to bring Kona to her through technology when she was still unable to see her.

Melanie spent her free time when she was done with her studies, reading through everything she could about dolphin rehabilitation, hoping to find something they might be able to do to help Kona. Her focus on the dolphin kept the dark thoughts at bay, gave her something to think about while the medicine attacked the cancer inside her. Sometimes nausea and pain made it hard to keep herself distracted, but Melanie fought through it the best that she could. Like today, when all she wanted to do was crawl under the covers and sleep the day away, she resigned herself to sitting on the porch journaling about all the things they were doing with Kona this week. Even if she was not there, she could pretend that she was still a part of it from the outside.

She was sketching Kona in her book when Grandma Mimi interrupted her, patting Melanie's arm gently as she sat down in the wooden chair beside her. "How are you feeling, Mel?"

Melanie sighed almost dramatically. "Same as always. Tired. Bored."

Grandma Mimi pointed to the drawing. "Is that Kona?"

"Yeah," Melanie grumbled softly. "Mom still won't let me go see her yet."

"You'll see her soon enough. She's right, though. You have to focus on you."

Melanie understood what her grandma was trying to tell her. She needed to pay attention to herself and make sure she was following every one of the doctor's orders. Still, her whole life did not have to be about cancer. There was so much more to her than that. "I am. I take my meds. I eat the food, even when I want to puke. My body is pumped with chemicals that make my skin crawl, but I'm doing it, Grandma."

A sadness crossed over her grandma's face, and Melanie instantly regretted it, but it only stayed there for a brief second. "I know you are, honey."

"I missed most of the summer. Now I'm missing my junior year. I just want to be normal for a change."

Melanie closed her book and looked down at the ground. Grandma Mimi seemed to be her closest lifeline this time around. The two spent many hours together. If Melanie ever needed help with her homework, Grandma Mimi was there. Some of it was over her head, but her grandmother tried to help her nonetheless.

"It will all work out, Melanie. I have faith." Grandma Mimi slid her arm across her back, and Melanie snuggled against her. "You are one of the strongest people I know, Mel."

Melanie smiled at her. "That's because you both raised me to be strong and not to be afraid of anything."

"No, you get that from your father." Grandma Mimi's eyes misted over.

Melanie closed her eyes and tried to conjure his face. It had been almost eight years since he had passed away. "I miss him,

Grandma."

Her father had been her hero long ago, even before he died protecting others. Melanie often stared at the small triangle that hung over the mantle, a flag wrapped up in his honor, with his detective shield sitting just above it. Losing him had been one of the hardest things they had ever had to deal with. Well, that was until cancer had reared its ugly head. Melanie liked to think of him standing by her side, sometimes like a guardian angel who watched over her. It was her way of holding on to him.

"We all do." Grandma Mimi had genuinely loved her son-in-law. The two of them had always been as thick as thieves, especially where her mother was concerned. All the pranks they had played on her were only outweighed by the surprises.

"Sometimes, I wish I could hear his voice again. That's selfish though, right, because Kimmie never really got to hear it." And yet, even though Melanie had heard his voice, sometimes she felt like she would never remember it. There were only a handful of videos taken of him.

"It's normal to wish for someone you lost." Grandma Mimi kissed the top of her head. "It's going to be all right, Melanie."

"How do you know?"

No one could really be that certain. Melanie wanted to believe it was true, though, because there was no other option for her. She was going to beat this. It was the only thought she needed to hold onto because the others were unmentionable.

"Cause we raised a fighter. We're going to knock this cancer out." Grandma Mimi raised her fists like she was going to box something.

Melanie fought the urge to giggle. "Yes, you did. And yes, we will."

She raised her hands and bumped fists with her. Melanie

appreciated the sentiment. It was as if her grandmother had realized how low she was feeling.

At that moment, Grandma Mimi's phone dinged. She pulled away and read the screen. A slow smile slid across her face. "Get your things."

"Why?"

"Your mother wants you to come to the aquarium."

"Wait; what?" Melanie's mouth nearly dropped down to the ground. "Are you serious?"

"She got your numbers. They look good. Time for you to get out a little."

"Yes!" Melanie nearly jumped out of her chair. She stopped herself and turned to look at her grandma. "What's the catch?"

"You have to wear a mask. Take your meds with you."

"That I can do."

Melanie raced from the porch and headed inside to get everything she needed. While the day had started out with a dark cloud, she was starting to feel the sadness disappear. She was finally going to get a chance to see Kona.

All the way there, Melanie had to stop herself from babbling to her grandma even with a mask over her mouth. Grandma Mimi was all smiles, too, though. The moment her grandmother dropped her off at the aquarium, Melanie quickly texted her mom that she was heading in to see Chase. High school seemed to let out earlier than the elementary school, which was why Grandma Mimi had to drop her off and head straight home. Melanie couldn't wait to surprise him. She had not seen him in almost two weeks, even though they texted each other every day.

Melanie fought the urge to sprint through the aquarium. She knew she would only end up paying for that later if she did. So, she walked the path leading to the booth she had shared with

Chase for such a short time. Walking around to the front where people purchased the fish, she waited until the line was closed. Then she popped her head into the booth and almost scared him. "Hey, stranger!"

"Mel! Why didn't you tell me you were coming?"

"Because I didn't know until this afternoon." She fidgeted with her mask as the heat bore down on her. Breathing into it over and over made her face overheat, but she'd put up with it as long as she could visit the aquarium.

"You look...." Chase nodded to her hair.

"Different?" Melanie was still getting used to the hairdo herself. "I guess you missed it in our chat the other night."

"I'm sorry I didn't notice. I thought you had just washed your hair or something." His grin was just as goofy as she remembered. "Did it start to fall out?"

Melanie did not mind his question at all. He asked a lot of them really, but she knew it was just him trying to understand what she was going through. She put a hand to her headwrap and gave him a half-smile. "Some started to. I had Amber shave it off this weekend. She would have shaved hers too, but Mom wouldn't let her this time."

"I could shave mine off," he offered in solidarity.

Melanie grinned at him. "I know a few people who'd pay to see that happen, but no."

"I'm down, though." He pulled his hair back so that the top of his head moved up, and his eyebrows raised.

This time Melanie could not help but laugh at him. "You look like a pig! Stop!"

Chase started to snort and somehow ended up choking on his spit. Melanie had to slap him across the back. She looked around to see if anyone was watching the exchange, and saw a few people giving them odd looks. "Are you on break now?"

"For a few. If I had known you were coming in, I would have asked for a longer break." He reached his hand out to hold hers. "I've missed you."

"I miss you too. I wish I wasn't just visiting. I miss this place, but I'm not cleared for work yet. It's my off week," explained Melanie.

"Off week?"

Melanie realized there were some things she might not have explained to him yet. She just did not want their entire relationship to revolve around her cancer. "When I don't have chemo appointments."

"Sorry. You've probably told me this already. Sometimes I think I understand everything." He looked away from her almost guiltily.

"You're doing great, though. But don't get used to it. I plan on kicking it to the curb anyway. You've been amazing, Chase."

"I'm just above average," he replied.

"Are you kidding me? How many girls are lucky enough to have a boyfriend who's willing to shave his head for her?" She teased him. "But seriously, thank you, Chase. It means a lot."

"You mean more." His eyes met hers, and she saw the truth in them. His love overflowed. Melanie was thankful for it.

"Mom said I might be able to start coming here on my off weeks if I promise not to overdo it." At least that was the conversation they'd had weeks ago, but she hadn't shared that with Chase yet as she hadn't wanted to get his hopes up. Melanie only hoped her mother kept to her promise. She had never not kept one before, but sometimes she could be overprotective.

"Do you want to go see Kona?" Chase asked her.

"That's a stupid question." Melanie shook her head and

rolled her eyes. "Have you met me?"

"Yeah, I should have known better. Let me make sure Leland's got this under control."

Melanie waited patiently for Chase. When he came out, she breathed a sigh of relief. Part of her was worried that he could not break away for a moment. When he came out from the hut, she wrapped her arms around his neck and moved her mask away long enough to kiss him on the cheek. She couldn't risk kissing him on the mouth just yet.

"So, you didn't come just to see Kona?"

"Nope. I get the best of both worlds. Better hurry up, though. Mom's put me on a short leash." Melanie was not going to be here for very long, so she wanted to make the best of it.

"Let's go then." He wrapped his arm around her shoulders and escorted her down the sidewalk that led to Kona's tank.

The two of them made their way over to where Kona was swimming under the surface. Melanie saw the way Kona barely skimmed the surface. The dolphin had been doing that when she was first brought to the aquarium. "She doesn't look happy."

"She's missed your face. I've tried to keep up with her training, but apparently, I'm chopped liver where she's concerned."

"It's the face," Melanie teased him.

"Hey now!" Chase looked as if he were about to push her in the water, but he stopped himself. That kind of clowning around they would have done before Melanie relapsed. She missed those times. Even though they still had a few, it wasn't the same as before. Melanie was afraid it might never be, but for now, she would take what she could get.

Melanie leaned over the side of the tank and tapped the water. She watched to see if Kona heard the sound. When the dolphin came to the surface several feet away, Melanie almost breathed a sigh of relief. "Hello, girl. I've been worried about you."

Kona made her typical greeting sound as if she recognized her right away. Then the dolphin started to chatter at her like she was telling her off for not being there.

"I know, I know. But I didn't have a choice. I promise to come more often. When I can."

"She still likes the rings."

"So I noticed. You were doing the beachball in the last video. I'm glad you're still working with her, but she still needs to play more."

Melanie nibbled on the inside of her cheek as her worries were staring her in the face. Kona was not doing well. Melanie felt sick to her stomach because she knew part of the reason was that the dolphin felt abandoned. It broke her heart to not be there with her.

"Agreed. I'm glad you came today."

Melanie's phone dinged, and she knew it was her mother calling her back to the office. She was only going to get a little time today. Melanie knew that, but she also knew her mother would be more lenient about her visits in the future. "Me too. Mom will send out a search party if I don't get to her office ASAP. She said I can come back in a few days if I behave."

Chase grinned at her. "You? Behave?"

"I'll have you know, I've been a model patient. Taking my meds and eating all the disgusting spinach. I think I'm going to turn into it soon." Melanie stuck her tongue out in disgust.

"Well, you do look a little green around the gills."

"Shush you. Flattery will get you nowhere." Melanie pushed his shoulder playfully. Chase did not seem to mind, though. He just continued to grin at her. Melanie reached over to pat the water one last time before she left. "Don't worry, girl, I'll be back before you know it."

Chase opened his arms, and she stepped into them. He hugged her so tightly she thought she wouldn't be able to breathe. It was nice. "I promise I'll take care of her. You take care of you, okay?"

"I promise," she whispered against his chest as she lay her cheek against it. She wished they had more moments like this, but they were limited, unfortunately. "I'll see you later, Chase."

"Count on it." Chase let her go, and she started to walk away. "Mel?"

She turned around and answered, "Yes?"

"I love you."

"I love you too."

Melanie felt a blush climb up her face at his words. She would never get used to it, no matter how hard she tried. His love carried her through on the days when pure will could not. Melanie would never forget it.

CHAPTER 17

Two days later, Melanie was dragging her feet in the morning. She had spent the night before dreaming things no one should have to dream about. Melanie saw the faces of her friends that had already left this world. They were reaching out to her, asking her to save them from the death that had been inevitable. Each time Melanie tried to reach her hand out to one of them, they would disintegrate into ash. When the last one disappeared, she was left with nothing more than a mirror to stand in front of. Melanie squeezed her eyes shut, refusing to look inside it. Even in her dreams, Melanie fought with every ounce of herself.

Just when her eyes were about to be forced open, Melanie awoke from her nightmare. For minutes after, Melanie stared at the ceiling and tried to get her breathing under control. The panic was real. It was the same gripping feeling anyone fighting for her life would feel. Melanie rolled over in bed and wrapped her arms around the dolphin that Chase had given her months ago. Her head fell into it right before the tears started to fall. She hated to lose control, hated the fear that seemed to have nothing better to do than torture her when she was so close to finding her way free from cancer. Melanie refused to think the treatments weren't working. They had to be. She was not going to be next. There was still so much for her to do.

"You all right, Mel?" Her sister called from the doorway.

Melanie didn't answer at first. She was having trouble finding words. Tears continued to fall down her face, making dark blue stains on the stuffed animal beneath her cheek. It wasn't the first time, nor would it be the last time she cried into it.

Amber slid into the bed next to her and curled up next to her. "It's okay, Mel. You're going to be okay."

Was she? It wasn't like her sister could actually promise her that. No one could. Melanie snuggled up against her sister anyway. She was reminded of how Amber had snuck into her bed when she was nine, comforting her when she cried. Melanie's tears dried as she lay there. "Don't you have to go to school?"

"Yeah, but it's still early." Amber stroked her head. "You know I'm still here, right? You can still talk to me."

"I know." She did, but voicing her fears just made them more real. "It was just a bad dream."

"Well, you're awake now. Nothing's going to hurt you."

If only that were true. Melanie sighed softly. "You better get ready."

"Well, isn't this a sight for sore eyes?" Mom called from the doorway.

"What are you doing home?" Melanie asked her. Her mom should have already been at work.

"I'm going in later today."

"Oh."

"Time to get moving, Amber. Your sister is already getting her shoes on."

"Miracles do happen." Amber hugged Melanie one last time before she got up from the bed. As she made it to the door, Amber looked back at her. "You owe me a game of Monopoly later, got it?"

Monopoly? It had been years since they'd played it. That was the game that had gotten her through a lot of rough patches before. Melanie knew it was Amber's way of telling her she was there for her. "You're on."

After Amber left the room, her mom walked to her closet and started to pull out clothes. "Get dressed."

"Why?" Melanie had not gotten up this early in forever, it seemed. She usually slept an hour after her sisters had left. Then she would get up and start on her school work.

"You're coming with me today."

"What?" Melanie fought the urge to jump out of her bed and zip into her clothes. She eyed her mother, speculatively. "What's the catch?"

"Nothing. I just thought you could use the fresh air. But if you'd rather stay home...."

"No way!" Melanie climbed out of bed and pulled the clothes out of her mom's hands. "I'll just be a few minutes."

Before she knew it, Melanie was at the aquarium breathing in the smells that had been second nature to her for as long as she could remember. When she was sick before, Melanie had come to work with her mom just like this. Amber had been in school, and her sister Kimmie was in daycare. Grandma Mimi had spent a lot of time with her during that time, but sometimes she had needed time to herself too. Melanie had been more than happy to spend the time at the aquarium with her mom. All that time had only increased her passion for the animals that lived there.

The moment that Melanie raced over to the dolphins, she was excited to see Julia, who waved her over. "Hey, Julia!"

"Mel! Your mom said you might want to help some today. Why don't you get changed into some clothes and come see

Kona?"

"Thanks!" Melanie smiled from her head down to her toes. The only thing that would have made this complete was if Chase were here too. She'd text him some photos later, though. He'd probably kick himself that she got to come while he was stuck at school, but she didn't care.

After changing into her junior trainer's clothes, Melanie raced back to Kona's tank and made her way over to the island. Melanie readjusted her mask over her mouth as she climbed onto it. The mask kept her a little more protected from the germs around her, just as the headwrap protected her scalp from the sun that was heating up the ground around them. While not as scorching as the summer temperatures, it was still pretty hot outside, especially directly under the sun.

"Go ahead and call her, Mel." Julia stood behind her as she leaned over the water.

Melanie tapped the water with her hand and encouraged to Kona to come closer. "Come here, Kona."

When Kona did not rise to the surface, Melanie realized the dolphin was upset with her. Not that she blamed her. Kona had come to depend on her early on, and when Melanie had gotten sick, it was as if her safety blanket had disappeared. Melanie felt horrible about it, but it was all out of her control. All she could do was fight to get better and be here for her when she could.

"I'm sorry, girl, but I'm here now."

She tapped the water with her hand again and waited to see if the dolphin would come around this time. When Kona rose to the surface, she whistled and clicked at Melanie as if trying to tell her how upset she was with her, but Melanie did not take it personally. It was going to be hard on both of them because it would still be impossible to come every day. When Melanie was on chemo, she had to have limited exposure to the outside world. The only times she would be safe to come would be her off week, when the chemo wasn't tearing her immune system apart. Even then, it could be risky, but Melanie didn't care. She could not stay at home all the time. Melanie wanted to be living her life, if only in those rare instances.

"Come on, girl, it's okay. It's still me," Melanie called to her.

Kona floated on the surface of the water and watched Melanie carefully. The dolphin swam closer and laid her head on the edge of the island. Her eyes seemed to look deep into Melanie's soul as if trying to read her thoughts. Melanie was afraid Kona would sense the fear inside her. Fear had a way of scaring animals away, but Melanie's fear wasn't for Kona, but one that she carried deep inside her every day of her life. Would the dolphin understand that Melanie's body was still attacking itself even with all the treatments that had been thrown at it? It was hard enough for Melanie to understand, and this was not her first rodeo with it. Why did cancer pick her? Was it in her DNA the moment she was born? Did something she did make her more prone to catching it? Melanie tried to keep those thoughts at bay, but the truth was they were always there — they probably always would be. Even small moments of happiness were covered in them.

Kona backed away from her after a moment, taking some water into her mouth. Just when Melanie thought the dolphin would turn away, she sprayed Melanie playfully, causing Melanie to shriek in laughter. Kona echoed her laughs with high pitched shrills. It was as if Kona had realized what was missing from Melanie's life. The happiness she felt from Kona's display was enough to chase away the thoughts that echoed inside her. Instead, she became focused on playing with Kona and raising both their spirits.

Melanie cuffed her hand in the water and splashed back at the dolphin. "Gotcha!"

Back and forth, they splashed, until Julia handed Melanie a ball. Melanie tossed the ball into the water, and Kona eyed it speculatively as if she was not quite ready to do full on play with Melanie. Kona approached it carefully, watching the way it bobbed up and down with the rippling water.

"Aww, come on. Kona. Chase said you liked the ball."

"She does, she's just being finicky." Julia smiled at her. "Keep trying. She'll warm back up to you."

"I hope so. I would have been here every day if…."

"We all know that. Don't let her shake you. Kona loves you. You're good for her."

"She's good for me too."

Melanie knew that having Kona gave her something to focus on during the hard times. There had been quite a few of them lately, especially when Dr. Strand changed some of her medication. Some of them made her feel like her skin was on fire. Some made her feel like she had swallowed a cotton ball. None of them was a picnic, but some were better to handle than others. All she had to do was get through this. Melanie knew there was a bright day on the horizon, the day when she was cancer free. This time she would beat it for good. She was bound and determined to never come back to this moment, never to have to feel like she would never have control over her life again.

In some ways, that was why she related to Kona. The dolphin had not asked to be captured from the free life in the ocean, just as Melanie had not wanted to be held captive to her illness. They were two souls being controlled by some other puppet master. Melanie wished there was another way to help Kona other than just helping her get used to her circumstances. That was a little like giving in really, but she was not sure what else she could do. If she had her way, Melanie would set her free in the deep blue ocean where she belonged. Melanie was pretty sure that it was as likely as snowfall in the middle of July in the hot Arizona sun. It would take a miracle, one that Melanie wasn't sure she could manufacture.

Finally, Kona inched forward in the water just close enough to push the ball with her snout. After the first tentative push, Kona started to zoom all over the pool with it. Turning, the dolphin bumped the ball with her snout so that it landed right in front of Melanie. Melanie smiled to herself as she picked it up to toss it back to Kona. The two began a makeshift volleyball game consisting of just one girl and a lonely dolphin.

Unfortunately, time was always limited. Melanie was only allowed to help in short spurts, even on her off weeks. Melanie understood why, but she still wanted to rebel against the rules. It was not fair that her cancer dictated every aspect of her life. She was more than ready to give the big-C its marching orders. Melanie looked down at the water before she stepped off the island. She didn't want to say goodbye, but she had no choice. If she didn't follow her mother's rules where her time here was concerned, Melanie might lose the opportunity. Now was not the time to push the boundaries.

"Bye, Kona. See you soon, I hope."

She felt the small splash of water hit her feet and knew that Kona still wanted to play. Melanie refused to turn around, though. If she did, Melanie would never leave. The resolve to keep moving was already a weak one. Tears threatened to fall as she walked away. Kona had become so much more than a dolphin to her. Melanie had never realized until now that Kona represented the future she wanted to have. To be able to help her and other animals like her was something that was deeply ingrained in Melanie. Part of her was afraid that she would never get the chance.

Melanie tried to shake those thoughts off as she made her way through the aquarium. When she walked into the office to find her mother, she was surprised to find her sister Kimmie sitting in one of the chairs. "What are you doing here?"

Kimmie mumbled something incoherent and looked down at the floor. Melanie knew that look. Her sister had gotten into trouble. It had only happened a handful of times, and Kimmie was the one sister who was more prone to that. Melanie sat down next to her and saw Kimmie shrink away from her. Melanie had an inkling that this had something to do with her.

"What happened, Kimmie?"

"They were saying horrible things about you. One of the kids called you a Ferengi."

"A Ferengi? From *Star Trek*?" Melanie snorted aloud. That was a new one. Last time it was Chrome Dome or Mr. Clean. Kids were brutal. Some of them had no capacity to think outside of their own egos to care about what another kid might be going through. What surprised her was the fact that a kid Kimmie's age actually knew what a Ferengi was. The bald creatures looked a lot like trolls with overextended ears. The only reason Melanie knew was that Grandma Mimi was an avid *Star Trek* fan.

"Yes...." Kimmie's lip trembled in anger as she crossed her arms in front of her chest.

"What did you do?" Melanie was almost afraid of the answer.

"Gave her a black eye."

Melanie snorted and coughed into her hand. Oh, to have had her to defend her years ago. "Nice!"

"No, it's not. Don't encourage her. She's not Laila Ali, and we are not to solve our problems with violence." Her mother's voice was a mixture of annoyance and exhaustion as she entered the room.

"So how long did you get?" Melanie whispered to her sister while her mom sat down to focus on an email on her computer.

"Three days," Kimmie whispered back.

"Bonus!" Melanie grinned at her.

"I heard that. And it's not a reward. It's a punishment. You're just lucky Grandma Mimi can be there with you, and I don't have to leave work. You're going to have to make up all your work too."

Kimmie mumbled under her breath, "It was worth every second."

Melanie sighed. "Look, kid. I'm a big girl. Sticks and stones won't break my bones. Don't let them get to you."

"But I'm not going to let them talk about you." Her lip trembled.

"It's okay, Kimmie. I'm going to be okay. Letting them call me a name here or there is not going to make me break. They can't touch me, kid." Melanie held her hand out to her sister and waited for her to grab it.

"I just...." Tears fell down her face.

Melanie felt her insides weaken their resolve. She did not want to see her sister worrying so much. It was bad enough that this cancer had taken a lot of her own childhood. She did not want it to take Kimmie's too. "I know. You feel helpless. We all do, Kimmie. But you know what?"

"What?" Kimmie's lip wobbled.

"Fear is not the enemy. Sometimes it makes us stronger. Sometimes it makes us weaker. Me...I picture it in my mind and tackle it one step at a time. One treatment, then another. Promise me you'll talk to me when you feel scared, okay?" Melanie held up a pinkie for her sister to make their pinkie pact.

"Promise."

A loud sniff made both of them look over at their mother.

"What? I've got allergies."

"Sure, Mom." Melanie shook her head.

"It's just...when did you get so wise? So grown?"

"Oh, don't worry. I'm still very immature. Lots of growing up to do." Melanie conjured a smile that she hoped would convince them both that she was all right. It was the same one she always plastered on her face to keep them from worrying. Melanie had to be strong for everyone else, even when she felt weak. Sometimes it weighed on her, but what choice did she have? If everyone were depressed around her, Melanie would never be able to claw her way out of this darkness.

"Yeah, she was watching *Sesame Street* yesterday," Kimmie added.

"Hey, they have a new monster. Can you blame me?" Melanie shrugged her shoulders.

"You two are something else. Well, Grandma Mimi will be here soon. Why don't you meet her at the entrance?"

Melanie nodded to her mother and saw the relief in her eyes. She knew it was because Melanie had been able to find a way to soothe her sister's angst. Melanie was a good buffer. She'd learned to be that way a long time ago. It was a side effect of being a survivor, and from being so strong that she became the glue that held everyone together. That nurturing part of herself was the same part that wanted to make Kona's life better. It all just took time, time that sometimes felt borrowed.

CHAPTER 18

The dark cloud hanging over her head was hard to conquer. It followed her around every second of the day. Yesterday, when she'd woken up, nausea had been debilitating. All she could do was lay in bed and pray that the moment would pass. Some days were like that. Some were good, some bad. She wished she could figure out when it would happen, but there was no warning. It was an unfortunate side effect of the high doses of medication she had to take. It was the price of fighting the cancer that wanted to take over her body.

By the time she had finally felt better, most of the day had wasted away, which was depressing and infuriating at the same time. She was supposed to go to the aquarium yesterday. Even her consoling texts from Chase did not make her feel better. She loved him, and he tried his best to understand. They all did, but would always fall short. Melanie tried to be patient with them, but they would never know what it was like to feel like her body was being devoured from the inside out. She prayed they never did. Melanie wouldn't wish this on her worst enemy, much less the people she loved.

Today was a different day, though. It was almost as if yesterday had never happened. Melanie refused to not take advantage of it. While her mother was determined to keep her at home, Melanie had used a little well-placed guilt to make her bring her to work with her. She had promised her mom that if she felt bad, she could take her home. Melanie had no intention of leaving the aquarium, though. She was going to power through, no matter what it took. Melanie refused to give cancer much of a thought today. Today was about living, not worrying about an outcome that might come somewhere along the road.

As much as her mother worried about her, it made her feel better to see Melanie making an effort to lead a normal life. Melanie knew it was hard to watch her on the days where it would almost be easier to give in to the sickness that plagued her. Kids like her, they had to have a fighting spirit to get through this, for cancer could easily whittle away one's reason for living. Melanie refused to give in to it, much like many others. Her resolve to not give up burned like a solar flare inside her. She had so much to live for, so many dreams to fulfill, so many new ones to make. Life was a gift, and she was going to live it the best that she could, even when she felt low. Melanie would live for all those that had been unable to live before her. Their memories pushed her forward, reminding her to take the time to enjoy the world around her as Lori had. Melanie had even taken to blogging her experiences the way Lori had, as an homage to her. It was as if her friend had passed the torch on to her, and Melanie was running for her life with it.

In the darkest of days, the only thing that made her feel better was seeing Kona again. Kona was a good example of surviving against the odds. While captivity could have completely broken the dolphin, Kona seemed to be thriving, doing well enough for more detailed training, which would help her assimilate with the other dolphins. Maybe it was the fact that Melanie had been able to see her more often, or that Chase had worked hard to pick up the slack when she could not. As it stood, Kona loved both of them enough to continue her healing. That was not to negate the bond that was growing between Kona and Julia, but there was a different connection between the teens and the dolphin. Julia was smart enough to recognize that. The trainer wanted the best for Kona, even if it overstepped her own duties to provide it.

Even though things were going better for Kona, Melanie was worried about her emotional well-being. Melanie hoped that her loneliness might improve if she had other dolphins with her. Deep down, though, Melanie knew the only thing that would really help her was her freedom. Kona belonged back in the ocean, where she had the room to breathe. She would give it to her in a heartbeat if that were within her power to do so. Melanie knew that was the only way Kona would ever be happy.

How could anyone feel good about profiting on the capture of such a beautiful creature? In most places, it was illegal to poach a dolphin from its natural habitat. Only a few morally corrupt areas of the world allowed it. The Solomon Islands, Faroe Islands, Peru, and Japan were some of these places. She couldn't believe how often it happened. She feared that someday they would be completely poached from the ocean. Extinction was always a possibility if humanity did not find a way to reattach itself to their morality. Detachment had become the status quo these days. Many people lacked the ability to have empathy outside of their small circle of life. Nothing else existed, but their day to day. For a girl trapped inside her own world and the disease that held her hostage, she had nothing but time to reflect on the state of the world and how she would one day like to change it if she were able.

Shaking away the depressing thoughts of the dolphin drives

from her head, she decided to focus on the one dolphin she could help. Kona needed her, just as much as Melanie needed the dolphin. Kona had become a bright light to Melanie, even on her most cantankerous days.

Melanie adjusted the handkerchief over her head as she glanced in the locker room mirror. "You got this!"

Melanie heard the door open and turned to see Julia enter. "Good morning, Melanie. I'm glad you came with your mom today."

"Mom wanted to make sure I'm not in your way, though." Melanie shuffled her feet as she waited for Julia's reply. According to her mother, Julia had been a little stressed with the inspections that were coming up soon. One of the trainer's jobs was to make sure every animal was being kept at the highest standard of care. There was a fair bit of irony there, considering they were being kept in the middle of the hot desert sun. Even though it was now fall, there was still a good deal of heat when the sun was highest in the sky. These animals had nowhere to go to escape those rays. In the ocean, they could swim deep into the open blue, which offered them more protection from the dangerous ultraviolet light.

"No, not at all. In fact, you're a lot of help. I could certainly use an extra pair of eyes today." Julia picked up one of the clipboards from the locker in front of her. Her eyes roamed down the list, taking in every word before she turned back to smile at Melanie. "You ready?"

"Of course! Bring it on." Melanie's head rose high as she put on a face of strength. The truth was she was only as strong as she pretended sometimes. While she was feeling better today, there was a fear that the tide would turn at any point during the day. Melanie tried not to let those thoughts rise to the surface, but the reality was they were there even when she was having a good day. That fear would probably be with her for quite some time, maybe even the rest of her life.

"Let's get started then."

Melanie followed Julia out of the locker room. She had no idea what an inspection detailed, but as a junior trainer, she was interested in all the aspects of the job. She would take mental notes along the way and compare them with Chase. The two of them were always making a running record for what they liked about the aquarium, and what they would change if they were given a chance.

"Okay. First thing, though, we have to check on the stingray lagoon."

"Fine by me." Melanie had always thought stingrays were interesting. They glided like watery kites with a grace that could not be denied. Melanie enjoyed feeding them when she got a chance too.

The pair of them made their way through the shaded sidewalks that led to the Stingray Lagoon, where the aquarium visitors paid to feed the stingrays each day. Outside the dolphin experience area, this was the second highest money maker. People loved to interact with animals, even if they were never meant to. Melanie was guilty of the same. Sometimes that was hard to manage. Of course, she would always want to see these creatures up close. She was human too, but her desires did not outweigh the rights of these animals to live the life they were supposed to. This was something she had been blogging about lately. Not that she'd had a lot of traffic on her blog yet. It wasn't a makeup tutorial, nor was it some lame-brained teenage challenge that everyone else seemed to think was the next hot rage. That didn't keep her from sharing her thoughts anyway.

"All right, Melanie. We need to make sure that all the stingrays are swimming today. One of them was hiding under a rock for most of the day yesterday. That's not a great sign." Julia looked down at the water, searching through the shaded rocks.

"Why not?" Melanie had never really asked any questions about any of the other animals at the aquarium. She had a laser focus on Kona for the most part. If she was going to work with marine life, it would be a good idea to take in as much information as she could.

"It could mean we have a sick ray." Julia was visibly counting the moving bodies as they glided through the water. "Twelve... hmm. We should have fourteen swimming. Do you see any near the rocks?"

Melanie put her face down closer to the water and let her eyes zero in on the rocks in the middle of the pool. She saw one stingray hovering in place, and another that was skimming the bottom of the tank under the rocks. "Julia...there's two right there. One is hovering, and the other is swimming on the bottom, under the rocks. Are they sick?"

"Possibly. We'll have to check the water levels. We've had this happen a few times. If one chemical is off even just slightly, they can get skin diseases and even infections." Julia took a small vial from the pack she was carrying. She opened the top and leaned over to fill it with water. When she was done, she put a strip in it. "Well, it doesn't seem to be the water. I'll have the vet keep an eye on them."

"Right. Good idea." Melanie did not know what else to say. It was not great to hear that the stingrays were prone to sickness. She imagined all those hands reaching in and feeding them. Who knew what kind of illnesses people brought into those waters? She shuddered at the thought.

"Okay, let's check on Hilo." Julia picked up her bag and clipboard.

"Hilo?" Melanie had never heard of Hilo before.

"Yes. Hilo. He's a young beluga whale who was brought in from Russia. He's a beautiful beluga." Julia was visibly excited. "We've put him with Lily."

"How is Lily treating him?" Melanie could not imagine it could be good, for that whale had been known to be temperamental from time to time.

"So far, Lily seems to be ignoring him. She seems more interested in Kona than Hilo."

Melanie was not surprised to hear that. She had noticed the way Lily seemed to keep an eye on the dolphin. "They are always calling to each other, aren't they?"

"At first, I thought it was a coincidence, but they come to the edge of their pools and talk to each other all the time. I've never seen it happen like that before."

"Lily must sense how lonely Kona is. Will Kona make her way into the tanks with the other dolphins soon?" Part of Melanie wanted to see her move in with the others, but the rest of her worried that a wild dolphin might not be as accepted in a tank of captive ones. Would they treat her the same as the others? Would they sense the wildness in her and reject her? There were so many things that could go wrong, and just one chance to make it right. Melanie nibbled on the inside of her cheek and tried not to let herself go there. She still had hope that Kona would be all right.

"Soon. We still need to get her used to humans a little more. Especially if they want to put her in with the experienced dolphins."

The experienced dolphins that Julia was talking about were the dolphins that people paid to interact with, the ones that

198

were right in front of the booth she had spent the first part of the summer in with Chase. While some people only spent a little money to feed them, there was another group of dolphins on site that they spent even more on. People spent hundreds of dollars just to get in the water with these dolphins. The safety of the animal and the customer were equally important. She was pretty sure Kona would not make it into that particular part of the exhibit. She was terrified most of the time, not that Melanie blamed her at all.

Melanie did understand the fascination with swimming with dolphins. They were such amazing creatures. Getting up close with them was a dream for many people. The more time she spent with Kona, the more she realized how intelligent and caring they could be. Kona seemed to have sensed her low spirits the other day when Melanie and Chase had been working with her. The dolphin helped to even out her mood by being even more playful than usual. By the end of her day, Kona and Chase had both helped lift her spirits.

If Chase had noticed the darkness inside her that day, he never commented. She was thankful for that. Most days, she hated talking about it. Talking only made her fears more real, not to mention they tended to deflate the air between them. It was the same with her family. Melanie did not want them to see her as anything other than strong-willed and determined.

Shaking her thoughts away, she glanced down into the tank and saw the new beluga whale. He was a third of the size of the others, which made him look quite small in comparison. "He's so tiny!"

"He does look smaller than others, but he is already weaned and fending for himself. He was born in captivity." Julia pulled her clipboard out and checked off a few boxes.

"What are you looking for?"

"I'm checking to see if he is swimming, sleeping, or any other behaviors. So far, he's done really well. He had quite a few infections in his last aquarium."

"That sounds dangerous. Can he make Lily sick?" Melanie was a little worried. She did not want Kona to lose one of her friends.

"I don't think so. His problem was the water in his former tank. The chemicals were off so badly that Hilo was getting respiratory infections as well as skin lesions." Julia wrote something else on her paper.

"That's horrible. At least that won't happen to him here." Melanie stomped her foot and stuck out her chin.

"Not on our watch, right, Mel?" Julia patted her on the back and hugged her close.

"You got that, right!"

Melanie smiled at Julia. She had grown even closer to her since she had started dating Chase. He was so much more than a boyfriend to her, though. Chase was her best friend, sometimes her only friend. Sure, she still had friends at school, but it seemed like the moment they started high school without her, their worlds had shifted further away from each other. In a way, Melanie began to feel like they had left her behind. Melanie had tried to accept that people grow apart, but it seemed to affect her life more than theirs. They all still had each other. They all had a normal life, the kind of life she wished she could have.

"Okay, he seems to be fine. Lily is staying away from him right now, but hopefully, she will warm up to him soon." Julia wrote something else down in her notes. "You ready to go see Kona?"

"Am I ever!"

As they walked away from the pool, Lily breached, and a large splash splattered them with water.

"Hey!" Melanie turned to the tank and shook her finger at Lily. "That was uncalled for!"

"But pretty funny." Julia chuckled slightly as Melanie tried to shake the water off her.

"Says you. You're wearing a wet suit. This is going to stick to me for the rest of the day." Melanie pulled her wet clothes away from her skin and tried to fan the water off them. As she started to walk across the sidewalk, a hobbling seal almost knocked her over. "What in the world?"

"Sammie! You devil you!" Julia tried to shoo the seal away. "How do you keep getting out? You're like a slippery, Houdini!"

The seal barked at them and dodged her hands. He scampered away and headed for Kona's pool. The seal climbed up the rocks leading to the pool and dove into the water.

"Wow. Did he just…?" Melanie blinked a few times as she tried to let her brain take in what she was seeing.

"Yes. The other night he escaped from his enclosure and spent the night in with Kona. They seem to like each other." Julia rubbed her hand over her temples. "I didn't need this today. We have a deadline, Sammie."

"Well, maybe we can work with both of them today," Melanie suggested.

"Looks like we have no choice unless I want to wrestle him out of the pool. That I would rather not do."

"I don't blame you."

Melanie followed Julia back to the employee entrance that led them to the island where they could work with Kona one-on-one. By now, Melanie had started to feel like a professional, as she knew the intimate nooks and crannies behind the scenes. It made her feel essential, like she had a higher purpose.

Melanie settled on the edge of the island and dangled her feet in the water. She tapped the water and called for Kona. "Come here, girl!"

Kona came to her in seconds, followed by Sammie, who already had his mouth open for food. Melanie giggled. "Silly, Sammie! I think he wants your food, Kona."

Kona turned to look at the seal, almost as if she understood Melanie's words. The dolphin flapped her tail in the water and splashed the barking seal. Sammie dove into the water and came up right in front of Kona, blocking her from any fish that would be thrown her way.

"We've got plenty for the both of you." Julia now stood beside Melanie with a pail of fish that they were using for training.

Upon seeing the pail, Sammie tried to climb onto the island. His front flippers reached for the ground, and Melanie moved out of the way just in time. The seal now turned to her with his whiskers twitching as he tried to sniff out whether Melanie was hiding any fish.

"Down boy," she told him. Melanie was not entirely sure what to do. She had never been this close to a seal before. She did not want to risk upsetting him, for while he was used to people at the aquarium, she was still a stranger to him.

"Here, take one of these." Julia handed her a fish.

Sammie waddled closer, and Melanie held up a hand. "What do I do?"

"Tell him to wait and hold your hand up." Julia gave her an example with her own hand.

"Okay." Melanie held up her hand. "Wait...."

"Now, when Sammie is sitting patiently, toss him the fish."

Melanie kept her hand up, and when Sammie was sitting

appropriately, she tossed him the fish. Sammie gobbled it up and stepped closer to her. He put his head in her lap, and Melanie felt trapped between wanting to run and petting his head. She took a chance and stroked his head. "Good boy."

Sammie lifted his head slightly and barked at her before he backed away. Melanie watched as Julia made a gesture with her hands and blew her whistle. Sammie dove into the water and waited for his next command.

"How do you know all of this? I mean, usually, you just work with the dolphins, right?" Melanie asked her.

"Yes, but I've pulled double shifts before. It's always good to know as much as you can about the animals around you. Now, how about some ring races? Let's see who can get the rings back to us first."

For the rest of the morning, they took turns throwing the colored plastic rings into the water. Kona and Sammie both zipped through the water after them. At first, Sammie was the clear winner, but now that Kona was figuring out the game, the dolphin was starting to beat him to them. While Kona was larger than Sammie, they both seemed evenly matched with their speed.

After watching the two play in the water, Melanie was thinking a lot less about her own problems and more about Kona's. The dolphin may have been having fun, but she had run into the walls a few times when she could not slow down fast enough. Melanie knew she did not imagine the fear and panic in her eyes. The dolphin did not belong in this aquarium. She wished she could do something about it. Kona deserved so much better. They all did.

CHAPTER 19

The day before Thanksgiving, Melanie sat near the edge of the feeding pool, where she watched Kona swimming slowly by herself. The dolphin had been moved in with the other dolphins last week. Their hope was she would become adjusted a little easier with the other dolphins around her. If she could not make it with them, the owner of the aquarium would be forced to ship her off to another aquarium. He only cared about making a profit from his investments, while Julia and the other trainers worried about what would happen to Kona if she were no longer in their care. Even Mr. Marcus was worried about her, which was saying a lot, as he rarely wanted to rock the boat. He had been there watching over the whole process as Kona had been moved from her tank into the new one.

Melanie wished she could have been there for it, but Julia thought it would be better for Kona not to affiliate her move with Melanie. Melanie was her rock, and even though she could not be there all the time because of her treatments, Kona had seemed to adjust to seeing her on limited days. Those were the days that were the best for both of them. Kona was happier when Melanie was there, and Melanie felt lighter every time she left. Focusing on Kona helped her get past all the rough spots that had become almost too many to count.

Melanie sat near the edge of the feeding pool, where she watched Kona swimming slowly by herself. Melanie had not been able to come as often as she would have liked. She had hoped that after a while, the chemo would slow down, and she would be able to come more than just on her off weeks. That had not been the case. Instead, her treatments were becoming more aggressive. Dr. Strand continued to monitor her white blood cells and check her scans for any changes. Melanie's faith in herself was starting to waiver. For months she had fought tooth and nail to keep strong and focused. She had her schoolwork to distract her some days; on others, it was not nearly enough. Those were the days when she just curled up in bed, feeling sorry for herself while the rest of the world seemed to turn around her. Any time someone came into her room then, she would fight the urge to rage against them just because their health came so easy to them.

Melanie had even pushed Chase away a few times, and while other boys would have taken it personally, he never seemed to. Melanie wasn't sure how he managed to care for her when she was so horrible to him. She didn't feel like she deserved him half of the time. It was probably a good thing he had school to distract him, even though part of her was afraid he would find another girl that didn't come with the baggage she did. Melanie tried not to be the jealous girlfriend, but some days it was hard not to wonder what he did when he was away from her. Then she would feel guilty for having those thoughts, for Chase would be the first to tell her no one else mattered to him.

Her mom was taking more evening hours since a lot of Melanie's appointments were during the day. Even though Grandma Mimi was there to help, Linda wanted to be the one there for the appointments. Melanie hated to admit it, but she wanted her mother there too. She would not have been able to get through this without her. There would always be a part of her that felt like a scared little kid who wanted her mommy. Melanie was not proud of those feelings, because, at sixteen, she should carry herself differently. So, she pretended to be aloof when her mother hugged her sometimes, even when she just wanted to snuggle in closer. When she was too weak to keep up her teenage pretense, Melanie would climb into her mom's bed and sleep against her. Melanie always returned to her own room before Amber woke up, though. She didn't want to be outed for her weakness, and her mom seemed to understand that.

Melanie tried not to think about where her life was headed right now. She wanted to just focus on the day to day. It was easier that way, especially when she never knew what the day would bring. Today though, all she wanted to do was play with Kona. Melanie tapped the water with her hand and waited to see if Kona would come over. She was worried that the dolphin would be too upset to do so. Melanie already knew she wasn't reacting well to her new environment.

"Come here, girl." Melanie repeated her movements. When the dolphin did not come over, she felt her heart sink to the bottom of her stomach. Kona was probably not adjusting to being in the tank with the other dolphins. Melanie only hoped this would change over time—it had to. Kona could not continue to be in isolation for the rest of her life. There were rules against that, not to mention what the owner would do to her if she continued to be a money pit. So much time and effort had been put into Kona, and he was still not reaping any rewards from it.

"Come on, girl, I'm still here for you." Melanie held her breath as she waited to see if Kona would even respond to her.

Kona turned to face her, but it was clear the dolphin was wary

206

of her presence. The other dolphins circled closer to her. One of them surfaced a few feet away as if to see whether Melanie had any fish in her hand, but when she saw that Melanie had nothing to give her, she dove into the water and zipped away.

"Sorry...no food for you, Lula. Kona...come on, it's time to play!" Melanie tossed one of the rings in the water, just to see what would happen. She watched it sink to the bottom of the tank. Watching for Kona, she realized Kona was no longer on the surface. She held her breath slightly as she waited to see what would happen next.

"That's my girl!" Melanie cheered as Kona burst from the pool with the red ring in her mouth. She swam over to Melanie and tossed the ring at her. Kona made the clicking sounds that greeted her and put her snout on the platform. She continued to chatter at Melanie as she waited for her to toss more rings into the pool. "Hi, girl." Melanie reached over and slid her hand gently over Kona's head. "I missed you. I know I've been away again. I'm doing the best I can, girl. But look at you. You made it to the big pool."

Kona echoed her thoughts with more of her shrills and clicks. As Melanie held up the rings, Kona followed her movements with her head.

"Okay, here you go!" Melanie tossed all six rings into the water and waited to see how quickly Kona would retrieve them. None of the other dolphins seemed to be interested in the least, especially since Melanie had not brought any food with her.

Before she knew it, Kona returned with the rings in her mouth. The dolphin tossed them up at Melanie, who barely had time to catch them. Even though Kona was playing the game with her, Melanie could see that her spark was gone. "Poor girl. What's the matter? Are the girls not treating you right?"

Kona turned to look at the other dolphins as if she understood Melanie's words. Melanie was always surprised by how much Kona seemed to know precisely what Melanie was saying. Her mom told her she probably imagined it, but Melanie did not think so.

"Don't worry, girl. I'm sure it will get better. A few more rounds?" Melanie held up the rings and waited to see if Kona was ready. When the dolphin lifted her head, she knew Kona was prepared to go again.

By the time they had played another ten rounds, Julia and Chase were both making their way over to the pool. Julia was carrying her pail of fish, while Chase was carrying a few other odds and ends with him.

"Glad to see her playing." Julia nodded to the water.

"She's missed you," Chase almost mumbled. "I do too."

"I know. I'm sorry I haven't checked in with you lately. Just had a lot going on." Not to mention she had felt like crap. Not a single inch of her was up to talking on the phone or spending time with Chase, no matter how much she would have loved to. Sharing that with him would only make him worry, though. She didn't want him to have to carry so much of that with him.

"It's okay. You're here now."

He grinned at her, and Melanie felt her heart beat faster. She always missed him, even if she tried to pretend she didn't. Melanie wished she had the energy to be the girlfriend he deserved.

"Looks like she's happy to see you." Julia stood near the edge of the island with a whistle in her mouth. The dolphins in the water started to swim fast circles around their enclosure. They all probably hoped Julia had brought them a few tasty morsels. "She's been so sad lately. She looks for you every day."

Melanie nodded her head. "I know, but it will be over soon."

She paused when she saw the panic on Chase's face. She held up her pinky as if to make a promise. "There are just two more rounds, and then I'll be back for good."

"That's the spirit!" Julia cheered her on.

"Giving up is just not something I can do. It's not in my DNA." Melanie gave her a small smile. "Is she going to be okay?"

"I hope so, Melanie. Right now, it's not looking so good for Kona." Julia reached into her bucket and tossed a few fish into the tank. The other dolphins raced to see who would get it first.

"You just need more time, right girl?" Encouraged Melanie.

"We sure hope so. Right now, it's not looking good." Chase sat down next to her. He handed her a water blaster to squirt Kona with. The two of them started to squirt water into the pool.

"Sometimes they turn around quickly. Sometimes it's a struggle. We're not giving up yet." Julia sat down next to Melanie. She reached for the rings and tossed them into the pool. Julia blew her whistle when Kona did not immediately return with the rings.

Kona rose from the surface and held the rings in her mouth just out of reach. Melanie smirked at Julia. "You know she's mad at you, right?"

"Yes, I'm sure she is." Julia snorted slightly. "I can take it, though."

"Maybe she's not meant to be an exhibit dolphin. The others barely acknowledge her. She was happier in her tank by herself." Melanie wanted to scream her frustration. She hated that Kona was trapped inside a tank. She should be out swimming free in the ocean. They all should.

"Well, I think if she doesn't perk up soon, I have somewhere she can go. Zoe's tank mate just got shipped to California. We can't leave her alone for too long. It's against the rules." Julia blew her whistle when Kona did not immediately return with the rings.

"Do you blame her for being so upset?" Melanie could not help the anger that rose to the surface.

"Whoa, chill, Mel. You know my mom loves all of the dolphins here." Chase stuck up for his mom.

"I know. I'm sorry, Julia. I know it's not your fault." Melanie's face paled. She didn't mean to snap at Julia. Sometimes her emotions were hard to get under control. Especially lately. Melanie never knew when they would rise.

"She's right to be mad, Chase. I'm angry too. I wish I could save her from this life. You know if I had a choice she would be free, right? All I can do is make sure she is well-cared for." Julia sighed aloud. "In a perfect world, all animals would be free from harm, especially from human reach. But we don't live in a perfect world."

"That's the truth. Why does Fillimore keep cutting corners?" Chase let out an irritated breath of air.

"Businessmen sometimes make financial choices without considering their impact on the animals here. We do the best we can to protect them."

"I know, Julia. You care more than some of the others. You practically live here. I bet you take them home with you at night." Melanie knew what it was like to take something home with you in your head. She did the same thing every time she left the doctor's office.

Chase snorted. "Sometimes, I think I'll find one of them in the bathtub."

"I have never brought any animal home intentionally. There was the one time a bird snuck into the car, though."

"I remember that one. Didn't you have to scrub bird poop off the seat for a week?"

Julia rolled her eyes. "Don't remind me."

"I wish there was something more we could do." Melanie felt slow desperation growing inside her. If she had a magic lamp, she would probably wish every captive animal could be safe in their natural habitat away from humans, but magic lamps did not exist. Neither did wishes. There was very little magic in this world, and she was already too jaded to believe it if someone said it was anything more than a system of tricks and illusions.

"I hear you. Sometimes it just breaks your heart, but I know if I didn't do this job, someone else would. And I can't guarantee they would do it right. If I can, I'll make sure Kona gets removed from this tank as soon as possible," Julia promised her.

Melanie gave Julia a half-smile. "I know you will, Julia."

Kona chose that moment to splash them both with her tail. The dolphin always seemed to know when she should lighten the mood. Kona tossed the rings at Melanie and waited for Julia to give her some fish.

"That a girl." Julia tossed her a couple of fish and turned to Melanie. "Listen, there are some people that are coming here today."

"Oh?" Melanie wondered why Julia was telling her this. She was never invited in for special meetings since Melanie was just a kid and did not work at the aquarium.

Chase seemed surprised. "That's today?"

"What is?" Melanie wondered what in the world they were talking about.

"You'll see."

Chase had a grin on his face as if he were up to something. Melanie was not sure she wanted to know what it was either. What had he done this time? He was always coming up with random surprises. *Please don't let it be a flash mob.* Melanie would never let him hear the end of that. She hated being the center of attention lately, but that's because everything in her family seemed to revolve around Melanie and her cancer.

"Okay…is it about Kona?" Melanie splashed the dolphin with her hand and waited to see if Kona would squirt her.

"No, it's…well, it's hard to explain. Better for you to come and find out, okay? I want your mom to come too."

"Am I in trouble?" Melanie felt her insides start to churn. It was the same kind of feeling as if she were being sent to the principal's office, which had only happened a handful of times when she was younger.

"Oh, no. Goodness. I'm sorry, maybe I should just tell you. I heard about this foundation called Charlie's Dream. It's for kids that are dealing with life-threatening diseases."

"Like cancer?" Melanie still hated the way the word rolled off her tongue. Cancer. It was a six-letter word that was the worst word in the human language. Forget the four-letter words. They were tame in comparison.

"Yeah, like that," added Chase.

"It's The Charlie's Dream Foundation. Charlie was a young boy who died of leukemia. His father, William, created the foundation in living memory of his child. People donate from all over the world to make children's dreams come true." Julia put her hand on Melanie's hand. "I'd very much like for you to have something special."

"Oh." Melanie felt her heart drop to her feet. "I see. Well, I don't need any wishes. I'm doing fine."

Chase looked down to the ground. His voice was almost shaking when he started to speak. "We didn't mean to upset you."

Melanie felt bad. He was just trying to do something nice for her. She should thank him for caring, she knew she should, but she just could not conjure the energy. So many people around her were sad on a daily basis. They may not vocalize it, but Melanie could sense it. It put a lot of stress on her shoulders. She wanted just to be responsible for her own feelings, but Melanie knew that was not an option. Cancer did not just rule her life. It ruled theirs too.

"It's okay, Chase."

"Chase and I, we just wanted a way to celebrate everything you do," Julia explained.

Melanie took a deep breath and tried to wrap her mind around the gesture they were offering her. She knew that deep down, this had come from a beautiful place. They truly cared about her, and that was not something she should just blatantly ignore. She took a deep breath and tried to keep her darker feelings out of her voice. "Thanks, I think. But you do know I'm not done yet, right?"

"Oh, we have plenty of time to train Kona." Julia waved away her concerns.

"No, I'm not done living. Aren't those for kids that aren't going to…?" Heaven help her, but Melanie could not stop the tears that clouded her eyes. Every day she was faced with the strength and weakness in her own mortality. Some days were easier than others. This kindness, it was sweet, but it was like a dark cloud looming over her. Kids that got wishes or dreams; they were the ones that most people thought would not make it. That was what she had always thought at least. Melanie refused to think someone else might pity her for the life she lived. She was a fighter. Nothing was going to keep her down. The idea that some corporation was going to give her any kind of special treatment because she was a cancer kid, it felt a lot like a nail in her coffin.

"This isn't about dying, Mel," Chase reassured her.

"Oh, no. No, no, no. Please don't think that's why we contacted them. A dream doesn't mean you are dying, Melanie." Julia's face started to flush. "What I mean is that they are for those who are fighting with courage, like you. I admire that about you, you know?"

"So do I," added Chase.

"I'm sorry. It's just half the time I feel like people are watching to see when I will fall if you know what I mean. The other half, I have to be strong enough to convince myself I'm still walking." Melanie could not keep her emotions out of her voice. She was almost trembling until Chase reached for her hand. It was her constant lifeline.

"You're still the strongest person I know."

His smile was sweet, but there were tears in his eyes. Melanie saw him fight to hold them back. She hated that her illness brought him so much pain. Melanie just wanted to wrap her arms around him and tell him everything was going to be okay. The only problem was, it was a lie. She didn't know that everything would be okay. Melanie wanted to believe it would be, but this time was harder than the others. She had a lot more to lose.

"Thanks, I guess." Melanie squeezed his hand, but kept a little distance between them, as she was barely holding it together.

Julia looked visibly shaken as tears threatened to fall. She sniffed for a second, then coughed into her hand to hide her sadness. "Just come talk to them, okay? Nothing needs to be decided today, all right?"

"Okay, Julia. Thank you." Melanie took a deep breath and tried to settle herself. It would not do any good to go into some meeting so emotional.

"No. Thank you. Every day our lives are better for having you. Just look at Kona." Julia nodded to the dolphin, who was eying them from the water.

"Mom's right. There's no way she would have made it this far without you."

"Aww. She's a fighter like me, though." Melanie pulled her hand from Chase's and patted the water. Kona swam up beside her. Melanie reached over and rubbed her head. "Good girl." She stood up and rubbed her hands on her pants. "Well, I better check in with Mom. I'll see you later, Julia."

"And what about me?" Chase looked as if he were trying to analyze her state of mind.

"Don't we have a movie date?"

"That depends...is it your turn to pick, or Kimmie's?" Chase looked as if he was getting tired of watching princess movies.

"Oh, it's totally mine. Kimmie has dance practice, and Amber is working. So it will just be you and me." When Melanie saw Julia's scrutinizing look, she amended her answer. "And Grandma Mimi."

"Good woman. Always liked her." Julia nodded to her son.

"I know, best behavior." Chase held his right hand up.

"Don't worry. Chase is a true gentleman." Melanie saw him blush and knew he didn't like where the conversation was going. "I have to get going now. I'll see you later."

CHAPTER 20

Just a few minutes later, Melanie was standing in the main office, wondering if she should just interrupt whatever her mother was doing. She took a chance and opened the door to find her mother was sitting at her desk. Sitting in one of the chairs next to the desk was a woman Melanie had never seen before, a slender woman with medium length brown hair. She wore a pair of sunglasses on top of her head as she rifled through a small accordion folder that was filled with papers. Melanie thought she looked like a classroom teacher who had stashed her papers inside in a mad dash out the door. Melanie was not sure what to think of her.

Melanie cleared her throat to get her mom's attention. "Mom?"

"Come on in, Mel. Have a seat. This is Jenna Marsh. She's from The Charlie's Dream Foundation."

Jenna Marsh stood up and offered her hand to Melanie. "Pleased to meet you."

At first, Melanie did not want to shake her hand. The woman represented a part of her life she was trying to keep hidden from the rest of the world. When she saw her mother's cursory glance, Melanie reached for Jenna's hand. She shook it briefly before she retracted it. Melanie pushed another chair closer to her mother's desk as if drawing a line between them. Melanie was not inclined to trust the woman any time soon.

"I hear you like to help at the aquarium." Jenna sat back down.

"Yes." Did the woman think she was going to get more from her than that? Melanie was not comfortable with this whole situation. Had it been her idea, it might have been different. Melanie was sure several other children needed a dream more than she did. Maybe Lori would have been able to see more butterflies if someone had nominated her. Melanie started to wish she had thought about it earlier. To bring her friend a little more peace in her life would have made her passing a little easier to handle.

"That must brighten your day." Jenna put her the folder in her lap and sat back.

It was a dance she recognized, the one where an adult tried to figure out just what to say to a kid with cancer. Did they praise them for how great they looked? Should they ask how they were feeling? Adults never really knew where the boundaries started. Kids were different. They either went out full force with all their questions, or they just shrugged their shoulders and treated her like it was no big deal. That was probably because most kids had no idea what cancer was or the toll it took on anyone who had it. This woman was probably a little better at it than most. She focused on other things, a tactic that only worked when the kid in question could not see through it. Melanie had x-ray vision on this woman and was not ready to fall into any traps of being a cancer poster child.

Melanie crossed her arms over her chest and glanced at her mother, who was giving her a look that told her she had better be on her best behavior. "Sure. When I get to come to the aquarium, soon I'll be able to come here more. Right, Mom?"

Her mother smiled at her. "You have another two rounds of treatment, but yes, I imagine you will spend a lot more time here."

"See. Almost done." Melanie held her head up with false bravado.

"Melanie is a fighter. She's been more of a rock to me than I have to her."

"Children have an unbreakable spirit. I've met quite a few, just like Melanie here." Jenna nodded toward Melanie.

"Why are you here?" Her tone was defensive. Melanie could not seem to help herself.

"Melanie Lynn Parker. Manners." Her mother's tone was a warning to mind herself.

Jenna smiled kindly at Melanie anyway. "The foundation often sends a representative to get to know the kids before we bring them in."

"Look, no offense, but I barely get any time with Kona. Do I need to be here?" Melanie was ready to bolt.

"Mel, please listen to her."

Jenna waved her hand in front of her. "No, it's quite all right. Actually, I wouldn't mind meeting your dolphin."

Melanie rolled her eyes. "Kona? She's not my dolphin. She doesn't belong to anyone. Or she shouldn't. Wild animals shouldn't be possessions."

"I see. Well, do you mind if I tag along with you?" Jenna's patience was stronger than her mother's, for Linda Parker was giving Melanie a glance that told her they would be having a long talk later.

Melanie sighed in defeat. "Fine."

Melanie pushed up from her chair and headed out the door. She could hear the woman following her. Her mother would probably want her to give her a tour of the place, but Melanie really did not want to have anything to do with her. She had never been one for the spotlight and hated to have all the attention on her. Maybe that was because she did not want the cancer to be at the forefront of her life all the time.

When they made it to Kona's tank, Melanie turned to Jenna. "You can stay here while I work with her. It's safer. Kona is not fond of strangers."

"I see. Well, I'm happy to watch from here." Jenna gestured to the viewing area that surrounded the tank.

Melanie made her way to the island and tried not to think about why Jenna Marsh was here. The Charlie Dream Foundation. She had heard of it before. When she was in the hospital, they had visited one of the kids on her floor. Adam. Melanie shivered as she conjured his sweet little face. The four-year-old had the brightest smile every single day. Melanie had almost been envious of that ability to smile even when he must have felt sucker-punched by the chemo. He had been given a dream himself but had passed away a week after having it fulfilled. It was a pattern she did not want to be a part of. She had seen enough loss to last her a lifetime. That might be why she felt so strongly about not having a dream granted. In her mind, she needed to just focus on surviving. NED was right around the corner, and this time she would not let go of it. Melanie hoped that her luck would continue long enough to be free from all the doctor's visits. That would not happen until she was in remission, and even then, she would have to go through periodic scans. Remission was not guaranteed, but she refused to think there was no way out.

"Back so soon?" Julia asked her.

"She wanted to see Kona." It was a half-truth. She did not want to hurt her feelings. Melanie knew that Julia and Chase were only trying to help.

"I knew you would be back," teased Chase.

"You know me. Can't stay away." Melanie was happy that no one brought up what they might have discussed in the office. Not much was discussed actually, but Melanie was a smart girl. She knew how it all worked. There was no need to give her the nitty-gritty details.

Melanie tossed out a ring for Kona to retrieve. As she did, she saw Jenna watching her with interest. Melanie smiled at her, knowing her mother would expect her to at least show some manners. "Kona has her good days and bad days. When she first came here, she wouldn't interact with any humans. Now she trusts a few of us."

Jenna put her elbows on the edge of the encloser and looked down at the water. "What happened to her?"

"She was taken from the wild and sold to the aquarium. Most of the other dolphins here were born in captivity."

As if to punctuate her point, the other dolphins rose to the surface in search of food. Two of them stopped in front of Jenna and started to make noises as if they were begging for food. Jenna stepped back slightly and grinned. "I see. So it's all they know?"

"Yes. But this girl...she misses her freedom. I don't blame her. She feels as trapped as I do." Melanie sighed softly and closed her eyes as she let her vulnerabilities rise to the surface.

"What do you mean?" Jenna asked her.

"She's trapped in her tank with no way out, and I'm trapped in a body that keeps attacking itself. Both of us want our freedom in different ways." Her words were strong as she emphasized what she rarely shared with anyone else. She felt the dark cloud float around them. The knowledge that living was a struggle for her was something that sucked the joy out of the air. She felt Chase withdraw next to her. She was sorry for it, but sometimes reality was hard to hide.

"That makes sense." Jenna had a thoughtful look on her face as she scribbled something down on her notepad.

"Good girl, Kona," praised Melanie. The dolphin had retrieved the rings that Melanie had tossed into the water nearby.

"She's lucky to have you." Jenna's voice was filled with a realness that Melanie could not deny.

"Yes, she is. We all are. She's one talented junior trainer," added Julia.

Melanie could not help the beaming smile she plastered on her face. Julia's opinion meant a lot to her. "Someday, I want to work with all kinds of marine life."

"At an aquarium?" Julia asked her.

Melanie knew that Julia loved her work, but Melanie had always been pretty vocal about wanting to work in a place that helped protect marine life. After working with Julia, though, she saw that was what the trainer tried to do. Even though these glorious creatures were trapped inside the tanks, it was Julia who made sure they thrived the best they could. Melanie was quite sure if Julia had not been there; some of these animals would have died a long time ago. "I don't know. Maybe. Maybe at a sanctuary or rehabilitation center."

"Sounds like you have a bright future ahead of you," Jenna commended her.

Melanie's eyes met Jenna's, and for the first time, a genuine smile rose to her face. It was as if the woman understood her whole point. Yes...there was a future. Melanie did not plan on leaving this world any time soon. "I do, don't I?"

"Well, I've taken up enough of your time. We'll be in touch, Melanie."

"Okay." Melanie smiled at her again. "It was nice to meet you."

"The pleasure was truly mine. Keep up the good work, Melanie." Jenna waved at her before she turned away.

Melanie sighed in relief. She turned to the other two and saw the concern on their faces. "I'm fine."

"I didn't mean to make you feel like...."

"I'm dying?" Melanie filled in the blank for Chase. "It's not a bad word, Chase. Some people do die from cancer. I'm just not going to be one of them."

"We didn't mean to imply that we thought you were." Julia's eyes were filled with sadness as if she were worried that their act had hurt Melanie in some way.

"It's fine. I'm not fragile. I don't break easily." That was not entirely true, but Melanie was not going to make them feel worse than they already did. There was no need for that.

"Good. Are you coming back tomorrow too?" Chase asked her.

"As long as Mom says I can." Melanie stood up and wiped her hands on the small towel next to her. "I guess it's about time for me to head back in. See you tonight."

"Count on it."

When Chase came later, his face looked conflicted. Melanie could tell that he was feeling bad for what had happened earlier. "Mel —"

"Shhh.... Don't ever apologize for caring." She put her finger on his lips and silenced him. Melanie put her head against his chest when he wrapped his arms around her.

"I love you," he whispered.

"I love you more," she answered. Melanie had had time to think about why he'd called the foundation. He cared about her in ways she was just starting to understand. His love felt eternal, and even if it didn't last forever, Melanie was going to hold onto it for as long as she could. She heard the slight cough from the other room and stepped away from Chase, who was now grinning sheepishly.

"Grandma Mimi," he greeted her.

"Chase. I'm about to make some popcorn. You kids need anything else?"

Melanie heard the slight emphasis on kids and fought the urge to giggle. While her mother was okay with her dating at her age, Grandma Mimi was still coming around to the idea. Good thing she hadn't found out that Chase had already kissed her. Grandma Mimi would have a field day with that one, but really, she had nothing to worry about. Melanie was not in a hurry to rush into more of a relationship with Chase. Both of them were happy with the speed at which it moved. Some things were best to wait for, after all.

"I'll get some drinks. Why don't you turn on the movie? I put a few choices on the stand," Melanie followed her grandma into the other room.

"It's good he had time to visit, Mel. Just make sure —"

"We behave?" Melanie filled in the blanks for her.

Grandma Mimi smirked as she pulled the microwave popcorn out of the bag. "I know what kids do these days, Melanie."

"We're not those kinds of kids. Besides, if you haven't noticed, I do have other things on my mind." Melanie pointed to the handkerchief covering her head, knowing it would make her grandma drop it for a little while.

"You're a good girl, Melanie."

"I know, Grandma." Melanie returned her smile and walked over to kiss her on the cheek. "Thank you."

"For what?" Grandma Mimi touched her cheek where Melanie had kissed her.

"For being here for me, in case I don't say it enough." Melanie didn't meet her eyes this time. Instead, she backed away from her and reached into the fridge to grab a few sodas.

"I wouldn't be anywhere else. I'll bring the popcorn in. I trust you'll behave if I retire to my room? Book club is kicking my butt." Grandma Mimi grinned at her.

"Of course."

Melanie was glad that they would have some privacy. The moment Grandma Mimi left them, Melanie snuggled up against Chase on the couch. The two of them were half-asleep when her mom returned home. While it would have been awkward for someone else, Linda simply smiled at them and joined them for the rest of the movie until Chase had to go home.

Later, Melanie lay sprawled out on her bed in the fluffy pajamas that made her feel like she was being wrapped in a warm hug. She had her head covered as she wrote in her journal. She was so absorbed in her thoughts that she did not hear her mother walk into her room.

"How you doing, kiddo?"

Melanie almost jumped out of her skin. "Gah! You scared me!"

"Sorry."

"I'm fine." Melanie answered her first question.

"What are you writing about?"

"I'm making a list of how I can help Kona and other dolphins like her." Melanie realized that her mother probably thought she would be writing about her amazing boyfriend, like other girls.

While she did love Chase enough to write about him, she chose to spend her time on the other thing that consumed her thoughts. Chase was her present, but the things she wrote about those were her future. Maybe it was a future he would be a part of, but that was something that was too soon to tell. They were still kids, after all.

"Oh?" Linda seemed surprised.

"There's so much good we can do, Mom. Shouldn't we at least try? Otherwise, what's the point of it all?"

"Are we questioning the meaning of life?" her mother teased her.

"Always." Every. Single. Day. Life was the thing she fought for, so of course, she questioned every aspect of it. Her mother had to have known that.

Linda moved away from the door and walked over to the bed. She sat down next to her daughter and rubbed her hand along her back. "Don't ever stop, Mel."

"I won't, Mom." Melanie knew that her mom was talking about more than her thoughts.

Linda fixed her headwrap then kissed Melanie on the forehead. "I love you, Mel."

"I know," Melanie whispered.

Her mom got up from the bed and started to walk away. "Amber's working the late shift, so don't stay up too late."

"Okay, Mom." Melanie turned back to her journal. She could feel her mother's loving gaze from the doorway. Her love was one thing that Melanie would never question. They had been through thick and thin together. Throughout the triumphs and the struggles, her mother was there for all of them just as much as her sisters were. Despite it all, Melanie knew she was one of the lucky ones. Their love was unconditional. Even when she felt like lashing out at them, they seemed to understand. Melanie was lucky to have it. She would never forget that.

CHAPTER 21

Just a few days later, The Charlie's Dream Foundation had already set up another meeting with them. Since it was a late afternoon appointment, Melanie had talked her mom into letting her spend most of her day with Kona. It was a big day for more than one reason. Today, Kona was going to be taken from the tank with the group of dolphins. She was going to be put in a tank with another lone dolphin, Zoe.

"So, what will happen?" Melanie asked Julia.

"First, we will bring Kona over and do our daily routine checkup. While she's lying still, I will give her a slight sedative. That will make it easier to wrap the hoist around her." Julia pointed to the wrap that would slide around the dolphin. "You aren't going to be near her when it happens."

"Why not?" Melanie crossed her arms over her chest, ready to argue for the right to be by Kona's side.

"Because she did not take to it last time. She was angry with me for a week. She needs one person she can trust."

"Fine. But I'm still watching." Melanie refused to not be there in some way for Kona right now.

"I figured as much. Go on the outside of the enclosure where you aren't right in the mix here." Julia nodded to the sidewalk, where people tended to line up to feed the dolphins.

"Okay," grumbled Melanie.

"Trust me, Mel. It's for the best."

Melanie left the small island and made her way through the maze that led from the back to the front. If any outsider made their way into the training area, they would easily be lost. Melanie was a pro at navigating it by now. When she made it to the other side, she watched as Julia brought Kona over to her. As she went through the checkup, Julia gave Kona a small injection in her dorsal fin. A large rectangular cloth was wrapped around Kona before a crane latched onto the hook. Before she knew it, Kona was hoisted out of the water to be moved to her new tank

Melanie watched with bated breath as she put her hand on the glass of the tank. She called out to Kona. "It's going to be all right, girl. It has to be. At least you'll be a little less stressed back in the other tank." Melanie shook her head and sighed to herself. "It's not the ocean, but it will have to do for now."

Melanie wished there was something else they could do for Kona. It did not seem fair to keep moving her from tank to tank when all the dolphin wanted was to head back to the sea. Melanie had calculated several different ways to get her there, none of which would actually work. It was not like she could steal a semi and set up a portable tank on a jailbreak. How would she even manage that? It was certainly hard to get her to an ocean when they were in the middle of nowhere. That was why dolphins did not belong in the desert. They needed the fresh ocean air, the chaos that came in the swelling waves close to the shore. Kona deserved so much more than she was given.

Melanie wished she could wait until Kona was awake, but their appointment at The Charlie's Dream Foundation was looming right around the corner. Her mother would be coming out of her office at any moment to search for her. Her siblings were going to come along too, even though it was a school day. Her mom thought this was important for them all to be involved in, and while Melanie did not want to go, she was giving in to keep her mother happy if nothing else. Linda Parker spent her time divided between working maddening hours at the aquarium and making sure every facet of her medical life was well under control, from the painstaking way she monitored her medication and side effects, to the way she soothed her when her stomach was rebelling. Melanie knew she was doing so much, so the least she could do was listen to what they had to say.

Melanie heard the familiar click of heels and knew without turning that her mother was already heading her way. Melanie sighed and leaned over the tank one last time. "I'll see you later, girl." Turning to face her mother, she plastered the happiest smile she could conjure and hoped her mother would not see through her cracks. "That time already?"

"Yes. Your grandma has already picked up your sisters. We just need to swing home and pick everyone up."

"Okay." Melanie swung her backpack around her shoulders.

"Mel...."

"Yes?" She turned to look at her mom.

"I'm really proud of you. I know this is not your ideal situation."

"As long as we understand, this is a celebration of life and not an expiration stamp." Melanie sighed when she saw the hurt in her mother's eyes. "I'm fine. Everything is good. I'm just more worried about Kona than anything else."

"She'll adjust, Mel."

"And what if she doesn't?" Melanie turned back to look at the tank. "She deserves better than this."

"I'm sure we'll figure something out. We need to get moving."

"Let's go then." Melanie did not feel like wasting any time. Better to just get this over with.

The trip home was quiet. Melanie did not feel like talking anymore. When the others piled into the van, she made it a point to shove in earbuds to crank up enough music to block them all out. At this point, her sisters were too excited to leave it alone, but Melanie stared out the window and ignored their excitement.

Maybe she should be excited, but she did not want to be stealing a dream from a dying kid. She was far from it herself, at least that was the mantra she held tight too. There were too many things she needed to do in this lifetime, things that could maybe change the world if she were given a chance. All she wanted to do was get back to a normal life so she could keep helping Kona. To say she was obsessed was probably putting it lightly. Melanie could not help the way she felt, though. There was an entire world unprepared to help a defenseless creature. It happened the world over with many species of animals. What Melanie knew more than anything was that there would never be any kind of change if someone were not brave enough to raise their voice and speak out against injustice. She was just trying to figure out the best way to do it.

Her thoughts turned inside her like a ballerina turning out from a pirouette, never staying in one place for too long, in case her mind traveled back to the reason they were being asked to The Charlie's Dream Foundation. Most days, her life was inundated with that reality as she adjusted from one med or another. Today, if she were honest with herself, she felt bloated and swollen, all side effects from her current round of treatment. She wanted to deflate her skin to let the air out so she could feel like herself again. She did not want to feel like a puffy marshmallow at all.

When they finally made it to their destination, Melanie followed her mother quietly. Her sister Amber swung her arm over her shoulders and pulled her tight against her. "It's okay, Mel."

"I know," Melanie mumbled. She did know everything was fine, but her thoughts were distracted by so many things.

As they stood in front of an elevator, Melanie almost rolled her eyes at her younger sister's need to push the button before anyone else could. "Have at it, kid."

"Thanks!" Kimmie pushed the button so hard, Melanie half expected her to start complaining about breaking it. Thankfully, she only shook her finger and laughed it off.

Melanie sighed to herself. That kid would be the first one to get a cast on everything in their house. She had already broken both arms — not at the same time, thankfully, because having one arm down for her had been more than a challenge for the rest of them. Melanie had had a few uncharitable thoughts about that, for when her sister was injured, at least the focus was no longer on her cancer. That had been a relief, even though she would never wish for her sister to be hurt. No one in their right mind would ever wish for that to happen.

She followed the others onto the elevator and tried not to feel like she was marching to her doom. Maybe other kids did not feel this way when they were given this opportunity. Melanie was just trying to focus on the good in her life, not the colossal C-sign that seemed to wave over her head everywhere she went. Yes, she saw people looking at her with curiosity. Some looked away the moment she made eye contact. Others were more subtle about it, glancing for a few seconds then looking somewhere else before they turned back to look at her again. She always wanted to rail at them that yes, she had cancer. No, she was not dying.

Yes, she had very little hair, but no, it did not bother her. She wore her baldness like a medal, knowing that it would always draw attention to her. Melanie did not care, though. She knew that bald was beautiful, even if it was unusual for everyone else.

As they walked toward the main office, she let her thoughts wavered slightly as she took in the walls around her. There were so many photos of other children that Melanie soon lost count. All those smiles immortalized on film. How many of them were still here after all these years? It was a thought she could not ignore. The same thought that almost everyone who walked these halls must think as they made their way to the front desk.

There was a small reception area at the front of the room, with a colorful plaque with The Charlie's Dream Foundation embossed on the front. An older woman was sitting behind it. She had short grey hair and was wearing a pair of glasses with a beaded eyeglass holder. Melanie was reminded of one of the ladies that worked at the diner with Amber. When she looked at her sister, she could see by her slow smirk that she thought the same thing.

Her mother checked in with the secretary and was directed to the chairs in the small alcove to the left. They each sat down, even though Melanie was not really interested in doing so, for the moment she did, her knee started to shake slightly. No one else seemed to notice, though, which was something she was thankful for. A TV hung from the ceiling, and Kimmie was already watching the cartoon that was blasting on it. Her grandma was sitting next to her mom, rubbing her arms as the two waited quietly. Amber's face was glued to her phone as usual.

When Melanie could no longer handle sitting, she paced back and forth in the tiny office. She was not quite sure what to expect. When Julia had put her name in for a dream, Melanie had wanted to turn it all away from her. That would have been a slap in the face to the people who were making this possible. So she had started to think long and hard about what it was she wanted, but so far she had everything anyone could ever want from life. Even though her body was riddled with disease, Melanie was doing things that most people could only dream about. She had far more opportunities than other kids in her position. Life was not measured in possessions for Melanie. It was the time she spent with her family, Chase, and at the aquarium that meant the most to her.

"I still think this is not fair." Kimmie stomped her feet and crossed her arms. "How come Melanie gets something special?"

Linda looked down at her nine-year-old daughter with the tired smile of a mother working hard to provide everything for her kids. Her husband had died shortly after Kimmie had been born, leaving her to take care of their kids and handle everything life threw at them. "Kimmie, that's enough."

"Well, if I were sick—"

"Kimberly Louise!" Linda's voice almost shook the office.

"Mom, it's okay." Melanie walked over to Kimmie and put a hand on her shoulder. "I don't know why I get anything special, either. You're far more talented than me, Bug."

Kimmie's lips wobbled slightly, and tears squeezed out of her eyes. "I didn't mean...."

Melanie wrapped her little sister in a hug and sighed. "It's hard on all of us, Bug. I understand that you get shuffled under the rug. Besides, if wishing people were sick made them sick, then the opposite would be true, too, right?"

Amber walked over to them and sat down next to them. "I thought I was supposed to be the wise one."

"Meh. Just 'cause you're seventeen doesn't mean anything.

I think you've lost a few brain cells to all that hair dye," teased Melanie.

"Highlights are hard to keep up. Maybe I should just shave it off." Amber winked at her sister.

"I hear it's trending right now." Melanie grinned.

"Girls, there will be no head shaving." Linda let out a sigh. "I think they're running late. What time was the appointment again?"

"Four-thirty, Mom. It's only been five minutes."

Melanie crossed her feet and uncrossed them. She tried not to let her nerves show, but Melanie was not entirely sure she wanted to be in this place. This made her feel like something was final. Her life was not over. Things were hopeful—at least she felt like they were.

At that precise moment, the door opened. A tall African-American woman walked through the arches and turned to look at them. Turning to Melanie, she smiled. "You must be Melanie."

"Yep. That's me." Melanie gave her a half-smile. Her nerves made her stomach do flip flops.

"I'm Regina Lewis. Come with me." She gestured for Melanie and her family to follow her.

Regina ushered them down a hallway that was covered with picture frames of smiling children. From riding horses, sitting in race cars, taking rides in hot air balloons, all the way to magical trips to Disney World, the children were all fulfilling dreams that they had. Each one seemed to have a medical condition of one kind or the other. A few seemed to have cancer just like Melanie, as they too showed the tell-tale signs of hair loss and what Melanie called chemo skin.

"These are most of our past recipients." Regina stopped briefly for them to look through some of the photos.

"Ooooh, Melanie, I want to go here!" Kimmie was pointing to Disney World.

"Or here." Amber was looking at a white sandy beach that stretched out to meet the bright blue ocean waters.

Melanie rolled her eyes at her sisters. Yes, they probably did want to do something that reminded them of a vacation, but what Melanie had in mind was something even more meaningful if it were even possible.

Regina opened her office door and waited for them to come inside. "Please have a seat."

"Thank you," Linda answered her.

"As you see, dreams come in every shape and size. William Cooper created the Charlie's Dream Foundation. He lost his son to childhood leukemia in 1988. William Cooper had spent his life amassing enough money to make all his family's dreams come true, but all the money in the world could not keep the billionaire's son healthy. His son's dying wish was for his father to make other children's dreams come true. Mr. Cooper created the foundation to do just that. It's grown over the years."

"Wow, that's fascinating, isn't it, girls?" Linda encouraged her children to answer.

"Yes!" Amber and Kimmie answered together.

"Sure." Melanie's voice was not cheerful. "If dying makes one more deserving. But what if I'm not dying?"

"Charlie's Dream is for any child fighting through their disease. It is not a death sentence." Regina smiled knowingly at Melanie. "You are not the first doubter I've met, Melanie. Most children feel the same way. That's the fighting spirit. Many of the children you passed in the hall are alive and well today."

"Right. So, I've been chosen to make one of my dreams come true?" Melanie chewed on the inside of her cheek and wondered what would happen if she just blurted it out.

"Yes. Do you have an idea of somewhere you want to go or something you want to do? A family vacation?" Regina waited for Melanie to answer.

Melanie waited a few seconds before answering. "I want to set Kona free."

"I'm sorry?" Regina seemed confused. "Who is Kona?"

"A dolphin," Amber answered for her.

"You could have anything, we could go anywhere, and you want to waste it on a dolphin?" Kimmie looked incredulous.

"Melanie, I'm not sure that's how it works." Linda tried to redirect her daughter.

"Why not? She said a dream. That's what I dream about day and night. If you paid attention to her, you'd know she's miserable. Captivity is killing her slowly." Melanie crossed her arms over her chest.

Regina shuffled the papers on her desk. "Well, that is quite the dream. I can honestly say no one has asked for that before, but after hearing what Jenna had to say, I'm not surprised. She was very taken with you."

"Does that mean you won't fund it?" Melanie was not ready to give up.

"You sure are a strong young lady. I tell you what—I'll put your request in to the higher-ups. Maybe we'll get some media attention involved. I'm not making any promises, though. If this falls through, do you have a second choice?"

Melanie looked over at her sisters and felt guilty. This illness had affected their lives too. Was she being selfish asking for something that did not give them a little hope for their future? "Guys?"

Kimmie and Amber both looked at each other and nodded

their heads. Kimmie turned to Melanie and put her fist up. "Ocean or bust!"

Melanie gave her a fist bump. "All right!"

"We got this, Mel!" Amber bumped fists with her too.

Their mom teared up as she looked at her children with pride. "That's my girls."

Regina was visibly impressed. A slow trickle of tears fell down her face, and she smiled awkwardly as she dashed them away. "I tell you what. I'm not going to sleep until we make this dream come true."

"Do you need us to do anything?" Melanie asked her.

"How are you with reporters? I have a feeling you girls just might be what we need to boost this to the top." The wheels were turning in Regina's eyes.

"The girls have been performing since they were teeny tiny. Ballet, gymnastics. I think they can handle it," Linda answered her.

"How about you?" Melanie crossed her arms and looked at Regina.

"Oh, it's on." Regina put her fist out and waited for Melanie to bump it.

Melanie giggled and bumped her fist against it. "Thank you."

Regina nodded at her. "Of course. Now, if you don't mind, I think I have maybe a million phone calls to make if I am going to make this dream come true."

Melanie and her family left the room as quietly as they had entered. She turned to look at her mother and was surprised to see her crying. "What's wrong?"

"I'm so proud of you, honey." Linda opened her arms, and Melanie walked into them.

"Thanks, I guess." Melanie closed her eyes and let herself be hugged. It was a rare occurrence lately since her medicine made her so moody.

"We'll make it happen, Mel. No matter what." Linda looked determined.

Melanie suddenly had a horrible thought. If things did not go well, her mother could lose her job at the aquarium. "Mom... what if you lose your job?"

"There are other jobs, Melanie. There's only one you." Linda straightened the cap on Melanie's head.

"And there's only one Kona," added Kimmie, who grabbed Melanie's hand and started to swing it.

"I love you guys!"

Melanie's heart felt light for the first time in weeks. Their willingness to help her did more than they knew. Melanie needed them to know she was going to be okay. The fact that they were willing to fight alongside her made it clear that they did not think she was at death's door. They were a family of fighters.

CHAPTER 22

Time moved slowly some days, but it still continued along. It was now February, eight months from when she'd started her treatment schedule. The days were a little easier to bear now that she was almost finished with her treatment. Since she was closer to the end, she could spend more time at the aquarium, as long as she got all her schoolwork done. While she might not be in school, the way her sisters were, the work she did at home was just as detailed and annoying. Melanie would much rather spend all her time with Kona, but there was no way her mom would ever allow that.

Today, Melanie had spent the early afternoon holed up in her mom's office, finishing the rest of her math unit before she could move on to spend some time with Kona. Mr. Marcus had been extremely lenient on her mother, dragging her to the office. That was probably because Melanie was helping with Kona so much. He may look like a bulldog at times, but the man was all bark and no bite. He was a big softy where Melanie was concerned too. Melanie was sure that would change when things started to kick into gear. They had been trying to find a way around making a huge headline first. Regina had a few cards up her sleeve that she was going to try first. Melanie only hoped they worked.

"I'm done now, Mom," Melanie called over to her mother, who was up to her neck with some accounting paperwork.

"Did you get your scores yet?" Linda turned to Melanie with an expectant look on her face.

"Yes," grumbled Melanie. While she had not done terribly, her mother expected her to get more than a passing grade. She had high expectations for her and her sisters, which Melanie would probably be thankful for later in life. Right now was not one of those times. As a teenager who would rather be doing anything else but schoolwork, Melanie spent nearly all her time grinding her teeth together. At some point, she was going to have fangs as her teeth wore down against each other.

"And?"

Melanie could almost hear her mother's foot tapping on the floor. "I got an 84."

"I see…well, that is an improvement, but if you want to be on track for next year, you're going to have to do a little higher."

"Higher? Are you kidding me? You know how much I hate math." Melanie closed her eyes and blew a hot breath. She would rather have a root canal then figure out algebraic equations or solve some kind of geometric proof.

"Mel…you can't fall behind. That was the rule when we decided to homeschool this year, right?" Her mother reminded her oh so casually.

For some reason, Melanie was more annoyed than usual. Even so, she decided that giving in to her mother's demands right now was probably the best course of action. "If I promise to study twice as hard, can I please go take a break now?"

"Yes. I think a break is a good idea." Her mom smiled at her and nodded to the door. "Better go before I change my mind."

"You don't have to tell me twice."

Besides, Melanie was pretty sure that Chase would be here by now. He took the city bus here after school on the days when he worked after school. That he hoped to change as soon as he was able to save more up for a car, at this rate, he would be twenty-one before he had enough for the car of his dreams.

After she made her way to the locker room, she quickly changed into spare clothes. She looked herself over in the mirror before she headed out. Today, she had chosen not to wear her cap. While her head had been clean-shaven for a while, now a small patch of hair was starting to come back in, as it was the color in her skin. She did not look as pasty as she had over the past few months. Melanie chalked this up to being almost done with her chemo. While she had high hopes that this would be it for her, she would not know for sure until she had more bloodwork and scans. Those were still a few months out, though.

When she made her way out of the locker room, she almost ran into Chase. "Hey."

"Hey." He leaned over and kissed her. "You look great."

"Thanks." Melanie gestured to his outfit and all the decorations that were hanging outside the locker room. "So, what's with all the red?"

"What, this? February is Heart Health Awareness month, didn't you know?"

"I guess that kinda goes with Valentine's Day. What are we doing today?" Even though she was in a relationship, she had not given Valentine's Day much thought; she had been so consumed with Kona and their campaign that was about to start. Maybe that made her a failure as a girlfriend since she had not even thought of what gift she would get him. Melanie just didn't pay a lot of attention to holidays much anymore. There were just days, weeks, months, and all of them seemed to bleed into each other even with her time here at the aquarium and the moments she spent with him outside the aquarium.

"Daily routines. I just did Kona's. She'd probably love you forever if you played with her," Julia answered her. "You look great, by the way."

"I feel great." Melanie favored the trainer with a smile that she actually felt for a change. She was having a good day, outside the grueling homework. And the fact that Chase was now here too already brightened the dull start to her day.

"Good." Chase nodded to the changing room. "Gear up. Let's get some time in with her."

"Definitely." She lived for these days when she could work beside him. A small dream was starting to form inside her, of a time when they might be able to spend their life together doing this very thing. Melanie knew better than to get attached to that idea. Nothing was permanent. That was something she had learned time and time again. Even so, she gave in to the daydream like most normal girls her age would. Did that mean she was doodling his last name next to hers in her notebook? No, she wasn't that foolish. It wasn't something she said out loud or put out there for anyone else to see. It was a secret longing she held inside her so that she would be the only one who was disappointed if it didn't come true. Her family loved Chase. She knew they hoped he would be in her life forever, but no one bothered to voice it.

Melanie sighed as she tried to keep those thoughts deep inside. When she finally was ready, she left the room and found Chase sitting on the bench by himself in the locker room. He had a small jewelry box in his hand and seemed to be fidgeting.

"Chase?"

"Mel...." He cleared his throat, and she had the feeling that he was about to do something serious, which made her want to head for the hills. But she stayed frozen in place.

"Chase?"

"I know it's not quite Valentine's Day, but I got this for you." He was clumsy when he opened the box. Inside was a small sterling silver dolphin on a chain.

"It's beautiful." Melanie breathed a sigh of relief. Thank goodness it had not been what she first thought it was. Any time a girl saw a jewelry box, it represented something greater, like a ring. She had just turned seventeen. There was no way she was anywhere close to thinking of marriage. Melanie should have known he wasn't either. Besides, he might not have the same dreams she did. There was always a chance that Chase would outgrow her, especially considering he was older than her.

"It's my promise to you." He stood up and stepped closer to her.

"Promise?" Melanie's eyebrows rose curiously.

"That I won't stop until we set her free," Chase promised her.

"Me either. And thank you. Can you help me put it on?"

Chase pulled the necklace out of the box and fiddled with the clasp. He walked behind her and placed the chain around her neck. When his arms wrapped around her stomach, she sank against him. She closed her eyes as he whispered, "I love you."

"I love you more," she answered.

"I love you to infinity." It was what Chase said to her every day. It was his way of telling her that no matter what happened to her, he would always love her. Every time he said it, her heart was full.

She sighed and let herself breathe a moment before she moved away from him. Melanie kept the tears at bay, even though inside she was crying like a little baby. Was it wrong to wish for a lifetime of moments just like this? She quickly got herself under control and turned to smile at him. "It's beautiful."

"So are you."

"Stop it!" She pushed on his arm.

"What?" He grinned at her.

"You don't want to make me cry, do you?" She held her chin up challengingly.

"Never."

"Good. Then let's get to work, shall we?"

He put his hand to his head and saluted her. "Yes, ma'am."

"Good boy," Melanie teased him. She moved to the exit and was happy that he followed her in silence. Right now, she wasn't sure she had any words to give him. What else could she say?

Melanie walked over the platform and called Kona forward. "Come here, girl."

Melanie splashed the water at Kona when she popped up to the surface. The dolphin talked back to her before she splashed back at Melanie. The limited joy that Kona displayed almost made up for the guilt she always felt inside. She wanted nothing more than to set Kona free, but her plans were taking much longer than she'd expected.

"How're the plans going?" Julia asked her.

Melanie's smile faded from her face. She peered down at the water and tried to find the right answer. Sure, they were planning a protest. There were a few interviews scheduled, but first, Regina was going to work a different angle, because those other options were going to be even more challenging. "Are you sure you want to know? What if you lose your job?"

"Then, I would say it was well worth it if Kona returns home." The honesty in Julia's voice was heartwarming.

Melanie felt tears brim in her eyes. "Yeah...."

"We'll be fine, right, Mom?" Chase interjected. He had been her ears for quite some time, the only other sounding board outside of her family. He had some pretty good ideas about how to campaign for support. Melanie was happy he was working behind the scenes. She did not want him to lose his job either.

"We will. If I lose my job, I'll find another." She nodded to Melanie. "Sometimes, it takes a small voice to remind you to have the courage to fight the good fight."

"By the time I'm done, they won't know what hit them." Melanie held her head up with an air of pride. She was ready to rage against the world if that would help set Kona free.

"That's the spirit," Chase cheered her on.

"You know you might lose your job too?"

Chase shrugged his shoulders. "It's not like there aren't a hundred other jobs out there. I could even flip burgers with Amber."

Melanie snorted. "You'd change one smell for another. Amber smells like a walking grease pot when she comes home."

"Great, then my cats will stop chasing me around the house." Chase smiled at her, and she was captivated by it.

Kona watched the exchange and scooted closer to the pair of them. The dolphin slid onto the island and put her head in Melanie's lap in an attempt to cheer her up. Melanie put her hand on Kona's snout, feeling at one with the dolphin, the way she usually did. The two were like soul sisters, even if their biology disagreed. Melanie was pretty sure Kona would protect her if given a chance, just as she would protect Kona with her last breath if she had to.

"Oh, Kona! You sweet girl. One day you'll have everything you deserve." No matter what it took, Melanie would never stop fighting. She might be young, but her voice was loud, and if she used it loud enough, people would start to listen. It would be the youth that would change the world. If they sat around and waited for the adults to do it, it would never get done. Not that adults did not care about wildlife; they were just so caught up in the everyday survival they did not stop to think outside of their small circles. The world was more than just the people they interacted with on a day to day basis.

Humans were not the only living creature that deserved the chance to survive. Someday, she would make sure to drive that point home. For now, she would focus on this one animal, this one cause, before she spearheaded the whole world's problems. She was sure to learn a lot about human nature along the way. Melanie would soak it all up and learn as much as she could. Now that the worst of the chemo was behind her, she was even more determined to push forward.

CHAPTER 23

On the other side of the country, Dr. Daniel Smith, a marine biologist, was sitting at his desk reading through some paperwork. He was working on a study near the bay, determining the effects of the overpopulated areas on the local marine life. His goal was to gather enough material to limit the number of boats allowed on the water at one point in time, a feat that was much harder to do than one might expect. Humans were too used to taking what they wanted from the world. Trying to bring it back was going to be nearly impossible, but Daniel was not afraid of the challenge.

His eyes popped up when his desk phone rang. He let it ring three times before he picked it up. "Dr. Daniel Smith...."

"Daniel, it's been a long time," Regina Lewis greeted him.

Daniel sat back in his chair and smiled. "Regina, it's good to hear your voice. Are you still granting children their dreams?"

"You know it!" Regina answered.

"Don't tell me you have a child whose dream is to tour our research lab." Daniel had not heard from her in some time. The last time was when he'd helped a child get closer to a humpback whale in the wild. Any tour could have worked, but this child wanted to see it through scientific eyes. That child was now working in the field, a young scientist with true grit. Alexander

Washburn had quite a bright future, one that Daniel had been proud to be a part of.

"Not quite. We have a special request that's right up your alley."

"What's that?" He was filled with curiosity.

"We have a teenager who has spent her time getting to know a dolphin at The Oasis Aquarium."

"The one in the middle of the desert?" Daniel shook his head. He had several thoughts on the matter, none of which were friendly. The people who ran that aquarium must have lost their minds if they thought they were doing any good for those animals. None of them belonged in the hot desert heat.

"The same one. They have a dolphin there named Kona, who was taken from the wild and forced into captivity. The girl's a natural with the dolphin, helping her to adjust to her life, but even Melanie knows that dolphin does not belong there. Her only dream is to set the dolphin free."

"And that's where I come in?" Daniel had a fair amount of clout. He had championed many causes. He had been itching for a fight with the owner of that aquarium anyway. Now was as good a time as any, he supposed.

"We thought if you approached them with a way out, we would not have to rock the waves too much."

"So, you have a backup plan?" Daniel knew it was a crapshoot, but he was willing to fly to California if it meant taking the wind out of some blowhard's sails.

"Mass media campaign with Melanie and her sisters. The three of them are already rallying online. I was hoping this route might work first."

"Well, let me give it a try. I'll get back to you soon."

"Perfect. Thank you, Daniel."

"Any time, Regina."

Daniel ended the conversation and pulled out a folder from his desk. It contained all the information he had already gathered on The Oasis Aquarium. He had been keeping his eye on it since it had gone under control of some real-estate tycoon who had no business running any kind of animal park, much less a marine aquarium in the middle of the Arizona heat.

He opened his email and started to type a letter that he knew would get his foot in the door with the corporate office. Daniel was well-respected in his field. All he had to do was string the right words together to get a meeting with the owner, Mr. Tyson Fillimore. Let him think that Daniel was bringing some kind of prestige to his aquarium. That ought to do the trick.

Days passed before Daniel received a reply. A week after that, he found himself traveling to California, where Mr. Fillimore's corporation was located. Daniel found it ironic that a man who lived near the ocean would not have opened an aquarium there. Then again, it was all about money. The lack of other aquariums in the desert made it a gold mine for the man. It was about supply and demand to him, something that drew people in from all over Arizona and the bordering states. It was easier to get there than it was to get to one of the coastal aquariums.

As Daniel walked through the front doors, he found himself in an over-decorated room with oversized plush furniture. He almost rolled his eyes at the ostentatious artwork on the wall. Yes, the man had money. Did he have to advertise it all over the place?

Daniel stepped up to the desk, where a secretary was filing her nails absently. "Excuse me," he interrupted her.

She set her nail file down slowly and gave him a once over with her eyes. "Can I help you?"

"Dr. Daniel Smith, from the Marine Research Lab. I have an appointment."

"One moment." The secretary picked up her phone and called her boss. "Mr. Fillimore, you have Dr. Daniel Smith here from the Marine Research Lab. He's in the lobby. Yes, sir. I know you are very busy, but he says he has an appointment. Right, yes, of course. I will send him right in."

Daniel stood there and waited for her to address him again. When she only rose and gestured for him to follow her, he tried not to take it personally. It was clear that she was irritated that she actually had to get up from her desk instead of working on her overpriced manicure. He really didn't understand this new generation and their work ethics. He followed her down the hall to Mr. Fillimore's office, where he found a man in his early forties sitting behind a cherry desk that looked as if it had never been used. What exactly did this man do all day? Count his money in his vaults like some kind of miser?

"Mr. Fillimore, this is Dr. Daniel Smith," the secretary introduced them.

"Thank you, Elizabeth. That will be all."

Daniel walked closer to the desk and extended his hand to Tyson Fillimore, who shook it lazily from his desk. So, it was going to be that kind of meeting. Daniel knew he would have to hit this one hard. "Thank you for seeing me on short notice."

"Please be seated." Tyson gestured to the chair at the front of the desk. When Daniel sat down, Tyson continued. "What can I do for you, Dr. Smith?"

Daniel Smith sat back in the chair and splayed his hands out in front of him. "You can start by letting the dolphin go."

Tyson frowned in slight confusion. "Pardon me? What dolphin?"

Daniel took a slow breath, knowing full well that Tyson knew which one he was talking about. How could he not know? He had requisitioned it, after all. "The wild one you have in captivity in your Phoenix aquarium."

"What right do you have to tell me what animals I can and can't have? Get out of my office and stop wasting my time." Tyson dismissed him as if he were an ant climbing on his arm. He must have expected to flick him away easily without any rebuttal.

"Now hold on here, Mr. Fillimore. This isn't right on so many levels. The water in Phoenix isn't compatible with their skin. She's prone to bacterial infections, not to mention the poor animal is stressed out."

"What I do or don't do with my corporation is none of your concern, Dr. Smith. You'll leave now, or I'll have you escorted out of here."

Daniel stood up, quite prepared to be tossed out at any moment. It would not be the first time it had happened. "This isn't over."

"Leave now, Dr. Smith, or I will be forced to call security."

"I'll go, but you should know we're just getting started here."

Daniel Smith turned and walked out the door. As he made his way down the hallway, he pulled out his cell phone and called Regina Lewis at The Charlie's Dream Foundation.

"This is Regina," she answered.

"Hi, Regina. It's Daniel."

"Hello, Daniel. Good to hear from you. Any news?"

"I just left his office. He wouldn't budge. He wouldn't even listen to what I had to say. Barely let me get two words in."

Regina sighed on the other end of the phone. "I was afraid of that."

"We had to try."

"Thanks, Daniel. Can we count on your support with the reporters and the picket lines?"

"You bet. It's time Mr. Fillimore gets a lesson in humanity." Daniel was already making plans in the back of his head. He would not stop until Kona was back where she belonged. He would make sure that the teenage girl stayed at the forefront of the battle, for her story would pick up more coverage than a middle-aged scientist fighting for the dolphin's release. Her courage and fierce loyalty should be at the forefront.

"I'll call you back when it's all been arranged."

"Looking forward to it. Keep me posted."

As Daniel hung up, the wheels were turning in his mind. There was still a long road ahead of him, but he would make sure that this dolphin returned to the ocean if it was the last thing he ever did. His second goal would be to find a way to shut down that aquarium for good. They had been on his radar for quite some time. One thing at a time, though; one thing at a time.

CHAPTER 24

Melanie was surprised at how fast time was flying by now that she had a new purpose. Even though she had to go through a few extra rounds of treatment, she had not let that take the wind out of her sails. Instead, she kept her eye on the prize ahead. With the support of local media and an ever-growing network of social media, the girls were all starting to pick up speed on their campaign to free Kona.

Melanie blogged every day, telling her followers about what it meant to be a wild animal contained in a small living space when it should be living free in its natural habitat. With each post, she was picking up even more traction. She spent time researching scientific articles she found on the Internet, as well as the massive database from the local library. Melanie was learning as much as she could about animals in all shapes and forms, ones that had been poached from their natural habitat and kept as living trophies all across the world. The more she learned, the more she realized that even if they were able to help Kona, there would still be many more animals to champion.

The networking she was doing soon became almost too much for her to handle. She was thankful that Regina Lewis from The Charlie's Dream Foundation was helping her make connections outside of the home base they had set up in their living room. A few college students volunteered to make phone calls to local and state officials to rally the support for their mission. #FREEKONA was starting to trend as their campaign picked up speed. So far, they had flown under the radar where Mr. Fillimore was concerned. The wealthy tycoon was more focused on his other endeavors, which was annoying and a relief at the same time. While Melanie wanted nothing more than to set Kona free, she still did not want her mother to lose her job, even though her mom was more than ready to find another one.

Melanie looked around the living room with pride. Their home base was filled with all of their hard work. Hundreds of protest signs already lined the back wall, each one painstakingly crafted with love. Everyone had pitched in, from the youngest Parker to the oldest, all the way to the handful of friends who had come out to support them. Even Chase had spent endless hours helping on the nights when he was not needed at the aquarium. The more they worked together, the more helplessly in love she felt. The future was no longer a dark shadow in the distance. The light of hope was overpowering it, making Melanie feel as if she would be able to leave her mark on the infinite landscape around her.

The huge whiteboard next to the television was filled with a list of local news stations and the interview schedules for each one. Some would be done by the college students, some by Melanie and her sisters. It was a community effort. All centered on her dream to free Kona from captivity. While Melanie did not like using her cancer as a hot topic, the fact that she had it seemed to spark even more interest in the cause. At this point, Melanie did not care what they said about her or her illness if it meant Kona had a chance at a happier life. That would be more than worth it.

"Ouch!" Kimmie gasped as she pulled her finger to her mouth.

"Paper cut?" Amber asked her.

"Yes…the fifth one this week! How many more fliers do we need to pass out? A katrillion?" Kimmie grumbled.

"As many as it takes." Melanie sat down next to her and started to make a pile of her own. "It was generous of the Millers to donate the paper and printing."

"Yeah…I wish they'd slow down on the generosity," Kimmie sighed. "At least they're pretty."

"You did a great job on the artwork," Melanie complimented her. All three girls had designed the fliers, but Kimmie had been the one to draw the dolphin at the center of them. The kid was only nine, but she was quite the artist. That, and it had made her feel like she was actually a part of the fight—nothing like growing a protester from the ground up.

Melanie looked over at the poster on the wall. They had made that when they first started the crowdfunding. With the research she had done and the conversations she had with other outreach programs, Melanie had tried to come up with a number high enough to give Mr. Fillimore the proper incentive to free the dolphin. Melanie did not think he would even bother to listen if they did not have enough money to make an impact, but it was still worth a try. Unfortunately, they were only a quarter of the way to their goal. It was slow-moving at this point, but at least there was some kind of movement. They would not stop until they reached the top.

Near the front door was the massive pile of T-shirts they had been making at the local screen printing shop. They had gotten quite a discount on the shirts, and the printing itself was free. All they had to do was get enough volunteers to go in and help when they needed new shirts pressed. Each one was a different color of the rainbow, with a white image of a dolphin and the words #FREEKONA printed in big letters. Things were all starting to come together now. Melanie knew they would get plenty of traction soon.

"Can you believe how many people keep calling us?" Kimmie was thumbing through the list of messages that the girls had been compiling from the cell phone they had purchased for their cause. At just under twenty dollars a month, they were able to stay anonymous from the outside world and still manage to have a place for those that wanted to volunteer to leave a message. They had also set up an email account. The girls were all learning how to market and run this campaign together. They were getting pretty good at it too.

"Yeah. If only they'd send money with their outrage," grumbled Amber.

"It all takes time. At least the shirts are selling." Melanie picked up an orange shirt and held it up. "These colors are amazing."

Amber nodded to the poster. "We're only a quarter of the way to our goal, though."

"And that's if that mean old Mr. Fillimore even agrees to let her go." Kimmie crossed her arms over her chest and pouted.

Melanie understood how she felt. It did seem hopeless, but Melanie refused to give up. "With the protest, we'll get enough coverage to make the world take notice."

"How are you always so positive?" Amber asked her.

"What choice do I have? Ocean or bust, remember?" Melanie held up a sign that has an ocean wave and the words Ocean or Bust painted on it.

Amber smiled brightly. "You got that right."

Melanie opened her laptop and dove into her work. Her sisters were busy finishing up their own tasks too, so they did not need her undivided attention. There was still so much to plan, like the protest that would be coming up before they knew it. Melanie only hoped that a lot of people showed up to rock the boat enough for Mr. Fillimore to take notice. Even if he did not, she would not stop until she found a way to free the one thing that had kept her going for so long.

Kona was so much more than a dolphin to her. She was like her soul sister, even though they were two different species. Melanie was reasonably sure that Kona understood her better than any other thing on this planet. The two had grown even closer over the past few months. She spent as much time at the aquarium as she could. Even though Melanie would miss her, she knew that freeing her was the only thing that made sense. It was everything they had been working for.

Part of her wondered what they would do at the aquarium without her. Melanie had spent as much time there with Chase as she could. Kona had become the one thing they had in common. Sometimes Melanie wondered what would be left when they helped Kona move on to the ocean. More than likely, Melanie would lose the ability to work with Chase at the aquarium. The time there with him had been almost magical. It was rare to have such a large thing in common. Melanie couldn't imagine not being able to spend her days there. What would she do with her time?

Those were worries that she couldn't afford to hold onto. It would all work out in the end—it had to. But doubts were something a cancer kid held onto deep inside. They never wanted to admit it to the outside world, because they were so busy pretending to be strong. Melanie didn't always feel strong. On the days when she felt low, Melanie held on to the one thing that kept her moving forward. Making that one change for another living being that would save its life was worth the focus. In doing so, some of her other fears fell to the wayside. Keeping them there was the challenge.

***

While the girls were at home, Linda Parker was still working at the aquarium. She had been called into the manager's office for a late meeting. Linda wondered what it could be about, but tried not to overthink it. When she saw the manager sitting behind his desk, she knew that this was not a social visit. "Raymond."

"Linda. Good. I'm glad you could make the time." He gestured to the chair in front of his desk. "Sit."

Linda did so, but very slowly. By the way his hands were clasped in front of him; she knew this was not going to be one of her favorite meetings. He looked as if he were trying to choose his words before he spoke. She crossed her hands in her lap and waited for the outcome. Thankfully, she did not have to wait long.

"Look, Linda, I'm not a cold-hearted man. I believe in what your daughter is trying to do."

"Do you, Raymond? I keep asking myself if there was something more we could have done to prevent this." Linda had not known about Kona until she was already purchased and on her way to the aquarium. As the assistant manager, she had very little voice where animal acquisitions were concerned, but she still should have said something at the very least.

"You know Mr. Fillimore only cares about our bottom line." He waved her words away without really letting them sink in.

"He's certainly not an animal person." Linda had always

258

thought she was an animal person, but she was nothing compared to her daughter. Melanie had taught her a lot about true caring and understanding. Her daughter had more compassion for animals in one finger than most people had in their entire lifetime. Melanie made her want to be a better person all around.

Raymond sighed loudly. "Agreed, but he pays the bills. And while I hate to admit it, I need this job."

"I understand."

"Do you, Linda? If your daughter goes through with this protest, you could very well lose your job. I have no control over that."

"It's just a job." Linda brushed his words off. She understood what he was trying to say. The two of them had been a team that had run like a well-oiled machine for so long. He did not want to lose her any more than she truly wanted to lose this job, but her daughter mattered more than anything else to her in the world. Seeing Melanie so alive and passionate about something throughout all her health struggles made her want to see this thing through, no matter the consequences.

"You have children to take care of."

"That's what I'm doing, Raymond. This dream, this goal, it's the one thing that has kept my daughter healthy enough to survive. That dolphin, she's a miracle worker." Tears brimmed in her eyes, even though she was trying to be strong.

Raymond took a slow deep breath as her words sunk in. "Good luck, Linda. Off the record, I hope it works."

"If that's all, I have a job to do here. While I still have one."

Linda rose from her chair with her head held high. She walked with a slow determination from the room. No matter what it took, Linda was prepared to help Melanie's dream come true. Heaven help the person who tried to get in their way.

CHAPTER 25

The morning of the protest finally arrived. So much work had gone into it that Melanie was almost exhausted, but it had been worth every single second. As she headed downstairs to get packed up, she saw her sisters already watching the news.

Kimmie almost raced over to her as she pointed to the television with excitement. "Look, Mel! There're so many people there already."

Melanie was shocked to see hundreds of picketers gathered outside The Oasis Aquarium with their signs. There was a long line of them marching as they shouted to let Kona go. News cameras were all around the parking lot, filming the growing crowd. A local newswoman was now reporting.

"Today, we're here documenting one girl's dream to release a dolphin back to the ocean where it belongs. When Melanie Parker, a cancer-fighting teenager, was contacted by The Charlie's Dream Foundation, she made one wish—to set Kona free from Arizona's Oasis Aquarium. If you look around, you can already see hundreds of early protesters."

Melanie smiled from ear to ear. "Will you look at that?"

Amber held up her cellphone. "#FREEKONA is trending in the millions!"

Melanie felt almost weightless for a change. Maybe today would be their lucky day. Even so, she tried to stay grounded in reality. "Good, but we still have a long way to go, don't we? One protest will probably not be enough."

Linda popped her head in the doorway. "You sure you have everything, Mel?"

Melanie tried not to roll her eyes. Her mother had asked her the same thing three times yesterday. "I have my meds, my snacks, my drinks, and my phone in case I need it. What about you? Do you have everything you need for your day?"

"I do, baby. Thank you for asking." Her mother smiled brightly. "Ready to roll?"

"Yep." Melanie felt like she was almost born ready. This was the moment she had been planning for so long now. She looked at her sisters and saw they, too, were ready to move on out.

"Let's go, then."

Linda ushered her daughters out the door and into the car. All of them were surprised to find Grandma Mimi already in the car. Their grandma just grinned from ear to ear. "What? I lived through the '60s. You think I'm afraid of a little protest?"

Melanie held her fist in the air. "Go, Grandma!

The ride to the aquarium seemed to take forever. All the way there, Melanie kept imagining what it would be like to see Kona swimming in the open sea. Would her friend race off, never to return? Melanie knew it was best for her, but she would be sorry to say goodbye. Kona had made it easier this time around. Focusing on the dolphin had taken her thoughts away from the chemo and other things that went along with her leukemia. The hope one small dolphin had fostered in her was something Melanie would forever be thankful for. Kona was one of the reasons why she felt like she could conquer the world.

The closer they got, the faster her heart started to beat. Melanie was nervous, excited, and afraid. There were so many emotions inside her that she felt like she would burst at any point. As the car pulled in past the picketers at The Oasis, Melanie was in pure shock at the number of people. The cameras had barely been able to capture the whole crowd there. Each and every one of them was holding up signs with various save Kona messages. Many even had the trending hashtag #FREEKONA written on them. Several of them are wearing the shirts that they had mailed out weeks earlier. There were even more shirts being sold from the back of the vans. The volunteers had come to pick them up the day before.

Melanie could barely contain her excitement. "Mom!"

Her mom smiled brightly. "Look at that! That's amazing, Mel. Look at what you've done."

"It wasn't just me. Regina did quite a bit. She's called every network in the area, every rescue shelter, any organization that could make even the slightest impact on setting Kona free."

Kimmie cleared her throat dramatically. "And what are we, chopped liver?"

Melanie grinned. "Are you kidding? I couldn't have done any of this without you two."

"If only the foundation had enough to make it happen." Her mom's words were almost a whisper.

"I know. Mr. Fillimore does not like to lose profits." Melanie looked down. Even all these people might not thaw his heart. Mr. Fillimore owned at least five dolphinariums. He profited from human curiosity by keeping aquatic creatures in tanks. He had no right to keep these animals boxed up like that, not that Mr. Fillimore cared. All he cared about was the money he could make. Melanie knew it would still take more than this protest to make a change. She would just have to figure out the next step from here.

Now, Mr. Marcus, who ran the aquarium, was silently on their side. He had allowed a few interviews on their cause before Mr. Fillimore had threatened to fire him. Thankfully, Mr. Fillimore had not figured out her mother's connection to the aquarium. Nor had they mentioned the work that Melanie had done there. They had made sure to keep her last name out of the media for their privacy. If they had not done so, chances were her mother would have already lost her job.

Linda reached over and touched her shoulder, soothingly. "Don't give up, Mel. All these people believe in you. We do too."

Melanie opened her car door and started to get out. "Okay. Don't worry. We'll call if we need you."

"Right. Good luck, kiddo."

"You too, Mom."

"Don't worry. We've got this," Grandma Mimi reassured her.

Linda waved at her family as she drove away. Melanie and her sisters now stood outside with their grandma. Melanie turned around and took it all in. This was almost too good to be true. It was a sea of people, each one taking a stand against the corporation that profited off the captivity of one single dolphin. If only their voices would provide enough force to get his attention. That would be amazing in so many ways.

As she looked closer to the entrance to the parking lot, she saw Chase standing there. He was wearing a red shirt with the #FREEKONA logo printed in huge letters. When he turned and saw her, he waved her over. He had been a blessing in so many ways. He had been so much more than a boyfriend. Chase had been the best friend she had ever had throughout the past year.

His level-headedness kept her focused when she was just a hair away from a meltdown. He seemed to know her better than she knew herself, which was crazy considering they had known each other for less than a year. Melanie was so thankful to have him in her life.

"There's Chase. Let's go." Melanie headed over to him right away with the rest of her family in tow. "How long have you been here?"

Chase smiled sheepishly. "The crack of dawn. I wanted to save us a good spot."

"Well, I'm glad you did."

Melanie turned around and was truly amazed at the turn out all over again.

Chase gestured around them. "Can you believe this?!"

"I know! This is insane!" Melanie felt her nerves start to melt away. The people around her began to recognize her and started to chant her name. She felt a blush rise in her cheeks. "Oh, dear!"

"Hey, take it all in. You earned it," Amber interjected. She held up her fist and started to chant her sister's name.

"If you start to call me your hero, I'm going to sucker punch you," Melanie threatened her.

Chase grinned at her. "Wow…you sure have a big fan club today. All the posters are gone already."

Melanie waved at the people, even though she wanted to shrink inside herself. "As long as they're here to help Kona, that's all that matters."

Chase held up his sign. "Look, I made a new sign."

"Under the Sea Is Where Kona Should Be? #FREEKONA." Melanie read the sign aloud.

"Yep, I thought it was appropriate." Chase shrugged his shoulders.

"I love it!" She threw her arms around his neck and hugged him. For just a moment, she forgot about all the people around her, until she felt him stiffen slightly. "Sorry."

"No. It's fine, but your grandma kind of gave me a look."

"Of course, she did." Melanie sighed as she moved away from him. "For someone who lived in the sixties, you'd think she'd be a little more liberal."

Chase shrugged his shoulders. "I can wait until we're alone."

"I bet you can." Melanie swatted at his arms. "Behave."

"Always," he promised.

As she looked around her, she realized that the protesters cheered for her just as much as they cheered for Kona. Melanie really did not want this to be about her at all. While it was her dream that had started this journey with The Charlie's Dream Foundation, the foundation itself did not have the steam power to make this come true. This was something the whole community around her had banded together to do. It had grown so massive; she was reasonably sure that these were more than just residents of Phoenix here with them.

They stood there in the middle of the humongous crowd for hours, their voices going strong. The media came and went, recording the protest at different intervals. Melanie could not believe how strong it had become. She was proud to know that she was not the only human who felt that dolphins had no place in the Arizona sun. With only hot desert around, animals that were not used to the climate could not flourish. Anyone who thought they could was out of their minds. All these people could have been paying customers today. Instead, they were spending their day in solidarity against the profiteering inside. Melanie just could not believe the intensity of the moment.

When she thought the crowd would falter, more people came.

With the news broadcasts, more people came out. Many of them stopped to say hello to Melanie before they joined the group.

"Can you believe this?"

Chase nodded. "It's amazing, Mel. I'm proud of you!"

"You too! Thank you for being here with me. I know your mom's job might be on the line too."

"I wouldn't miss this for the world. Besides, what kind of friend would I be to not stand by you?"

"Excuse me, are you Melanie Parker?" A woman Melanie had never seen before walked up to her. She was holding a large envelope in her hand.

"Uhm...yes...." Melanie looked her over and wondered who in the world she could be.

"I'm Valerie, and I work for someone who wants to help you." She put her hand out and offered it to Melanie, who shook it slowly.

"Okay...who?"

"Well, that's the thing. I'm not at liberty to say, but let's just say she has a lot of money, and she wants to buy Kona from the aquarium." Valerie held up the envelope. "In fact, here are her terms. I've made a meeting with Mr. Fillimore and wondered if you could join us. I think if he could see the world through your eyes, he might just give in."

"Where?" Melanie was not about to leave here with just anyone. Her mother had not raised an idiot.

"Inside the aquarium office. Mr. Fillimore flew in when he heard about the mass protest out here today." Valerie gave her a cheeky grin. "Good on you!"

"Oh, this?" Melanie gestured to the crowd. "This was a team effort. A lot of people made this happen. I'm just one voice."

"Well, I think you need to give yourself more credit." Valerie put the envelope under her arm. "Shall we?"

Melanie turned to her sisters, grandmother, and Chase. "Would you mind coming with me?"

"Sure. I'll just give your mom a quick text too." Grandma Mimi fished her cell phone out of her bag and sent a quick message to her mother. Within a few seconds, she was given a response. "Your mom will come too."

"Great! The more, the merrier. Shall we?" Valerie motioned for them to follow her.

Kimmie started to chant. "V-I-C-T-O-R-Y...victory, victory, that's our cry!"

Amber nodded to Kimmie. "You said it, sister."

Melanie turned to see Chase grin at her, and butterflies started to churn in her stomach. He threw his arms around her and hugged her. She closed her eyes and took a deep breath.

"You got this, Mel. Ocean or bust," he whispered into her ear.

Yes. Ocean or bust. Melanie smiled as she thought about all the people around her who had rallied behind something more than just the cancer that was deep inside her. For months she had gotten used to the sadness that echoed around them. Now they all had a new purpose, which had taken some of the pressure off her shoulders. Instead of pretending to be good to keep them all grounded, she had put her energy into the campaign. Melanie knew that this was saving her life, even if only for the moment. She was not blind to its effects. There was no guarantee that the medicine was doing its job, but it didn't matter. Not right now. Being able to fight something else gave her a renewed purpose to live for. Melanie refused to give up on Kona or herself.

"Let's do this!" Melanie held her fist in the air and watched her sisters do the same. They were in it until the very end.

The time it took to get to the offices made Melanie's stomach churn. She hated confrontation, but if Kona's life depended on it, Melanie would find a way to get through it.

Her mom joined her and grabbed her hand. "You can do this, Melanie."

"Okay, Mom."

"I second that. I'm Valerie Monteno. I'm here to help secure Kona's freedom. Shall we?"

"Sure. Why don't you all wait out here?"

Her sisters, grandmother, and Chase nodded their agreement. Chase gave Melanie a thumb's up, and she nodded to him. They were behind her all the way. Even though they were not going into the room with her, she knew they would walk through fire with her.

Linda Parker opened the door to the main office, where Mr. Marcus was almost pacing outside his own office. Mr. Fillimore has taken up his office at the moment, displacing him from his comfort zone.

"Raymond."

"Looks like you've rocked the boat a bit." His smile was filled with quiet respect.

"Looks that way."

"We have an appointment with Mr. Fillmore," Valerie interrupted him.

"So you do. He's not in such a good mood. Be careful, Linda," he cautioned her as he nodded to the door behind him.

"I'm not afraid of a little confrontation." Linda opened the door and sauntered right in with the entourage behind her. She swept her arm for Valerie to come forward.

Mr. Fillimore was sitting behind the desk as if it was crafted just for him. He peered up at them through his eyeglasses with a grumpy smile on his face. "Well, if it isn't my little troublemaker. You're the cancer girl, right?"

Melanie bristled slightly under his stare but stood as tall as an oak. There was no way she would let him knock her down. She had so much to do. She was about to tell him so, but her mother beat her to the chase.

"Excuse me? That's my daughter you're talking too." Linda was already on the defensive before they even started.

"Mom—" Melanie tried to cool her off.

"I'm not going to let him talk to you like that, Melanie. After all you've been through." Tears clouded Linda's eyes.

"This is not about me, Mom. This is about Kona." Melanie stepped forward to face him with her fists at her side. "Mr. Fillimore, my name is Melanie. I've been working with Kona for a while now."

"I see. Well, we'll have to put a stop to that if this is how you repay us," he grumbled.

Melanie felt the red rising to her face. "Do you know that Kona is the only thing that saved my life?"

The room got very quiet. Even Mr. Fillimore had the decency to blush. "Look here, now—"

"You look here. My name is Valerie Monteno. I may have the perfect solution for you. My client has asked me to make an offer for the purchase of Kona."

"I see. May I see your papers?" Mr. Fillimore held out his hand to read through the proposal.

"As you can see, we are prepared to offer more than you paid for the dolphin, as well as some compensation for the loss of income she might provide." Valerie waved her hand at the line that Melanie could not read, although several zeroes were showing.

"So, I just sign this over here, and then what?" Mr. Fillimore tilted his head at her.

"We arrange for transport of the dolphin to a rehabilitation organization of our choice. Dr. Daniel Smith will be more than happy to spearhead it."

Mr. Fillimore shuddered slightly. "That man is a pain in the—"

Valerie coughed discreetly. "So, what's it to be, Mr. Fillimore?"

Valerie stared him down, but he seemed to not care about the offer. He set the paper down and pushed it away as if to reject it.

This small act enraged Melanie. "Mr. Fillimore, if you do not sign these papers, I will not eat or sleep until everyone in our community, in all of Arizona, in all of the world, knows that you had the chance to set her free and you chose not to. Look outside your window, sir." Melanie crossed her arms over her chest and put her foot down in front of her. It was now or never. Melanie only prayed that there was still the same large crowd out there. "It's about to get even larger."

"You're bluffing," he snorted at her.

Melanie glared at him before she glanced over to her sister Amber. The two of them shared a meaningful glance. "Amber?"

"On it." Amber's fingers started to type something furiously on her phone.

Melanie uncrossed her arms and tried to relax a little. She did not need to look as nervous as she felt right now. "If you think that crowd is bad, we have only just begun. This *cancer* girl is about to bring it on like *Donkey Kong*."

Mr. Fillimore stood up from his desk and opened the blinds. As far as the eye could see, people were standing with their signs held high. He squeezed his lips together in deep thought. "If I sign, I'm the hero, and if I don't...."

"You're the villain." Melanie put her hand up to have her sister pause in her texting tirade. Melanie tapped her toe impatiently, waiting for his answer. "Well?"

"Fine, give me a pen."

Mr. Fillimore sat back down at his desk and read the proposal through from start to finish. Melanie thought he would change his mind with the amount of time he took, but when he started to sign and add his initials to different places, she knew he was a man of his word.

Melanie almost breathed a sigh of relief when he handed it back to Valerie. "Thank you!"

"Whatever," he grumbled. "One last thing. You are no longer welcome here. And you're fired, Mrs. Parker."

Melanie gasped and flung her hands at her side. "But you can't—"

"It's okay, Melanie. We'll be quite all right." Linda grabbed her hand and pulled her close to her. "You have your dream, Melanie. That's all that matters to me."

Melanie's eyes teared up as she hugged her mother tightly. They had fought a hard fight together, and finally, something was going their way. While they did not have tons of money at their disposal, her mother was as much a fighter as she was. With Melanie on the last stage of treatment, the bills would get a little easier. The future was far from bleak. Even though she had no guarantee that she would be in remission, Melanie had everything she really wanted at this moment. She could not be any happier.

CHAPTER 26

The weeks passed quickly for Melanie as she waited for the day they would take Kona to the sanctuary. It was killing her not to be able to visit Kona, but she had always known Kona was not hers to keep. She was a free spirit that deserved the right to swim away into the wild blue oceans she had once called home. Melanie had no idea if Kona would ever make it back to where she came from, but she knew the dolphin would be infinitely happier in any ocean.

Today, Melanie was heading into the Charlie's Dream Foundation to meet with Regina. Her sisters were staying home with Grandma Mimi as her mom took her to the meeting. Melanie turned to look at her mom, who was focused on the road in front of her. "What did Regina want?"

"Just to talk about our trip, I think."

Did her mom know something she wasn't telling her? "You sure?"

"Well, I might also be checking into an open position." Linda conceded.

"Really?" Melanie smiled to herself. How nice would it be for her mom to get a job helping other kids like her? Her mom certainly had experience with cancer, more than most people should ever have to deal with, and not only that, she knew how to work with moody teenagers who thought they had everything in the world figured out for themselves. Melanie was quickly learning that life ebbed and flowed in so many different directions. It was almost impossible to know where her path would end up.

"Yes, I was considering it, at least. There's so much left to do for other families."

"I think it's a great idea."

"Good," Linda answered as she put the car in park. "We're here."

So they were. Melanie looked up at the building where her journey to save Kona had really started. Had she known how it all would have turned out back when she first stepped into the building, maybe she would have left her attitude at home. Thankfully, she had been rational enough to change her attitude. Her desire to live outweighed her need to obsess over her illness, and her need to save Kona had driven her even further.

"You ready?"

"Always," Melanie answered.

The two of them walked together in silence, each with different thoughts swirling in their heads. Melanie didn't feel the need to share what this place meant to her. She wasn't sure she could vocalize it even if she was asked to. When they made their way into Regina's office, the woman was already talking to an older man who Melanie thought looked a little familiar to her.

"I'm sorry. Are we interrupting?" Linda Parker apologized for their intrusion.

"Well, there they are. Come in, you two. I have a friend I'd like you to meet." Regina gestured to him. "This is Dr. Daniel Smith."

"Dr. Smith?" Melanie extended her hand and shook his

enthusiastically. "I'm Melanie Parker. It's nice to meet you, sir."

"Sir?" Daniel chuckled. "I wouldn't go that far, but yes, I'm pleased to meet you too. It's not every day I get to meet the voice behind the resistance."

"Resistance?" Melanie snorted. Wasn't he a little extreme? It's not like they were a huge army plotting the destruction of some kind of governmental infrastructure.

"Well, yes. That's how I see your whole entourage. Look at what you've done. I've been trying to take down that Fillimore for years now."

"Oh, well, it was a huge team effort." She shrugged away his compliment. The way she saw it, she had very little to do with it all. Her entire community had banded together for a united purpose. All those people, they were the ones who had given them enough momentum to put their faces on the map. Melanie was just one person, a small piece of a much larger puzzle.

"And it could be the start of something even greater. Just think, from releasing one wild dolphin to springing them all. I've been trying to shut Fillimore down for quite some time."

"I don't understand." Melanie eyed him speculatively. Was he suggesting they try to free all of them? That seemed impossible. How many rich people would it take to make that happen? She was fairly certain that was the only reason that the owner had agreed to release Kona as it was.

"Your voice carries weight, my dear. The people are watching you to see what's next."

"The only thing I have planned next is getting Kona to her rightful home. That and kicking the rest of my cancer to the curb."

"That's a lot for her to focus on," her mother interrupted with her knowing voice.

"Well, yes, of course, but you have a chance to set others on

274

that path. All you have to do is use your social presence." Daniel suggested.

Melanie nibbled on her bottom lip. He was right. She had started with Kona, trying to send her back to the ocean, and he was also right that no dolphin belonged inside an aquarium with the hot desert sun sweltering their skin. She didn't have to stop with Kona. All she had to do was put the others into action. It would take a little work on her part, but really all she was doing right now was waiting for Kona's release. Maybe this was part of her footprint on the earth. There was still a lot of good that she could do. "We do have quite a few students in the colleges around the area. Let me see what I can do, Dr. Smith, but we'll have to be careful. I don't want this to ruin Kona's release."

"That's the spirit. Don't worry about Kona. Her release is already guaranteed. He can't legally back out now. That agreement is ironclad."

"It better be. If Kona gets hurt, you'll have to deal with me." Melanie crossed her arms over her chest and held her chin in the air with a determination.

Daniel grinned at her before nodding to her mother. "I like your spirit. You've got quite a fighter on your hands."

"She sure is." Linda put her hand on Melanie's shoulder.

"Well, what are you waiting for? Fillimore's going down," Melanie declared.

The meeting ended faster than it began. Melanie sat down in the chair in the lobby while her mother focused on her first interview with one of the other office managers. Melanie sat there with her legs folded under her, already working out a plan of action that could help continue the work that they had just started. First, spring all the dolphins from the aquarium. Then maybe they could think of something more global. Then again, if the dolphins deserved freedom, what about the whales and other large aquatic life. There was a lifetime of work before her, something she was just realizing would become part of her future no matter how much time her body gifted her. This focus, it tossed the fear to the wayside and let her live her life with purpose and focus.

When they left the office that day, Melanie was stronger than she'd ever been. New goals, new dreams, new memories were just over the horizon. Her family had helped her with her new outreach, doing their best to spread the word wherever they could. Melanie was proud of everything they had achieved, all that they had survived together. Her family had become a rock together, leaning on each other whenever the wind shifted in different directions. Melanie had always thought she was the one that held everyone together when her cancer had come back. It had been so easy to feel that she was the only one who had suffered, but the thing was they were all living through this in one way, shape, or form. They were always fighting through life together so that no one person was left out of the equation. Melanie would always remember it as one of the hardest times of her life, but she would never forget the love that had helped her rise above it all.

Where the sadness ended, happiness sprouted. She could not believe that today was finally the day! The anonymous donation had paid for moving Kona to The Mariner Rescue in the Caribbean. While they had paid for the trainers, The Charlie's Dream Foundation had paid for Melanie and her family to join Kona on her journey to the sanctuary. Melanie had never been so far from her home before—none of them had. Even Grandma Mimi was coming along.

"I can't believe I get to fly on an actual plane!" squealed

Kimmie.

"What else would you be flying on?" Amber rolled her eyes jokingly.

"A helicopter, duh!" Kimmie stuck her tongue out and shook head at Amber.

Melanie let out a quiet sigh. Sisters! At least they had remained constant, even if sometimes they were annoying. Then again, they had certainly put up with a lot from her over the past year. Dealing with all the ups and downs of her leukemia all over again had been more than anyone should be able to handle. These two had been her rocks through it all. They all had. Melanie was thankful for that, for now, that Kona was leaving her life, all that would be left would be her fight for her own life. Melanie was not sure how she would do it without Kona. The dolphin had given her the will to fight through it all.

Melanie tried not to think about it, but the truth was it was always under the surface this whole time. Even though she had distracted herself with her fight to free Kona, she had only been kidding herself. Last week, Dr. Strand had done another set of scans and a blood panel. Melanie had a bad feeling about it all, but she refused to let anyone else know her doubts. She had been so confident in her need to press on through it all, but it was always an outward show. Inside, the doubts were like a dull roar in her ear. She had been trying to block it out with the noise of a busy life, but now that the scans had been done, Melanie was having trouble focusing on it all.

"Isn't this our line?" Grandma Mimi interrupted the quiet.

Melanie reached down to grab her bag, but her mother put a hand on her arm. "You're not going with us."

"What?" Melanie felt her stomach churn. What was her mother talking about? She was cleared to go — Dr. Strand had given her blessing. "But I have to go with you. I need to see her, Mom!"

"And you will." Linda nodded to behind Melanie.

Julia was standing behind Melanie. "Hi, kiddo!"

Melanie ran toward Julia and almost knocked her down with a hug. "Julia!"

Julia hugged her extra tight. "I've missed you too."

Chase moved around his mother and gave her a teasing smile, one that he had been wearing a lot lately. "And what about me?"

Melanie shook her head at him. "I just saw you. How in the world did you keep this from me?"

Chase shrugged his shoulders. "You never asked."

Melanie glared at him. "Likely story!"

"You guys act like you're an old couple or something," teased Kimmie.

Amber punched her in the shoulder. "Shut up, Kimmie."

Chase grinned at Amber. "You owe me two dollars."

"Two dollars?" Melanie narrowed her eyes on them.

"I told him you would figure out that they were coming," Amber answered.

"I told her I was good at keeping a secret." Chase shook his head at Amber. "She didn't believe me."

"Wait; what?" Kimmie looked at Melanie, then Chase. "Why didn't you let me in on it? I would have doubled down."

Amber sighed loudly. "I always thought you were the bright one."

"I am bright. Loud too, at least that's what Melanie always says."

"Especially when you sing in the shower," teased Melanie. She turned to Julia. "How is Kona?"

"Come see for yourself." Julia held out her hand.

"Wait...what?" Melanie turned to face her mom. "Mom, what is going on?"

"Well, Julia called yesterday and asked if you could ride along with Kona to help keep her calm."

"Me? I get to fly with you? This is amazing!" Melanie was so excited. She had not been able to see Kona for weeks, ever since Mr. Fillimore had banned her from the aquarium. Melanie could have used her pull with the media to get in to see her, but she did not want to jinx Kona's release at all.

"Go on, Mel. We're right behind you. Everything you need is in this bag." Linda handed over a small carry-on bag.

Melanie raced over to her mom and kissed her on the cheek. "I love you, Mom."

"I love you more." Linda wrapped her arms around Melanie and kissed her on the cheek. "Have fun. We'll catch up with you there."

"I will!" Melanie waved at her mom as she walked away. She walked with Julia, her heart in her throat. "Do you think she missed me?"

Chase flung his arm around her shoulder. "Don't worry. I've been keeping her distracted when I can."

"She was looking for you this morning," Julia added.

"She was? Aw...poor Kona." Melanie felt a tiny tickle at the back of her throat as her smile started to fade. She looked off in the distance as she imagined her world without Kona in it. It suddenly seemed like a much smaller place.

"It's okay to be sad, Melanie. We're all going to miss her," Julia tried to reassure her.

"I know, but it's the right thing to do. Keeping her there just because we love her would have been selfish." Melanie squeezed her eyes shut and tried to stifle the tears. There would be time to cry later after she was sure Kona was free.

Melanie followed them through the terminal, barely taking in the sights around her. All she could think about was the inevitable end that would come.

They walked over to a smaller freight plane. As they made their way into the tiny belly of the aircraft, Melanie could hear the distressed calls coming from the large box Kona was inside. The box was to keep her from rolling all over the plane during the flight, but Melanie knew it must have felt confining for her.

She raced over to Kona and called out to her. "It's okay, girl. I'm here."

A happy chatter erupted from Kona at the sound of her voice, and Melanie felt her heart melt into a tiny puddle. Reaching inside, she stroked Kona's head and crooned to her as a tear fell down her face. "That's right, Kona. We're going home."

The flight was a little bumpy and longer than Melanie liked, but it was all well worth it. Kona did well, though, with the extra love and attention throughout the flight. They each spent time soothing the lethargic dolphin when she thrashed in her small container. Julia was on hand with a veterinarian who had volunteered his time to help make sure that Kona made the trip to the sanctuary with more ease.

Every once in a while, Melanie would lean her head over on Chase's shoulder, taking a break from pouring water over the dolphin. He held her close and rubbed her back as she relaxed against him. She was still trying to figure out what it meant to have a boyfriend in a world that was filled with chaos and uncertainty. Melanie wished she could promise more than a few moments, but her life was still not entirely in her own hands. Her stomach churned as she thought about the test results that loomed around the corner.

"It's going to be all right, Mel." Chase seemed to notice her nervousness.

"I know. She'll be fine." Her eyes met his, and she tried to smile at him, but she just could not conjure one.

"So will you...." His words were what she needed to hear, even though she was still trying to figure out how he knew what she was feeling.

Melanie gave him a half-smile. "I'll just miss her."

His eyes met hers. "We all will, but I wasn't talking about Kona. I was talking about—"

At that moment, Kona made a few clicking sounds, and Melanie was happy for the distraction. She moved back to her spot by her side and pushed his words from the forefront of her mind. Melanie did not want their relationship to be encased by the unknown. Sometimes, part of her felt guilty for even agreeing to become his girlfriend. What if something did happen to her? What if the cancer refused to let go of its control over her body? Chase had been with her through the worst of it this year, by her side when most people would have found a way to back away from her. She could not help thinking he deserved better. Then again, as her mother had said, not all high school romances lasted. Her mother had a handful, none of which were substantial. Linda had not met her father until she was in her senior year of college. So, Melanie knew that this could just be a phase for both of them.

At seventeen, it was not like she was making decisions that would impact the rest of her life. Well, except one: her will to live. Even if her tests came back with unfortunate news, Melanie planned to continue fighting with every last breath. There was no other choice, really. Melanie had learned that all life was precious. She had reached out to her network of volunteers to grow the next fight with The Oasis. Even though she cared about many of the trainers there, Melanie had to do what she felt was right. These beautiful creatures did not belong trapped in the desert heat. Her followers had agreed with her, and a new surge of protests started to form. While she wasn't able to be at the forefront of this movement with all the things she was trying to manage in her life at the moment, she was able to get the ball moving.

The more her movement had grown, the more animals had come to light. While she might not be able to help every single one of them, she would continue to be at the forefront of the fight, assisting others in creating similar campaigns that could make a ripple of change throughout the world. They were still trying to find a way to shut down The Oasis, even though it would take away one of the city's favorite destinations. The place had given her many happy memories throughout her life, but now those were tainted with a selfishness she had not known existed at the time. Sure, interacting with such amazing creatures was a dream many people had, but it was one they were not entitled to and was one that came at a high cost to animals that had no voice to speak for them.

Change was still happening at The Oasis Aquarium. Mr. Fillimore was still taking heat from the press, even though he had looked like a decent human being for setting Kona free. That was the thing with a hero's cape—it only lasted as long as good deeds continued to flow through. Hilo, the whale they had purchased over the last year, was growing sicker by the day, and Mr. Fillimore was doing very little to change that. His idea of self-preservation was to sell him to another aquarium, shifting the blame from his own to another. The public was on to him though, for ever since Melanie's campaign, the world was watching. #SAVEHILO was now lighting up the watch boards right along with #NODESERTDOLPHINS. It was amazing what could be accomplished with the right people on her side. It was a road she would continue to travel for the rest of her life.

This time, her mother planned to walk with her. With no ties to Oasis now, Linda Parker was blossoming more than ever. She had nailed the interviews and landed a job at The Charlie's Dream Foundation. Her management skills were an asset to the team, and the cause was one she could wrap every inch of herself into. Her experience with childhood cancer was something that made it easier for her to relate to the families that came through the door. That was something that her mother had in common with most of the employees. The CEO of the foundation preferred to hire those that had been through it. Not all of them had stories with happy endings, but even those were finding their lives filled with a new purpose. Melanie was extremely proud of her mother and glad that she had first stepped into that office so long ago. If she had known where it would lead her, Melanie would never have rebelled against it. The Charlie's Dream Foundation would always hold a special place in her heart, and if—no, when—she was older, she would find a way to donate to them in some way.

After a while, the time passed much faster. Her thoughts turned to how to help Kona as they got closer to their destination. She felt excitement race through her. This was everything they had all worked so hard for. Kona was going back to the ocean where she belonged. This gentle creature would be able to live her life in the open blue the way she always deserved.

As they landed, Melanie was filled with nervous excitement. "We're here, girl!"

As the plane landed, Kona's eyes opened, and she looked around her. She made her small clicking sounds, and Melanie rubbed her snout. Melanie had been telling her over and over what they were going to do.

"Good girl. We're just going to put you in the van now, Kona."

The plane was filled with a bustle of commotion as everyone started to make the preparations to remove Kona from the aircraft. Melanie stood by helplessly as the trained professionals took over. Chase grabbed her hand and gave it a gentle squeeze, and she looked up at him to see that he, too, felt helpless at the moment. Melanie knew he was just as attached to Kona as she was, even though he pretended to be strong.

She squeezed his hand back and leaned against him. "It's going to be all right."

He smiled softly. "I know."

The two of them waited to the side as the others loaded Kona onto the van. Melanie felt her heart stop as she realized this might be one of the last times she saw her friend. She bit back the tears and reminded herself that she needed to be strong for Kona. Melanie knew she would be sad, but her heart would heal over time. How she felt was unimportant really, for this was not about Melanie. This was about setting Kona free once and for all.

When the van was loaded, Melanie and Chase both squeezed in beside Kona. She could tell that Kona was nervous. Melanie could not blame her. All of this must remind her of the first time she had been taken from the ocean. If only Melanie could help her realize that this time, she was being returned to the sea.

Melanie drenched a towel and covered Kona with it. "Look, girl. We're almost there. Just a little further, and you'll get to see the ocean again."

It took close to an hour to get to the sanctuary. By the time they made it there, Melanie had butterflies in her stomach. This was it, the moment when her dreams finally came true. It had been a long road to travel, but now that she was here, Melanie was filled so many emotions, it was hard to hang onto one. As they made the preparations outside the dock, Melanie remained inside the van. She drenched a towel and covered Kona with it. Melanie turned to Julia, rattling off questions she really already knew the answers to. It was the nervous energy racing through her.

"So, she'll be in the ocean now?"

Julia turned to face her. "For the most part. She will be in captivity for a short time."

"I thought she would be free." Melanie felt doubts swarming inside.

"Oh, she is, Melanie. The enclosure is made from the ocean itself. The floors are covered with natural life. Fish come in and out through the holes in the walls. The only reason they will keep her there is to make sure she can fend for herself. Once she can, they will release her."

"So, she will feel like she's home from the start." Melanie felt a little more relieved. Even though she had read up on Kona's new home, her nerves were making her forget some of what she had learned.

"I believe so, yes. Looks like we're here." Julia's face was filled with quiet excitement. This was a dream for her as well, even if she never voiced it. Melanie knew exactly how she felt.

"You ready for this?" Chase asked her.

"Definitely." Melanie felt like she was born ready.

Several men came up to the van as the doors opened. They hoisted Kona out of the van and carried her on a stretcher. Melanie walked by her side, soothing her the whole time. Kona looked leery of the men around her. Melanie did her best to soothe her. "It's okay, girl. They're here to help."

When they made their way to the water, they started to lower the stretcher to let Kona get accustomed to the water. Melanie thought it would take much longer for the dolphin to adjust, but Kona surprised them all. As soon as they stepped away, she darted through the water.

"That's my girl!" Melanie cheered her on.

From where she stood, Melanie could see Kona checking out her new home. The dolphin swam through the shallow water and headed out to the deeper part of the enclosure. When she stopped at the wall, Melanie felt her heart lurch. Would Kona be sad that she could not go out there yet? She hoped the barrier wouldn't make it harder for her to adjust to her new life, but it was just a temporary measure.

Melanie looked over at Julia and Chase, who were standing just a few feet away. Julia's nod encouraged her forward. Melanie had never been in the water next to Kona before. She had always spent her time on the island next to Kona. Today though, Melanie took a chance and waded further into the water, hoping Kona would come up close enough for her to say a proper goodbye. She did not have long to wait, for Kona swam up against her. Melanie put her hand on her fin and tried to fight the tears that came to her eyes. She was going to miss her friend, more than she cared to admit, but Kona was never hers to keep. The dolphin belonged here, where she could be free from those that wanted to make a profit from her.

"It's okay, girl. You'll be out there soon. I promise." Kona slid under her arm and let Melanie hug her tight. "I know, Kona. I love you too. You're home now, sweet girl."

The dolphin chattered happily before darting away from Melanie and swimming through the water. She stayed there in the water, taking in each and every moment of the view before her.

Joy saturated the air as Kona's happy chattering greeted them all. The net that kept her enclosed in this area went out far enough for Kona to go deeper into the water. Melanie watched as the dolphin dove deep under the water, only to return in a graceful arc moments later. The water seemed to welcome her with a warm hug as she touched back down into its crystal depths. The sunlight glimmered on the surface, and the magic of the moment hit her. This was a miracle to be a part of, and Melanie would always be thankful for that.

As she returned to the beach, she sank her toes into the sand, trying to take in every inch of this moment. Her family was sitting on the beach looking out at the ocean. Melanie plopped down beside Amber and hugged her close. "Can you believe we made it happen?"

"We sure did!" Amber smiled.

"Hey! Don't forget me!" Kimmie launched herself at Melanie and tackled her to the ground.

"How could we ever, squirt?" Melanie squeezed her sister tight. She knew how lucky she was to be so close to them. Melanie only hoped she had a lifetime to watch her sisters grow into strong, mighty women. A tear sprung to her eyes, and she tried to fight it. This moment was filled with so much joy; she wished she could bottle it up for eternity. She saw Kona leap into the air again with happy peals of glee that echoed in the air around them.

When she tired of sitting, Melanie took a walk along the beach, watching the other dolphins swimming in the next safe enclosure. This was going to be the best thing for Kona. They were already chattering to each other as if they had always been friends. Kona had never been so social before at the aquarium.

Melanie was so lost in thought; she barely heard the others

walking beside her.

Her mother came racing toward her with tears in her eyes. She held her phone in her hand. "Melanie."

Melanie had an empty feeling in the pit of her stomach when she looked at her mother's face. There was a mixture of emotion on her face that Melanie could not quite interpret. "What's wrong, Mom?"

Kimmie shrugged her shoulders. "Got me. The phone rang, and she clammed up."

Melanie zeroed in on her mother with her eyes. "What is it?"

"I just got off the phone with Dr. Strand." Linda wiped the tears from her eyes.

Melanie closed her eyes and took a deep breath. They had been waiting on the results, something she had pushed to the back of her mind. The fact that Dr. Strand had called probably meant the worst. Melanie tried to stifle the doubt that raced through her, but it was pounding in her ears like white water rapids. She opened her eyes and looked down at the sand between her toes, trying to will the panic to subside.

"The treatment didn't work?"

"No…it's gone, baby. No evidence of disease." Linda opened her arms, and her daughter flew into them.

Melanie laughed and cried at the same time. This was the news she had only dreamed of before. Her sisters squealed as they threw their arms around them. Melanie jumped up and down with her sisters, each of them shrieking with excitement. Kona heard from the waters and started to sing along. It was almost as if the dolphin knew Melanie was going to be all right.

Grandma Mimi looked up to the skies above, then out to the sea. Tears were falling from her eyes. "Miracles are everywhere."

Chase walked up to her with a curious look etched across his face. "Everything all right, Mel?"

"Better than all right. It's gone, Chase."

"The cancer?" His eyes searched hers.

"Yes! NED!"

"Yes!" He threw his arms around her and picked her up in the air. She almost shrieked when he swung her around. When her feet touched the ground, she put her head on his chest and listened to the sound of his heartbeat.

"I knew it! I told you!" She whispered against him.

"I'm so happy for you, Mel." His head rested on hers briefly before he lifted it to check his phone."Guess what's happening right now?"

"What?"

"This…" Chase showed her a video of thousands of protesters in front of The Oasis with signs. "This one is even bigger than the first. Fillimore will have to concede soon."

Melanie turned slightly in his arms and called out to Kona. "Hear that girl? We're all going to be okay."

Kona called to her from the water, almost as if the dolphin understood every word.

Melanie smiled and waved. "Goodbye, Kona! Welcome home, girl!"

CHAPTER 27

Seven Years Later

Kona dashed through the waters near the sanctuary. She had returned to the ocean a few months after she had been brought there, but Kona had not gone too far from its reach. There was plenty of life, fish, and freedom out there for her. Besides, sometimes she checked in with the workers, especially since Julia had started working there when her son had entered college.

Julia stood on the dock close to the beach with a few other people. She kept her hands on her hips as she monitored the water below. Turning around, a smile lit up her face. "They're finally here, girl!"

Melanie could see Julia from here. Her heart raced in her chest as several emotions washed over her at once. She would never forget the day they had brought Kona home once and for all. The dolphin had earned her freedom, and Melanie had learned that her cancer was gone. Her cancer had not returned since that day. That day had been a miracle in so many ways.

Melanie looked over at Chase. "You ready for this?"

"Always." Chase grinned at her.

Melanie could not believe they were finally here. The two of them had been thick as thieves since that summer seven years ago, even attending the same college and earning degrees that would allow them to do even more for dolphins like Kona. The world was still as imperfect as ever, but having more youth ready to protect defenseless animals would help them all make a better impact. Melanie was still spearheading protests around the world, hoping to make a change one step at a time. With Chase at her side, she was sure they could tackle any challenge ahead of them.

"You guys picked a good day to start. Come see." Julia waved them closer to the dock.

Chase and Melanie made their way slowly across the dock. When Melanie peered down, she saw her friend swimming near the top of the water. She would recognize Kona anywhere. Melanie squealed in delight. It was almost as if Kona knew how special this day was for her. She never knew when Kona would be there, even though she had visited several times over the years.

"Kona! Hello, sweet girl!"

Kona rose to the surface near the dock and seemed to give her the biggest smile as she chattered to Melanie. Rising in the water, Kona turned circles in the air as if saying hello with the grandest of gestures. A dolphin calf rose to the surface near Kona as if trying to get a better look. She was the spitting image of her mother.

Melanie clutched Chase's arm in excitement. "Chase, look! Kona has a calf!"

Chase wrapped his arms around her shoulders and hugged her close to him before kissing her on top of her head. "Looks like everyone had a happy ever after."

Melanie held her hand up in front of her and let her ring sparkle in the sunlight. "Yes, they did."

Julia zeroed in on her hand, and a broad smile filled her face. "Excuse me? When were you going to tell me?"

"How about now?" Chase teased his mother.

Julia crushed them in a bear hug and squealed with happiness. The dolphin calf mimicked her and started to sing a little song up to Melanie. Melanie smiled down at her as she hugged everyone tighter. Melanie saw Kona wave her fins at her before diving back into the water, knowing that this was just the start of a new adventure for all of them. Her life had been a journey from start to finish, but even now, Melanie knew it was the love of one lonely dolphin that had changed it all for her. Melanie would always be thankful for that. Kona had taught her to be brave, stand tall, and fight for the things that mattered most in this world. Melanie would spend a lifetime doing just that, and it was all thanks to the courage that had blazed inside her during her darkest hours, to never give up, no matter the costs.

About the Author

Erik Daniel Shein is an American writer, visionary, film producer, screenwriter, pet enthusiast, zoologist, and animal health care advocate. Mr. Shein co-wrote and produced the CG Animated Fantasy/Adventure Feature Film, THE LEGEND OF SECRET PASS, distributed by Lions Gate Entertainment 2019.

About the Author

Melissa Davis - Born in Southern Illinois, Melissa Davis fell in love with reading from an early age, so much so that she started writing when she was in the second grade. From poetry to short stories, she has a love for it all. When she was in high school, she attended Illinois Summer School for the Arts at Illinois State University, which led her to attend the university. After graduating with a Bachelors in Education, Melissa taught for several years until her children were born, allowing her to fulfill two dreams at once: motherhood and penning her first books.

CPSIA information can be obtained
at www.ICGtesting.com
Printed in the USA
BVHW080106070820
585651BV00001B/15